THE DEFLOWERING OF RHONA LIPSHITZ

For Pete,

who influenced my adolescent years in a most important way.

With gratitude,
Lisa

The Deflowering *of* Rhona Lipshitz

Lisa Lieberman Doctor

ELDERBERRY PRESS

Copyright © 2004 Lisa Lieberman Doctor

Cover Design by Kaja Blackley

All rights reserved. No part of this publication, except for brief excerpts for purpose of review, may be reproduced, stored in a retrieval system, or transmitted in any form or by any means, electronic, mechanical, photocopying, recording, or otherwise without the prior written permission of the publisher.

Elderberry Press, LLC
1393 Old Homestead Drive, Second floor
Oakland, Oregon 97462—9506.
E-MAIL: editor@elderberrypress.com
www.elderberrypress.com
TEL/FAX: 541.459.6043

All Elderberry books are available from your favorite bookstore, amazon.com, or from our 24 hour order line: (800)431-1579

Library of Congress Control Number: 2003114091
Publisher's Catalog—in—Publication Data
The Deflowering of Rhona Lipshitz/Lisa Lieberman Doctor
ISBN 1-930859-87-2
1. Jewish—Fiction.
2. Coming of Age—Fiction.
3. Romance—Fiction.
4. New York—Fiction.
5. Women's Fiction—Fiction.
I. Title

This book was written, printed and bound in the United States of America.

In loving memory of my mother, Rebecca Dean.
And for my children, Andrew and Jamie, who fill my life with love and light.

Wednesday, August 11, 1971

If Millie Rosenblatt hadn't bitten into that empty frankfurter bun without realizing the boiled meat had quietly slipped to the floor and rolled under the table, I might never have left my husband Stuie.

Millie and I had a lot more in common than one might suspect, particularly if one were basing an opinion on outward appearances. Where she was somewhere past fifty, I was barely eighteen, where she was short, rotund and brassy blonde, I was tall and slender with dark brown hair. But we shared more important qualities than looks. What united Millie and me was the fact that we truly believed we were taking huge bites out of life when the sad truth was, our lives — much like Millie's roll — were actually quite empty. There was no real meat for either of us to taste, but no matter. We were determined to conceal what was missing with mustard and sauerkraut and convince ourselves that everything was totally fine.

All this became clear to me in that perfect moment, as Millie took the bun into her mouth and ran her tongue across those full lips, savoring the phantom hot dog that by now had come to a full stop under Gertie Bernstein's chair. On that hot and sticky Thursday night at the weekly Temple Beth Shalom bingo game, I knew I was meant to soar like a falcon above the badlands of northeast Queens, New York, and there was no way in hell Stuart Martin Weiner was coming along with me.

I knew Stuie from the day I was born, although nobody ever called him Stuie, except for me and his mother and the principal at P.S. 206. In our neighborhood, the Walnut Garden Apartment complex just off the Long Island Expressway, he was known as Skully because he had such a preposterously big head. Sometimes Selma, my former mother-in-law, would be hanging the wash out the window, and without warning she'd scream, "Stu-eeeee," kind of like a pig farmer calling in the herd, and after a few efforts that always ended in vain, she'd give off one loud "Skull!" and he'd stop whatever he was doing and shout back, "What do you want, ma?" from the stoop, or the gutter, or wherever he happened to be hanging out, usually with me, his steady girlfriend since the third grade.

The Weiners — Sam and Selma, Stuie and his eleven year-old sister Nola, lived at the end of the block in the building right over the garbage room. Every night after dinner I'd haul two bursting trash bags to the windowless room with the big metal cans that smelled of rotten herring and decaying banana peels, and as soon as I'd swung the bags into a bin and slammed the lid shut, I'd call Stuie's name and he'd pull back the green and blue plaid curtains in his bedroom and give me a half-hearted wave, not unlike the Queen of England acknowledging her subjects as her carriage rolled down Buckingham Palace Road.

I don't think there was ever a time when the sight of Stuie poking his head between the curtains or coming down the block excited me, at least not since junior high. Back then I actually thought he was cute with his curly brown hair and dark eyes, and I especially liked the way he could make the kids laugh in Mrs. Pullman's ninth grade science class by flinging pieces of dissected frog across the room. In junior high the names 'Skully and Ro' went as naturally together as 'bagels and lox' or 'cookies and milk,' and that made me feel cared for and safe, the way my mother said girls were supposed to feel. Most of the guys couldn't commit to what they wanted for lunch at Manny's Deli let alone who they would marry, so the fact that Stuie was willing to spend his life with a girl he'd known since infancy separated him from the others, at least a little.

Once we got to high school my feelings for him cooled quite a bit, and by eleventh grade I was aware of the fact I didn't love him the way I assumed I was supposed to. But it never occurred to me to do anything about it. He was Stuie, the only boyfriend I'd ever had, the first and only boy who wanted to marry me, and at Walnut Gardens, that was a big deal. My mother had always stressed the importance of marrying within the faith and within the neighborhood. She wanted me to marry a person with whom we were well acquainted so there'd be no unwelcome surprises later on. Like the other parents on the block she stayed out of her daughter's business but every now and then she had something important to say, like who I was supposed to spend my life with, and she expected me to listen.

Stuie went along with the whole thing and never questioned our engagement, either, behaving right from the beginning as if I belonged to him. Even in the fourth grade he enjoyed putting his hands all over my body, groping me beneath my undershirt. He was understandably thrilled when I graduated to a training bra at age twelve and he was even more excited when I moved into my first B cup three years later. Stuie loved fumbling with the triple hooks on my bra and the buttons on my blouse, but he hated kissing. He'd shut his mouth as tight as he could, screw up his face and hold his breath until it was over, as if I were his bearded grandfather or worse, his bearded grandmother. Stuie was so repulsed by the act of kissing that we avoided it altogether, turning our faces away from each other's during our intimate moments, thus never having to pretend we were enjoying it when the truth is, I would have preferred doing just about anything more than kissing Stuie, even playing bingo with the women on the block.

On our block, bingo was the highlight of the week, the night when the women piled into my mother's brown Chevy Biscayne and made their pilgrimage to the temple. Sadie Hochberger, Gertie Bernstein, and my own particular favorite, Millie, were usually in their best housecoats from EJ Korvettes, often in their bedroom slippers, always with plastic curlers beneath their kerchiefs. My mother prepared for the game several days in advance.

"Don't forget we're having scrambled egg sandwiches on Thursday."

"I won't, ma."

"Don't forget I'm leaving early for bingo."

"I won't, ma."

She talked about the game for days afterward, and I was amazed by her memory. "I can't believe he called B9. I was one away from winning the Round Robin." Bingo was a sacred word in our apartment, spoken with reverence, almost a prayer, and when I turned sixteen the women deemed me worthy to sit beside my mother as she spread her cards across the long wooden table. I was only too eager to tag along, Thursday night being the only real time my mother and I spent together, since she was the cashier down at the hospital and spent every waking minute at the job she loved. The caller, Morty, would shout, "G54" and my mother would spring into action, stamping like a crazy person with her bingo-player's broad stamping pen, repeating G54, G54 with every card she scanned, trying to avoid a potentially humiliating mistake. If Morty called the same number twice in one evening, Gertie, never the shy one, would yell out, "Hey Morty, shake your balls" and everyone would whistle and cheer their approval.

I learned a lot about reverence at the Temple, not during the High Holy Day services, but on bingo night. Morty, the ersatz Rabbi who by day worked at the Kosher butcher shop, would take his seat on the stage. The room would fall instantly into a hush, with no more laughter, no more chatter. Just the sound of his commanding voice bellowing "O68" or "N36" and the dull thumping of the ink pens and occasionally the crow of a lucky winner shouting "here!", her fleshy arm flapping above her hairnet. The voices in the room would rise in unison, an angry chorus from the sanctuary.

WEDNESDAY, AUGUST 11, 1971

"...I needed N35."

"...He should've called N37, the putz."

"...He called N36 last game. Hey Morty, you got a problem tonight or what?"

I watched the players, part of the sisterhood now, and I wondered, if Sadie wears her curlers on the biggest night of the week, for what event does she actually show off her hair? Then came the defining moment that set my life on a different path. Millie slathered mustard on her Kosher dog and leaned across my mother with that big laugh of hers, oblivious to the fact the frank had slid under the table. She took a hefty bite and rolled her eyes in what looked to me like sheer ecstasy, breaking her reverie only to brush breadcrumbs from her enormous bosoms. I watched as she chewed in slow motion, wiping her lips with the back of her hand, her mouth open and filled with roll and mustard, the meat on the floor hidden beneath Gertie's chair. I was riveted. And I became painfully aware, right then and there, that a whole world existed of which I knew nothing about, where people were different from the ones who surrounded me at the bingo table. There were people who stayed in school beyond the ninth grade, unlike my father. People who aspired to more than assistant manager of the Expressway Lock and Key Shop. People who had actually traveled west of the five boroughs, who woke up eager to greet the day, who had questions they wanted answered. I thought about my boyfriend Stuie up at the schoolyard with his slothful friends, cupping a smoldering Marlboro and taking a long, deep drag. I had a feeling he wasn't my destiny, but I wasn't quite sure how to change it.

The week after high school graduation Stuie and I chose Sunday, August twenty-second as our wedding date. Stuie didn't give much thought to what our lives would be like after the wedding. He wasn't fond of discussions about the future, and he certainly didn't want to hear about any dreams I might have for a better life. As far as he was concerned, this was the life we were born into whether it satisfied us or not. Changing its course didn't exist in his lexicon; nobody in his entire family had asked for more than they'd been given and Stuie was certainly not about to play the pioneer.

He didn't question who we were or what we might expect from life. He wanted to know how the Mets would hold up this season, or should we get one slice of Sicilian or two, or what's wrong with the TV and how come everyone's face looks so green? Those were questions whose answers came in black and white, not in shades of gray. The harder questions, the ones like, do you believe in miracles?, he left for minds far more curious than his own.

At least that's what Stuie would have said had he ever allowed himself to think in the abstract, which of course he never did. So rather than annoy my fiancée with talk of leaving Walnut someday in search of a richer, more satisfying life, I chose to busy myself instead with plans for the upcoming wedding, finding just the right dress in the clearance rack of Alexander's department store, choosing an affordable dinner menu with my mother, crossing names of second cousins off the guest list because they'd insulted my parents years ago, although nobody could remember the actual circumstances. In my family it was common practice to hold a grudge for twenty or thirty years. My father hadn't spoken to his brother George or his sister Bessie since the nineteen forties, before I was even born. A few years back my father saw a familiar-looking man walking along Eighth Avenue. 'Excuse me,' my father said. 'Aren't you my brother?' They shook hands and exchanged a few rounds of small talk, then they both continued on their way, never to speak again. It was pretty safe to assume that George Lipshitz and his children, none of whom I'd ever met, would definitely *not* be invited to my wedding.

In April, on my eighteenth birthday, I was presented with a half-carat diamond ring that Sam Weiner had been keeping in a safe deposit box down at the bank. It was the third piece of jewelry Stuie had ever given to me. The first was a silver-plated ID bracelet with his name engraved in block letters along the front. At age twelve, this signified that we were officially going steady. Eventually the ID found its way to the back of my drawer, to be replaced by a delicate ankle bracelet with two initialed hearts surrounded by tiny pearls for my Sweet Sixteen. But this, too, ended up in the drawer, as the pointy hearts caused the skin on my ankle to chafe and bleed. The

WEDNESDAY, AUGUST 11, 1971

third piece of jewelry was different. It was an important family heirloom, one that would stay on my finger forever. As the story went, Sam had cut the ring off some dead German woman whose body he had encountered while stationed overseas during the war. Sam was proud of the ring and the fact that it made him feel like a war hero, as if he'd single-handedly conquered the Germans and shown them who was boss. The ring was his prize, the medal he couldn't have otherwise received, and over the years it took on mythic proportions. Stuie handed it to me with great pride, telling me I'd better be a good wife or his father would have to cut it off my finger, too. I laughed and said very funny, and then Sam raised his glass and we all drank a toast to my becoming Mrs. Stuart Martin Weiner.

The ring was given to me in front of both Stuie's parents, and Sam kissed me so hard on my left cheek that I developed a canker sore and wasn't able to eat anything spicy for almost two weeks. Selma, on the other hand, simply nodded with tight lips as if it were her duty but certainly not her pleasure to acknowledge me as her soon-to-be daughter-in-law. She told me in a clipped voice to take good care of the family's most valued possession and I promised I would do just that. We all sat down to a celebratory dinner, the four Weiners and me, at the fold-out bridge table they set up in the living room whenever a guest, like me, joined the family for a meal.

Nola started complaining right away that her lamb chops were burnt and she hated sliced carrots so could she just have some bananas and sour cream instead? Selma was too busy sucking the pungent juice from the round bone of her chop to respond, but when her daughter whined even louder, demanding her mother's attention, Selma finally put down the meat and began to get up from the table. "Sit down," Sam said harshly, equally angry with his wife as he was with his daughter. "This kid's going to eat what's on her plate and that's that." Selma frowned at Sam but said nothing while I just stayed focused on my dinner, pretending not to notice Selma's glaring, disapproving eyes on me.

The next morning I brought the diamond ring down to Walnut Jewelers for a cleaning since it had been sitting at the bank since 1945. The jeweler frowned and took one good hard look at it and said it was worth almost nothing. I told him it was European, and an antique to boot, but he said, "Let me show you something, sweetheart," and he handed me the loop so I could see close-up why my ring was so irreparably flawed.

"See that?" he asked, and he pointed to the bottom of the diamond with the stubby point of a pencil. "There's a hole right here so it's worth maybe a couple of hundred on the open market. Why don't you bring your boyfriend in and I'll show him what a real stone looks like and we'll get rid of this piece of junk." I thanked him and left the small and cluttered shop, touching my ring protectively as the security screen door closed behind me.

None of my friends were engaged, making me the source of their envy, even though they wouldn't have married Stuie if their lives depended on it. The point was, I would definitely have a husband, which meant I would definitely have kids, which meant I would definitely have a life, the quality of which was inconsequential. But Stuie and I had no money for an apartment of our own, so after the wedding we'd be moving in with his parents, into the small bedroom he currently shared with Nola. The single bed, with its engraving of cowboy hats on the headboard, housed a trundle underneath which we would pull out and push together, enabling us to sleep as husband and wife while Nola took up residency on the sofa bed in the living room. It wasn't an ideal arrangement but it was what Stuie wanted and I felt it was my obligation as his future wife to go along with it.

I always tried to go along with whatever Stuie wanted since he had a terrible temper that he must have inherited from Sam and Selma, who hadn't spoken to my parents since Stuie and I were in kindergarten, right before Nola was born. There had been some kind of fight during the men's weekly pinochle game. Words were exchanged that could not be rescinded and from that night on the two couples never spoke to each other again, which made things a little awkward when trying to arrange a wedding. My father called Sam all kinds of names in the privacy of our apartment and sometimes if the two men happened to be in the garbage room or the barber shop or just on the block at the same time, they'd turn their

WEDNESDAY, AUGUST 11, 1971

heads away and my father might even spit on the ground.

For the women it was just as bad. Selma wasn't a bingo player but I think she would have been part of the sisterhood if only she and my mother spoke to each other. Selma avoided my mother like the plague and if they saw each other at the Kosher butcher or on open school night or at the beauty parlor they, too, would turn their heads away as if the other didn't exist. I thought their mutual hatred would have been a reason to prevent me and Stuie from getting married but I was wrong. In some sick way they enjoyed planning the event despite each other. It gave the whole thing an added dimension, a sense of drama, something else to complain about when they'd run out of reasons to hate the world.

So Stuie and I entered our senior year of high school knowing that come June we'd begin planning our wedding at the Temple, the very place I had been spending my Thursday evenings with my mother and the women from the block. The main sanctuary started to take on a different flavor once our plans got underway. There would be no bingo balls blowing in the big metal canister on August twenty-second. On August twenty-second there would be a chuppa fashioned out of colorful flowers, and my two best friends, Rochelle Davis and Marsha Kotner and Stuie's sister Nola would be in their identical pink bridesmaid gowns, identical except for the sizes.

Rochelle, a size twelve, was big-boned and curvacious, zaftik and sexy like Marilyn Monroe, with the same full, sensuous lips as the late icon. She was more experienced than any girl I knew, having tried just about everything with her boyfriend Sal DiMatelli who was six years older than us and a guitarist in a real band. Rochelle loved having sex and craved it constantly, so naturally Sal was always eager to drive his beat-up Pontiac fifteen miles each way from his parents' house in Maspeth to Rochelle's apartment in Walnut.

Rochelle and Sal made love practically every day after school in her double bed, and it wasn't unusual for him to stay there all night, since the Davises didn't impose a bunch of silly rules for their daughter to follow. Rochelle loved to spend the afternoon lying naked in that big bed with Sal, the two of them doing it over and over slowly and sensually, enjoying the taste and the feel of each other's bodies until they'd finally fall asleep in each other's arms at day's end, damp and exhausted and totally satisfied.

Marsha, on the other hand, was a size four bean-pole with tiny breasts and practically no hips. The boys on the block teased her mercilessly, calling her the Titless Wonder, but she maintained her dignity and never resorted to a padded bra in order to please them, and I respected her for that. The constant taunting eventually took its toll on her self-esteem, although she would never admit it. She liked to say she wasn't interested in the jerks from our neighborhood and was happy to wait for a mature man to come into her life, one who would treat her the way she deserved to be treated. She didn't need a boyfriend right away and she certainly didn't need actual sex to satisfy her, either. There were plenty of other pleasures that were just as fulfilling, like the pleasure she derived from reading one juicy novel after another. She usually chose sweeping romances and she often became so excited with a particular book that she'd leave it on my stoop with a note that said, 'You *have* to read this right now,' then she'd call me the next day to see what page I was up to. Sometimes the books were required reading in Marsha's advanced English class, like 'Wuthering Heights' or 'Madame Bovary,' but many of the novels were much too racy to find on the shelves at school. Those were the books that came only in paperback with realistic drawings of large-breasted women and hairy, muscle-bound men on the covers. I looked forward to every one of those books and gobbled them up as soon as they arrived, wondering if the women we knew in real life savored sex as much as the insatiable fictitious characters in Marsha's paperbacks with their aching loins and quivering lips. If they did, I certainly never saw any evidence of it at Walnut Gardens, where the women would rather play mah jongg on the front stoop than hop into bed with their own husband or for that matter, anyone else's, and the men seemed too exhausted after a day at the factory to think about sex at all.

Marsha's other passion was chocolate, and she consumed great gobs of the stuff without ever altering her tiny frame, thanks to an

WEDNESDAY, AUGUST 11, 1971

over-active metabolism she'd inherited from her maternal grandmother. On a daily basis Marsha would plow through entire boxes of Ring Dings, Devil Dogs, Yankee Doodles, Yodels and Suzie Qs with a big glass of cold, whole milk to wash it down, so of course she was the first to run out of the house when the Good Humor truck lumbered up the block in a ritual that was much-loved and eagerly awaited at Walnut Gardens all winter long. The old truck was synonymous with summer, arriving every evening at around seven o'clock, just as the sun began to dip behind the red brick buildings and the fragrant air became cool and breezy. By then the kids on the block were finished with supper and ready for dessert, lining up to buy root beer ices or chocolate chip pops or strawberry sugar cones from the truck that stopped at the curb in front of the fire hydrant right across from my building.

• • •

It must have been past seven, and I hadn't left the house all day. I turned the volume way up as the opening strains of "In A Gadda Da Vida" filled my room. I was feeling lazy and tired, melting on my bed in the middle of a ferocious heat wave, listening to New York's best progressive rock station on the FM band, the station I stayed tuned to night and day.

My favorite disc jockey, a man as old as my parents named James Ziegfried but known throughout the five boroughs as Ziggy, was on the radio from six to ten every evening except Sunday, and I was his most faithful listener. Ziggy and I had a secret which I had never shared with anyone, not my mother or Stuie or even Marsha and Rochelle: he was my friend. When I was in the eleventh grade I had called Manhattan information and got a listing for a James Ziegfried on East Fifty-third Street. I called the number before I could think about how scared and crazy I was, and to my utter amazement that wonderfully familiar voice answered the phone.

"Ziggy? Is that you?"
"Who's *this*?"
"You don't know me but my name is Rhona Lipshitz from

Queens and I bet you hear this all the time but I'm your biggest fan."

"Well, hello Rhona Lipshitz from Queens," he said cheerfully. From then on I called Ziggy once or twice a week after school. We'd talk for a couple of minutes and he'd ask if there was a song I wanted to hear and then he'd play it on his show that night. Ziggy wasn't in the habit of dedicating songs to his listeners, which was just as well since nobody at Walnut would've believed it was me even if he had announced my address right down to the zip code. I was happy keeping the whole thing a secret, anyway; it felt good to have this special friendship with somebody as important and famous as Ziggy.

Suddenly the familiar calliope music of the Good Humor truck clashed against the heavy metal sound of Iron Butterfly. I peeked through the Venetian blinds in my bedroom, thinking about a nice cold Neopolitan sandwich, luscious ribbons of chocolate, vanilla and strawberry ice cream between two slabs of sweet chocolaty cake. Marsha wasn't around – the chocolate maven called earlier to say she'd be visiting her grandparents in the Bronx and would see me tomorrow. Only Iris Sinitsky next door, thirteen years old but not running out of baby fat, was at the curb. Iris, whose best friend was Stuie's sister Nola, was always the second one out of the building when the ice cream man came along, right behind Marsha, her pudgy fist bursting with nickels and pennies. But tonight she was alone except for her mangy dog Scampy who was panting and drooling into his matted dog hair.

The usual vendor was a kid named Billy who had terrible acne and an unfortunate hook to his nose that made his lips look plastered to his face. To make things worse, he was always overcharging Iris, telling her it was five cents extra for a spoon or two cents more for a napkin. Iris wasn't very well liked on the block so no one told her she was being conned, not even me, although I always felt guilty about it.

There were still fourteen minutes left of my song, so I could grab a quick Neopolitan without missing too much of the guitar riff in the middle. I hurried to the kitchen, dug through the change drawer for a bunch of nickels and dimes, and jumped down the three steps of the stoop and over to the old white truck. That's when I saw him.

Oh, Jesus. In place of Billy, with his perverse sense of humor and nasty smirk, the most gorgeous boy I had ever seen was poking his hand into the freezer for a chocolate eclair pop. His jeans were low on his narrow hips, and his white tee shirt, tucked into his white pants, was tight enough to reveal a sculpted torso, not unlike Charles Atlas or Jack LaLanne, just lean and right. He had light brown hair cut short, green eyes and a smile that spread across his face with a perfect dimple on each side. He handed Iris her eclair and looked me over with an appreciative smile. "Can I get you something?" He didn't have a trace of a New York accent. I had never met anyone who didn't sound like me, not in real life, anyway.

I sucked in the evening air, hypnotized on the spot by the sound of his voice, thrown into a stupor, suddenly deaf to the words that spilled from his beautiful lips. "Excuse me," he said when I didn't respond. "Would you like something?" How melodic that voice was, flowing like warm honey, blanketing my body with its gentle tone. He cleared his throat and tried again. "Hello there, anybody home? Do you want some ice cream?"

"Ice cream?" The words had no meaning; they were foreign syllables from an alien tongue.

He pointed to the illustrated menu on the side of the truck, but I was lost. I didn't know who I was or where I was or why I was standing there at all. "O-*kay*," he said. I couldn't take my eyes off him, which felt wrong and scary and absolutely wonderful.

"Hey, you forgot the money," Iris said, handing over her nickels and taking a bite of her eclair pop. The ice cream man handed her a napkin and she awkwardly pulled two pennies from her fist but he refused to accept them.

I cleared my throat. "What happened to Billy?"

"At last, she speaks!" He smiled at me and I found myself smiling back, my heart pounding so hard I was sure my arteries would give out and I'd end up collapsed and dead on the ground the way my Aunt Estelle found my Uncle Henry on the bathroom floor three years earlier. I took another deep breath, pulling myself together, trying not to be distracted by the eyes and the dimples and the smile. "Billy called in sick so I'm taking over for him tonight."

"Just tonight?"

"I quit in a few days. I go back to school a week from Sunday."

"The twenty-second."

"Very impressive. How'd you know that so fast?"

"I just knew it. So where do you go?"

"Washington University."

"Great place. In Washington, obviously."

He winced, careful not to embarrass me. "Actually, it's in St. Louis."

"Of course it is. I knew that. I must've been thinking of the other Washington University. The one that's in Washington...where it belongs."

He laughed. "You're funny," he said. "Now that you're actually talking."

"I've never seen you around here before." I regained something like composure and was starting to enjoy the conversation.

"I don't usually come home for the summer but I got summoned by my parents." There was a hint of disdain in his voice as he smiled wickedly and gestured to the truck. "Although this isn't exactly what they had in mind."

"What *did* they want you to do?"

"Be a law clerk downtown thanks to my family connections." I nodded, not knowing what a law clerk did. My mother had applied once to be a file clerk at the hospital but I suspected that was different. "Any luck deciding what kind of ice cream you want?"

"I'm not really hungry. So what's your name?" I asked, filling the silence before he could question why I had run to the curb with change jingling in the pocket of my short-shorts if I didn't want any ice cream.

"Jeffrey. What about you?"

"Rhona. But I really hate it. I like Ro a lot better."

He nodded. "Ro. I like Ro, too."

"Thanks for not singing row, row, row your boat."

He smiled. "Now why would I do that?"

"Because everyone does," Iris said. I had forgotten she was there, and then forgot again immediately.

"Do you live around here when you're not in St. Louis?" I asked.

"Not too far. What about you?"

"Oh, not too far."

"Let me guess." He gestured toward my building. "Right there."

"No wonder you're in college," I said. "You're pretty smart. Unless you made up the whole thing about Washington University and you really went to Good Humor School."

He looked at me with a slow smile. That's when Florence Sinitsky poked her head out the kitchen window, yelling as if masked bandits were robbing her. "Iris! Get in here!"

"I'm eating."

"Don't give me that! You left your whitefish bones in the sink and the whole kitchen stinks to high hell. I'm nauseous from you already." Florence slammed the window shut. Iris winced and made her way toward the steps of her ground level apartment, her head down, the empty popsicle stick in her pudgy fist and Scampy by her side. I felt sorry for her, but relieved to be alone with Jeffrey.

We watched until Iris' door closed, then turned back to face each other. I thought of something Rochelle once said, telling us about the moment she and Sal first locked eyes: *If looks were weather, we would've been lightning.* Jeffrey spoke first. "So."

"So. What's your favorite subject in school?" He blinked. *Why am I so stupid?* Who wants to talk about school during summer vacation?

"I'm a European History major."

"No kidding. Must be a lot of work."

"It's not really work if you're having a good time. I just spent my junior year in Barcelona."

"Did you love it?"

"It was amazing. Most amazing year of my life. I was *supposed* to stay for the summer and rent a beach house with a bunch of friends on the Costa Brava." His smile faded. "But my finances got cut off and I had to come home."

"To be a file clerk."

"Law clerk."

My cheeks flushed red. "That's what I meant."

"I did it for a week and quit. It wasn't a job I was interested in."

"So what kind of job *are* you interested in?"

"You sound like my parents. They ask me that all the time."

Oh, no. I didn't mean to challenge him. I just had no idea. I'd never met a history major before. Then again, I didn't know a whole lot of people who'd gone to college, except for a few of the older kids at the schoolyard who tried Queensborough Community for a semester or two before dropping out to get a *real* job. "I'm so sorry. I'd hate to sound like anyone's parents."

"Especially mine, believe me. They actually think I'm going to law school next year which is just about the last thing I'd want to do except for maybe joining the Marines."

"They don't want you to do *that*, do they?"

Jeffrey laughed. "No, but it's almost as bad. My mother's got my entire life mapped out for me. First the law degree, preferably Columbia, then join a big firm and make partner, get married, have two kids, buy a house in Connecticut — unless I kill myself first and ruin her plans for weekend visits with her adorable grandchildren."

I didn't get why he was so annoyed. It sounded like a pretty good plan to me. Maybe he didn't like Connecticut. "What would you rather do?"

"If it were completely up to me and they stopped threatening to disinherit me?"

"Yeah."

"I'd travel around Europe for a couple of years. Maybe even live there indefinitely."

"Wow. Do people actually do that?"

He laughed again. "You really are funny, Ro."

He leaned back against the truck, arms folded across his chest, the hazy light of sunset making his hair shimmer. His eyes took a walk along my body, strolling from my chest down my bare legs to my bright red toenails. On the trip back up I saw his gaze stop at my left hand. "What's that?"

WEDNESDAY, AUGUST 11, 1971

"What?"

"That. You're wearing a diamond ring."

"I am?" Guilt swept over me like a hot breeze.

"What are you, engaged or something?"

"Engaged?" I laughed a little too heartily. "This is a souvenir from the war. Germany, I think." I laughed again, hoping he wouldn't see the lie smeared across my face like the yolk of a soft boiled egg.

"Germany," he repeated, clearly intrigued.

"So where do you live when you're not in St. Louis or Barcelona?"

"You already asked me that."

"And you didn't answer."

"Sure I did. I said not too far."

"Where exactly is that?"

"Nearby."

"Where? Glen Oaks? Bayside? Whitestone? There are a million neighborhoods around here."

He sighed. "You're pretty persistent." He smiled when he said it, like he wasn't complaining.

"I'm just curious."

"Why?"

"Now *you're* asking the questions," I said. We smiled at each other. "I've just never seen you around here before."

"I live out on the Island. Does that satisfy you?"

"*Where* on the Island?" I was teasing him now. I didn't know why he wouldn't tell me what town he was from. Was it someplace bad, like Levittown?

He rubbed his face uncomfortably. "Great Neck." He looked embarrassed, like it was a crime to be rich. He shouldn't have been embarrassed on my account. I always heard you can fall in love with a rich boy just as easily as a poor one, and I believe every woman on the block would have said amen to that. Jeffrey glanced at his watch. "I'd better take off." He looked up, catching my eyes and holding the gaze. "I enjoyed meeting you, Ro."

"You're leaving?"

"I still have my own route to do."

"But what if Billy gets sick again or what if whatever he's got gets worse?" *Jesus, how desperate am I?*

"Billy's fine. The Mets are playing Pittsburgh tonight at Shea." He surveyed my body once more with those green eyes, glancing briefly over my shoulder at my old apartment building where the paint was peeling and the living room window screen hung askew. I could see him thinking. "But that doesn't mean I can't come down here after work, right?"

I nodded hesitantly, wondering how it would look if the ice cream man came over without his ice cream. "Do you ever go into the city?" he asked.

"Sometimes," I said carefully. "Why?"

"I thought we could go there tomorrow night."

"You mean together?"

"It'd be a lot more fun than going separately."

"I don't think so."

"Why not? Are you busy?"

"It's not that."

"Then what?"

I felt my face tingling. "I just don't think it's a good idea."

He moved closer and touched my cheek gently, his fingers cool from the freezer. "You're scared, aren't you?"

I shrugged. "Maybe a little."

"Don't be. We'll just hang out, walk around, get something to eat and then I'll take you home. What do you say?"

I opened my mouth but nothing came out. Jeffrey watched my face carefully. "I'm not sure." *Convince me. Please.*

"Come on, Ro, you need to relax and have a little fun." He winked and it sent a chill through my body. I felt womanly and desirable in a very grown-up way.

"Okay," I said in a small, far-away voice that seemed to come from someone far more audacious than me. "I'll do it."

"Great. I'll come over at six." He flashed a fabulous smile before I could change my mind, then he jumped into the truck, threw it into drive and took off. I watched the boxy white back as it stopped at the corner, flashed its blinker and turned left toward the Expressway, leaving me alone at the curb, raging rivers of excitement, terror and remorse converging in my body and bursting the dam of restraint.

Thursday,
August 12, 1971

I had less than twenty-four hours to hunt down the ice cream truck and tell Jeffrey forget it, this slightly less than perfect ring I'm wearing is a symbol of my commitment to Stuie Weiner, a decent guy who lives at the end of the block and who would happily kick the butt of any guy stupid enough to ask me out.

Or I could've tried the truth from a different angle. I could've told Jeffrey it felt heavenly when he touched my cheek, but Stuie and I were getting married in less than two weeks and there was no take-backsies. But I didn't take the high road. I took the detour — the dead-end path of total duplicity.

I locked the door of my tiny bedroom and sat there all day Thursday, except for two trips to the kitchen for a Hershey bar and a bologna sandwich, and played with a thread on my chenille bedspread, keeping the world at bay while I anguished over the crime I was about to commit.

I had never told a lie in my whole life, at least not with any malice. In my house the white lie was a completely permissible and even necessary means of survival. Returning a dress to May's department store after wearing it a couple of times was a white lie. Telling my neighbor Solly he looked thin when he'd actually packed on an extra thirty pounds was a white lie. Sneaking off to the storage room with Stuie was a white lie and telling my mother that Rochelle was still a virgin so she wouldn't hassle me about our being best friends also qualified. But accepting Jeffrey's invitation to Manhattan didn't seem like a white lie at all, even with my limited exposure to dishonesty.

I couldn't decide if I was truly evil or just following my heart, allowing romantic thoughts of Jeffrey to waft through me uncensored. Until recently I had never even thought about being with another boy, mainly because all the boys at Walnut were no better than Stuie. But lately, now that I'd turned eighteen, I found myself fantasizing about adult relationships with romance and possibly even real sex, the kind that sounded so good in Marsha's books. I used to laugh when I read things like, *He touched her in that place where she was woman*, but I wasn't laughing anymore. I wanted to be touched in that place where I was woman. I wanted it a lot.

The problem was, I couldn't share my fantasies with Stuie since they didn't include him: they were about me and someone else, an unknown gentle person, a faceless, mature man who would take me in his arms and kiss me the way I longed to be kissed. Suddenly I could put a real face on my fantasies. Jeffrey's face.

Just the thought of being with Jeffrey made me feel like I was naked in cool water, but swimming right next to me was the shark of fear that I would hurt Stuie in a way nothing would ever fix, something I didn't want to do for all the money in the world. Poor Stuie. It wasn't his fault he couldn't thrill me. He'd tried to be a decent boyfriend and as far as everyone else was concerned, he succeeded. He had never even looked at another girl since the third grade and when my mother suggested we get engaged he said yes without a moment's hesitation. "Don't take it for granted," my mother had whispered to me so Stuie couldn't hear. "Most high school boys don't know from such commitments."

THURSDAY, AUGUST 12, 1971

Sitting alone in my room in the middle of the empty candy wrappers and the soda bottles, my scalp burned when I thought of myself as the betrayer. But here I was, letting my heart open for the first time in my life, and to a boy other than my betrothed. I wasn't proud of what I was doing but these strange thoughts weren't my idea — they jumped me when I wasn't looking. I wondered whose happiness I was responsible for, Stuie's or mine. Was I supposed to sacrifice my own to make sure he got his?

My mother knocked only once, to ask if I wanted to go with her to bingo. I told her I'd be going out with my friends later and she said there were a couple of hard-boiled eggs and a bagel waiting for me in the refrigerator, and I thanked her and said I wasn't hungry and wanted to be left alone. Except for the broom closet of a bathroom I shared with my parents, my room was the smallest in the apartment, but I loved it because it was mine and mine alone, my sanctuary where I could think and read and listen to the radio and write poetry long after the world had gone to bed. I didn't know where I'd be without my poetry. I'd filled so many notebooks that I was running out of places to hide them. Every time I opened the closet I held my hands over my face, fearful a notebook might fall from the shelf and conk me on the head, knocking me out cold and sending me off to the emergency room. I could see the headlines of *The New York Post*:

POETRY GIVES LOCAL GIRL CONCUSSION.

Marsha called six times and Rochelle banged on the door practically every hour, but I told them I was sick and couldn't see anybody today. I needed solitude, even if it meant dodging the two best friends I'd previously trusted with every secret. But this one was different — I was about to make a decision that might affect my entire future, and I had to make it myself, without the benefit of my friends' wisdom.

My bedroom, with the bright orange walls I'd once painted out of sheer boredom, was illuminated by a single overhead light. There was gold shag carpet on the floor, the narrow closet in the corner, and a small casement window facing the street. Stuie banged on it once while I was hiding out but I told him I was coming down with the flu. He accepted the rejection easily and ran off with Buffa and Larry, who were far more interested in a game of stickball down behind the laundry room than hanging out with Stuie's girlfriend, who would no doubt want to talk about the menu for the wedding. Our guests, it had been decided, would be eating chicken with rice for dinner, which at Temple Beth Shalom meant ninety per cent rice and ten per cent chicken. I wanted to go with the more expensive prime rib but it wasn't within my parents' allotted budget so chicken and rice would have to do. "If they don't like it," my father said, "let them stop for a hamburger on their way home."

I sat on my bed all day, listening to the radio and wondering what other women would do if they faced the same dilemma. Maybe they'd go where destiny took them without so much as a parting glance; but they weren't me. I knew the meaning of commitment, I had heard the words "duty" and "responsibility" every day, even if I couldn't give a dictionary definition. There was no way I'd go out with Jeffrey without analyzing the situation first, turning it upside down and inside out and looking at it from every angle. Let other women blithely put their future in jeopardy. I needed time to muse, journal open on my lap, pen poised in my hand, while I tried to quell the guilt with iambic pentameter.

By four-thirty I needed a break from so much thinking, so I called Ziggy, who was friendly and charming as usual. "How's everything in Queens?" he asked once I identified myself. I always made a point of telling him it was Rhona Lipshitz from Queens right off the bat just in case there were other Rhonas in his life, or even another Rhona Lipshitz.

"Pretty good, except it's still really hot out."

"Summer in New York," Ziggy agreed. "I'd rather be in Paris."

"Or Barcelona," I added. "Lying on a beach on the Costa Brava."

Ziggy chuckled. "Now you're talking. So what can I play for you tonight?"

"Could you play it between six-fifteen and six-forty-five?"

"No problem, Rhona Lipshitz from Queens. What do you want to hear?"

"I'm kind of in the mood for Led Zeppelin. What about 'Heart-

THURSDAY, AUGUST 12, 1971

breaker'?"

"Funny you should pick that. Robert Plant called last week from London."

"Are you serious? He actually *called* you?"

"Yeah, he always calls before he comes to New York. He likes to stop by the station."

What a life Ziggy must have. London, Paris, rock stars calling on the phone. He probably goes to parties in long white limousines and gets into any concert he wants for free. I thought it would be great to meet Ziggy in person, but my life was getting too complicated already so I just thanked him and hung up the phone. I had made my decision: I would throw caution to the wind and follow my heart wherever it would lead me. I was ready for romance and adventure, two things that had never blipped on the radar screen of Stuie's life.

My romance-free fiancé preferred to bypass the mushy stuff and cut right to the sex, begging every time to leave third base behind and go directly to home plate. But I always said no way, I'm not giving it up until we're officially married.

"But none of the girls is a virgin except you!"

"Not true," I would respond. "Marsha Kotner's a virgin and she has every intention of staying that way."

"Yeah, but that's only because no one wants to do her."

He first began pestering me about sex back in the tenth grade but I flat-out refused: "The answer is no and it's gonna stay no until the gold ring has been slipped onto my finger and the Manishewitz heavy Malaga has been sipped from the silver-plated cup." If my parents taught me one lesson over my entire eighteen years, it was that a woman gives herself to the one man she instinctively knows will be her soul mate for life, and she does it in holy matrimony.

Until then Stuie would have to be happy with third base, which for us meant me dipping my fingers into the tubs of Pond's cold cream both our mothers kept in their bathroom cabinets. I'd get a good glop of the stuff and caress Stuie while he touched me awkwardly beneath my bra, making sure there were plenty of tissues on hand. The first time we tried it, shortly after Stuie's Bar Mitzvah, it was so illicit and exciting that I wanted to do it again and again, which was just fine with Stuie. We called our newfound diversion a 'creampuff,' and Stuie would say he was in the mood for one right in front of my parents. We'd sneak off in plain sight to the storage room under my building where bicycles and dirty little secrets had been kept for generations. It wasn't unusual to find a used condom behind a rusted-out two-wheeler; one time Buffa found a forty-six double-D bra and put it on over his winter coat to the amusement of everyone on the block. As far as my parents were concerned, Stuie and I had gone off to Cappy's Bake Shop for a real creampuff, never realizing we were down in the storage room while their future son-in-law was enjoying the forbidden fruit of our sexual act. But like most new things, the novelty of the creampuff started to wear off, at least for me, after the five or six hundredth time, leaving me to wonder if real sex would lose its luster over time, too.

I would have asked my parents if this were true, if sex becomes obligatory and uninteresting for everybody, but they believed good girls like me didn't think about sex or talk about it. My father warned me over and over again not to embarrass him. I never knew what he meant, but I had a feeling we'd all be a lot more than embarrassed if he found me in New York City with a boy I'd met the day before.

I stared at my flawed diamond ring in the glare of the overhead light. If I wore the ring with Jeffrey he would ask more questions and eventually learn the truth about my engagement. There was only one solution: the unthinkable.

I am not a bad person. I am not a bad person. I took a deep breath and removed the half-carat ring from my finger, wrapping it in a Kleenex and placing it carefully behind my beloved FM radio on top of the cherry wood bookcase we had bought with green stamps from the A&P that now housed an outdated set of World Book Encyclopedias and a family of pink ceramic kittens. It was a terrible act, one that repulsed even me. I felt dirty, like one of those women in the movies who plots to murder her husband and run off with the insurance money.

I filled the tub with cool water and slipped in, letting my mind drift to the worst possible scenario if I were caught with Jeffrey. I'd

THURSDAY, AUGUST 12, 1971

have to face Stuie and my parents and all my neighbors at Walnut and admit the truth: I had betrayed every one of them and yes, I had embarrassed my father. Rabbi Marks would be asked to counsel me, and the women from the block would shake their heads every time I walked out onto the stoop, cautioning their own daughters about Rhona's cataclysmic mistake. Selma Weiner would hate me even more than she already did, and Stuie would run away in shame, maybe even to Canada to join some of the boys we knew who were living in Montreal to avoid the draft. My parents would be forced to move back to Brooklyn, the land of their birth. They'd never see Jeffrey as a fine boy from a good home, only the bum who had stopped a marriage ten years in the making. I would be infamous at Walnut forever, the subject of hushed stories told at sleepovers and at the bingo tables. I got out of the tub, shivering despite the heat.

It was all too horrible to imagine. Luckily, that didn't stop me from trying on everything in my closet in preparation for my date. As my ringless fingers deftly sorted through mini-skirts and skimpy sundresses, I realized that my usual wardrobe, fine for the schoolyard, would not reflect the refined tastes of the woman I wanted Jeffrey to greet at the door. Tonight I had to look sophisticated yet demure, tantalizing yet innocent, Audrey Hepburn at her best. The only contender was my graduation dress. White and lacy with a pink dirndl sash, it was probably too fancy and too scratchy, but it fit the bill better than anything else in the closet. I put my hair up in a French knot and fastened it with an ivory comb, just like I did on my graduation day back in June. I remembered my mother saying I looked like her little kewpie doll in that dress, and hoped it wouldn't have the same effect on Jeffrey. *Not tonight. Tonight I'm a woman.* I twirled around and around in front of the living room mirror, my arms over my head ballerina-style, my pointed toes propelling me into the air.

As I stepped into my pink high-heeled pumps I pondered how I was going to avoid one of Stuie's boys or God forbid, even Stuie himself while en route to Jeffrey's car. And what about little Iris Sinitsky? She was the only one who could point out Jeffrey in a line-up. If he showed up in a clean shirt and his own car she'd know in a flash what we were up to, and her childish envy knew no bounds. She'd be so mad he was going out with me and not her that she'd run to Nola and tell her everything before Jeffrey's car had even turned the corner. Then Nola would share the hot gossip with her parents and her brother in two seconds flat.

I sniffed the spray bottle of White Shoulders cologne my mother had bought herself at Walnut Drugs the previous Chanukah with her accumulated bingo winnings. I spritzed the sticky-sweet stuff behind my ears and along the inside of my thighs, praying I would make it safely from my front door to the curb without those treacherous obstacles, Iris or the guys from the block, getting in my way. *This must be what it's like negotiating land mines in Phnom Penh.* I gently rubbed a bit of Revlon pancake into my face, some creamy rouge above my cheekbones, then carefully painted a thin black line with a little tail that looked like a tadpole above my eyelids, finishing the whole thing off with an exuberant application of black mascara.

It was an amazing transformation. I looked like a slut, like the hitter chicks who hung out at the candy store long after my friends and I had gone home and crawled into bed, with their painted-on slacks and teased up hair and ghost-white lips. They always scared me a little, those girls with no curfew who rode around in open convertibles deep into the night. I certainly didn't want Jeffrey to think I was one of them. He was a college boy at a real university I'd never heard of before, who knew about masters degrees and junior years abroad in places like Barcelona which was either in Spain or possibly Portugal. Geography wasn't one of my favorite subjects but the point was, I couldn't let Jeffrey think I was nothing more than a sleazy hitter chick from the Walnut Garden Apartments.

I licked the end of a Q-tip and erased the eyeliner, tightened the comb in my hair and dared myself to imagine what it would be like to have Jeffrey kiss me. I took the dare, which made the blood drain so fast from my head I had to hang onto the bathroom counter for support. As I blotted my glossy lips on a Kleenex I felt my heart race at the memory of his green eyes looking right through me while I

THURSDAY, AUGUST 12, 1971

stood breathless at the curb.

I told myself sternly for maybe the billionth time that it was okay to go out with Jeffrey. My interest in him was perfectly normal behavior for a healthy woman like me who had had so few experiences and was just beginning to live. *Better to live now than when I'm too old to enjoy it.* I ran to answer the door, taking a split-second in the kitchen to check my reflection in the toaster-oven. I wasn't going to look any better than this no matter how hard I worked at it. I peered through the peephole at Jeffrey's perfect face.

"Good luck at bingo," I called to my mother's bedroom, shutting the front door behind me before she had the chance to pop out and ask where I was going in my graduation dress. Jeffrey stood in the hallway wearing a denim work shirt, his hands thrust into the pockets of his faded jeans. He smiled with surprise when he saw me in my fanciest outfit, my hair piled high above my head.

"You look adorable," he said as my own smile faded just a little. He extended his arm and escorted me to the gleaming white Cadillac Coupe de Ville at the curb, holding the passenger door open while I climbed in. I made a mental note that my fiancé had never held a door for me in his life (although my next thought was that nobody had ever taught him to).

My eyes scanned the block nervously. No neighbors were out in the heat to witness my indiscretion, except for Lila across the street who was hanging her clean wash out the window, reaching into the big pocket of her apron for wooden clothespins. I ducked low and stayed that way while we passed Stuie's building, my stomach jumping into my throat as Nola came out of the apartment with two heaping bags of garbage.

The Cadillac turned the corner and I heaved what must have been an audible sigh of relief because Jeffrey raised a curious eyebrow in my direction. "Everything okay?"

"Just fine," I smiled, my face frozen with fear, my heart racing. He smiled back as the car swung onto the Expressway toward the Fifty-ninth Street Bridge. I noticed his hands on the steering wheel. He had beautiful fingers with groomed nails that looked as if they had never been bitten. I thought of Stuie's fingernails, ragged and chewed down to the nubs, the tips already discolored from nicotine. The dashboard read quarter after six. "Oh, can we listen to Ziggy?"

"Sure." He reached over my knees and turned the knob. I began to relax a little when I heard the sound of Ziggy's voice, as if my dear friend was next to me on the black leather upholstery, reminding me to sit back and have a little fun. At six twenty-three my requested song by Led Zeppelin came on without fanfare and I smiled to myself. *Just watch me, Zig.* For the first time in her life Rhona Lipshitz from Queens was going to have herself all kinds of fun.

Traffic was heavy in the other direction but our side of the highway was clear and we sailed through Queens in no time at all. As we neared the bridge my heart began to race again despite my futile attempts to stay calm. I wanted to tell Jeffrey that going from one borough to another gave me panic attacks, so if it was all the same to him could we just turn around? But instead I just gazed at the tall buildings of the city like a tourist from Moosehead, Idaho, anxious about being so far from home amidst the strange faces and smells and sounds.

"I have a surprise for you," Jeffrey said as we made our way up First Avenue. He reached into his shirt pocket and pulled out two tickets.

"What are those?"

"Tonight's the opening of the Post-Impressionist Exhibit at the Guggenheim. My mother can't make it so she said I can have them."

I smiled nervously. The last time I'd been to a museum was during our sixth grade field trip when I was so preoccupied with giggling and gossiping that I'd totally forgotten to look at the paintings.

"Ever been to the Guggenheim?" Jeffrey asked, and I knew there was no way I could tell him I'd never heard of it.

"Maybe once or twice. I don't remember."

"Oh, you'd definitely remember. Frank Lloyd Wright designed it. It's one-of-a-kind."

"Really." We turned south on Eighty-ninth Street and found a parking spot on the street. Jeffrey opened the door and took my

THURSDAY, AUGUST 12, 1971

hand as I climbed out of the seat like a lady, mindful of my dress and my high-heeled shoes. We approached the imposing white building where a long line of art lovers in their evening finery was wrapped around the street. Jeffrey breezed past it with an air of confidence and I followed, whispering over his shoulder, "Shouldn't we go to the back of the line?"

"My mother's a patron," he said, handing our tickets to a uniformed guard and leading me into the hushed silence of the museum, the smell of expensive perfume lingering in the foyer. Most of the women who gathered about in small groups were older than me by at least ten years, and I marveled at their casual elegance, gold bangle bracelets hanging from milky-white wrists, jewel-encrusted pins holding silk scarves precisely in place. Unlike me, these women probably had no problem finding the right outfit among the hundreds that lined their closets, their lavish accessories neatly tucked into mahogany boxes. They were creatures from another planet, aliens so different from anyone I'd ever encountered that I found myself observing them more than envying them. Then it hit me: These are the people in Marsha's books, the jet setters who have torrid affairs in Paris and Rome, who spend their year-long honeymoons sailing around the world on their sixty-foot yacht.

Beyond the foyer were elaborately framed paintings on curved walls that spiraled up toward the top of the building. "Wow," I said, stunned by the breadth and the beauty of it all.

We took an elevator to the top floor and started a leisurely stroll down the spiral. "I told you it was special." *No, it's magical*, I thought as Jeffrey took my elbow, his hand soft and warm. We walked slowly, admiring the art. He pointed out pertinent details in a quiet voice, explaining how each piece of art tied in with its period in history. I nodded and tried to absorb as much information as I could but I was distracted by his green eyes and the fact that he had more knowledge on the tip of his tongue than I had in my entire set of World Book Encyclopedias.

"How do you know all this stuff?" I finally asked with awe.

"I'm minoring in Art History. It's interdisciplinary with the History department."

We stopped at a painting of worn brown work shoes, the laces untied and draped on the floor. "Hey, look at this," I said with a laugh. "Someone painted his shoes."

"That's van Gogh. He couldn't afford to hire a model so he painted whatever he saw in front of him, like his bed or the fields outside his window. Or himself."

I was quiet for a moment. "He was that poor?"

"Right till the end."

"Why didn't he paint his friends?"

"He didn't really have any. He lived a lonely and tortured life and then he killed himself when he was still in his thirties."

"Wasn't he the one who cut off his ear?"

"That's what people remember about him but there was so much more. He was a really complicated man." Like you, I thought. I reached a tentative hand toward the canvas but Jeffrey gently guided it back to my side. "They don't like when you touch the paintings," he said softly.

He turned to walk up the ramp but I wasn't quite ready to follow. There was something about those shoes, something that wouldn't let me take my eyes off them. The guy who painted them clearly needed to express everything that was boiling inside him, to fill his canvas with a piece of himself. I imagined him looking around his sparse room with frustration before settling on his own shoes as the subject of his next painting. I wondered if he recognized his own natural ability to take his God-given talent and use it to create art out of ordinary things. How resourceful he was to look at those shoes with such a fine eye that they came to life on the canvas, even in browns and grays, every crimp in the shoelace, every crease in the leather intricately and carefully depicted. Who would ever think to look for beauty in the everyday? I wanted to ask Jeffrey more about the shoes and the man who made them so real it choked me up, but I was afraid he'd think I was stupid. I couldn't tear myself away.

After a minute Jeffrey leaned in close and whispered in my ear. "Van Gogh died before his art had value to the world. Those shoes and the rest of his paintings had value just to him, which is pretty amazing when you think about it."

THURSDAY, AUGUST 12, 1971

I looked at Jeffrey and a smile came to my lips. He had read my mind, he knew exactly what I was thinking. Nobody had ever understood me like that, or seen into me so deeply.

Jeffrey smiled back and guided me up the ramp to the next piece of art, this one by Paul Gauguin, one of his favorite painters. He pointed out Gauguin's unique way of distorting nature, explaining to me how meaningful it was for the artist's contemporaries to be given the opportunity to express themselves in a way they had never known. I listened intently as Jeffrey told me about the art scene in France back in those days: how painters would hang out together in cafes and talk about their latest projects, sharing names of art dealers and galleries and wealthy enthusiasts.

"You know what I'd love to do?" he asked. "Go back in time for just one day and sit in a Monteparnasse bistro, drinking wine and eavesdropping on their conversations." It had never occurred to me to wish for something like that, but now it seemed like a wonderful fantasy.

"Do you think they'd like it if we turned them on to the Grateful Dead?" I asked. Jeffrey laughed, and I liked myself for the first time that day.

When we reached the ground floor again, Jeffrey said, "Hey, let's go to the Village and get something to eat." He took my hand and we ran across the street to the Cadillac while taxi horns blared and buses spewed exhaust. I felt excited and happy to be part of such an extraordinary city, but as the car made its way down Fifth Avenue and into Greenwich Village, anxiety invaded my body, sending adrenaline coursing up my arms and into my brain.

"Does it scare you being down here?" I asked as we headed into the bowels of the Village. "So many weird people and we're so far from home..."

"Actually, it's my favorite part of town. It's good to get away from all those uptight assholes in the suburbs." He glanced over at me. "Why, are you scared?"

"Of course not," I lied. "Scared of what?"

Jeffrey patted my bare knee. His touch zipped through me, settling somewhere deep in my belly. We parked the car in a lot on

Sullivan Street and walked south to Jeffrey's favorite Italian restaurant. I wished we could have found a place to eat uptown near the Guggenheim where everything seemed a lot more normal, and there weren't all kinds of strange people leaning over fire escapes or out of open windows for relief from the muggy night. I stayed close, afraid Jeffrey might disappear and leave me stranded in this dark, crazy world where groups of men, their eyes wild and demented, hid in corners passing bottles of Thunderbird wine.

These were the drunken bums my mother warned me about every time I left the house at night, and now I understood her warnings. As we walked, the smell of falafel and deep-fried fish and marijuana and scented candles hung heavy in the humid air, adding to my panic, and Jeffrey must have sensed it because he draped an arm around my shoulder, his hand dangling over my chest. I held onto his draped hand and he stroked my fingers as we walked. I inhaled deeply, feeling the full impact of his touch as my legs grew weak.

"Isn't this great?" he asked mostly to himself, breathing in the scent of the hot summer night. We settled into a booth at the back of Lombardo's Italian Cafe, the air warm and garlicky, the large standing fan working overtime for show. Jeffrey slid next to me in the booth, sitting close, his leg touching mine. "You'll love this place," he said.

I smiled, overwhelmed by the whole adventure, the Guggenheim and the Village and the promise of romance. A tired-looking waitress around my mother's age with a pencil behind her ear and a bouffant hairdo dyed black came over and dropped two worn menus on the table before moving on to the coffee machine. Jeffrey opened his menu and placed it between us so we could peruse it together.

"How hungry are you?" he asked.

"Not very."

"You want to share something? The portions are huge."

"Sure. What do you have in mind?"

"Let me surprise you." Jeffrey signaled for the tired woman who sauntered over as if she were doing us the greatest favor by taking our order at all. "Do you have baked ziti tonight?" Jeffrey asked.

"If it's on the menu it's in the kitchen," she said with some

THURSDAY, AUGUST 12, 1971

annoyance, staring at my outfit with curiosity, like she'd never seen a high school graduation dress before.

"That's what we want," Jeffrey said, undaunted by her rudeness. "We'd like to share one order."

"That's an extra buck fifty for the plate," the waitress said.

I leaned in close so she wouldn't overhear. "Isn't that a lot of money for an empty plate?" In my neighborhood a buck fifty at the corner luncheonette bought an entire meal from soup to nuts.

"Don't worry about it." He looked up at the waitress. "And two Cokes." She stuck the pencil in her apron and strolled away. Jeffrey waited until she was gone before turning his full attention to me. "I'm glad you liked the exhibit."

"I loved it. I can't stop thinking about van Gogh. Do you think he was happy while he was painting?"

Jeffrey seemed thoughtful. "That's a good question. His happiness probably came in spurts. Brief moments of it before he fell back into a depression."

We were silent for a minute. "So he never found out that people put on their fanciest clothes just to look at his old shoes."

Jeffrey laughed and put his hand over mine. "He would have been flattered to know how much you appreciate his work, that's for sure."

"You know what else I loved? The dance hall painting by...what was his name?

"Toulouse-Lautrec."

"That's the guy. All those beautiful women in their underwear with feathers in their hats."

Jeffrey smiled. "You look beautiful yourself even without the feathers."

"I do?"

"I like you with your hair up. You have such a nice neck." He let go of my hand and ran his index finger along my jaw line. Just then the waitress came over and plunked two glasses of Coke and two glasses of water on the table with enough gusto to make me jump out of my skin.

"Welcome to Lombardo's," Jeffrey said after she'd left.

"Reknowned for its crowd-pleasing service."

"Is it always like this?"

"Oh no. Sometimes it's worse. But the food's always good." The waitress returned with two plates, one containing a steaming portion of ziti, the other plate empty. She dropped them onto the table with a loud, angry thud. "You're in for a treat," Jeffrey said, picking up his fork. "Dig in." He brought the plate of pasta closer to us. The fragrance was heavenly and suddenly I was ravenous. The red sauce, the noodles and the baked mozzarella beckoned and without waiting for Jeffrey I dug right in and took a huge forkful, strings of melted cheese dripping from my fork. It was delicious. I drank my Coke in seconds flat and Jeffrey slid his own glass my way. "What'd I tell you about the food?" he asked, delighted by my appetite.

"I just hope there's enough for you," I said through a full mouth, the extra plate remaining untouched. Jeffrey grimaced and pointed to my chest. I reluctantly followed his finger and gasped at the sight of a quarter-sized blob of red sauce right in the center of my dress. I squeezed my eyes shut, humiliated.

"Don't be embarrassed, it'll come right off," he said comfortingly as he dabbed his napkin into a glass of water and handed it to me. I rubbed the stain gently, then a little harder, then harder still, succeeding only in turning the quarter-sized glop into a half-dollar.

He looked at me with compassion. "I do that all the time. Tonight it's your turn." I smiled gratefully, my humiliation dissolving into the warm, pungent air.

"I know just how to fix it," he said, helping me to my feet and placing some cash on the table. We walked out into the muggy night, the sweet and slightly scary smell of incense thick in the air, but instead of going to the dry cleaner's Jeffrey pulled me into a little boutique and bought me a string of love beads, purple, orange and green in an alternating pattern despite my coy protestations. He slipped it over my head and stood back to admire it. "Now all you can see is the necklace, not the sauce."

"Thank you," I said, smiling into his eyes, the moment frozen in time as shoppers jostled and pushed us out of their way.

After a while we walked back to the car, his fingers laced through

THURSDAY, AUGUST 12, 1971

mine, both of us tired and happy after our perfect evening, which was probably a little less perfect for Jeffrey since he didn't get any dinner. We drove all the way to Queens in peaceful silence, the lights of the city twinkling behind us beneath a black summer sky. Jeffrey parked the car in front of my building and shut the engine. "What happened to your souvenir from Germany?" he asked with a nod toward my hand.

"I guess I didn't feel like wearing it."

Jeffrey's gaze moved from my eyes to my mouth, and I watched his lips part slightly as he moved toward me. He kissed me softly and sweetly, then he pulled me toward him and allowed the kiss to deepen right there in the front seat of the Cadillac. I don't know how long we kissed, our arms wrapped tightly around each other, but by the time he moved his lips to my neck I was sure I had stopped breathing. I had never been kissed like that and I wanted more. I wanted kisses like that every day for the rest of my life. Jeffrey leaned back and held my face gently in his hands. "Tonight was fun, wasn't it?"

"It was wonderful."

"And you don't even have to be scared of me anymore."

"Me? Scared of you? You've got to be kidding."

He smiled and pulled me toward him for a hug, his breath warm on my neck. "Let's do something special tomorrow," he whispered.

"Tomorrow," I breathed.

"I'll come over around seven?"

"Seven." He moved back into his seat and started to open his door. "That's okay," I said, glancing around nervously. "You don't have to walk me."

"Are you sure?"

"I'm fine." I gave him a bright smile and ran up the stoop quickly, my feet barely touching the pavement as I breathed in the warm night air, the street dark and quiet. How utterly amazing, I thought, that a few short hours ago I was a mere child from Walnut Gardens, unschooled about the complexities of life and love and art, oblivious to an entire world that existed on the other side of the Fifty-ninth Street Bridge. This was the start of a new and wonderful life, a life I had secretly wished for but until that moment seemed hopelessly out of my grasp. And I knew I was teetering on the brink of being touched in that place where I was woman.

Friday,
August 13, 1971

I woke up at noon in a sweat, exhausted from the unrelenting heat wave and my own fevered dreams. I was on a tall wooden platform, a noose around my neck, waiting to be publicly hanged. There was an angry throng cheering below as the female executioner, who looked a lot like Selma Weiner, approached, a sinister smile on her face. Fully awake now, I reached for my neck and found the love beads instead of that nasty rope.

There was a note from my father tacked to the Fridgidaire. "Take garbage now," it said threateningly. I threw on a sundress and hauled the two smelly bags down to the garbage room, tossing them into an empty can and getting out as fast as I could. The plaid curtains parted above me and a large head poked between the panels. "Hey, Ro. Where ya been? I called for you this morning."

Damn. There was no escape. I gasped at the sudden realization I had forgotten to put my engagement ring back on, and clasped my hands behind my back. "Sleeping late," I called.

"I came over."

"I didn't hear you."

"Where were you last night? Wait a minute, I'm coming down."

The curtains swung back and my mind raced with excuses while my cheeks flushed with fear. I had developed a twelve-hour bug. I was in the middle of a really great book and I couldn't put it down. My favorite movie was on TV. I had to wash my h...

"What's going on with you?" Stuie asked. "Why weren't you at the schoolyard last night?" Stuie enjoyed showing me off at the schoolyard, marveling at the fact I was smart and pretty, as if the two were mutually exclusive. In the summer I'd wear my short-shorts with a little stretchy halter-top and he'd have his arms around me the whole night, rubbing himself against me from behind as he joked and laughed with his friends. By the time the evening was over he'd be so turned on from all the friction we'd have to make a quick stop at the storage room or go over to the electrical towers for a hasty creampuff on the way home. I'd bring a travel tube of Pond's and keep it in the zippered section of my shoulder bag. Stuie would lean against the wall or the fence holding onto my hips for support until he was finished, then I'd hand him some tissues and he'd zip up his fly and walk me home, patting my shoulder fraternally instead of giving me a good-night kiss. "So what were you doing?"

"Reading."

"Reading?" He said the word with loathing. "School's over." This was an alien concept, reading in August, and alien concepts frustrated him. He had no interest in trying something new unless it was some new weed that Buffa had scored from his cousin Paulie in Staten Island. New things required effort, and Stuie hated anything that required effort, like opening a book or noticing that a string of love beads was around his girlfriend's neck.

"What are you doing the rest of the afternoon?"

"Nothing," I said, unable to find a more creative answer on such short notice.

"You want to come over? My mother's at a Girl Scout meeting with Nola."

"I can't. I'm really sorry." I blew him a kiss and hurried back to

FRIDAY, AUGUST 13, 1971

my apartment, my head swimming with things to do. I had to wash and condition my hair, put on make-up, find the right outfit...not to mention the most important task of all: convincing myself I had every right to spend another perfect evening in Jeffrey's arms.

• • •

I started getting ready at four thirty, brushing my teeth over and over, lying down in front of the air conditioner to zip up my skin-tight dungaree short-shorts, trying to stay fresh until Jeffrey arrived. I might have chosen an outfit less revealing than the one I wriggled into, but the unbearable August heat was a great excuse to show off my body, especially now that Jeffrey had already seen me in my lacy dress and had concluded I was a fine and well-bred girl. Rochelle called twice, once just to say hi and tell me about her new earrings, the second time to invite me to Sal's band practice in Maspeth. I told her to go without me and have a great time, hanging up before she could ask about *my* plans for the evening or detect the anticipation in my voice. I went back to primping in the bathroom mirror and jumped at the sound of the doorbell.

"You look great," Jeffrey said as I opened the door, his eyes devouring me right down to my platform sandals. I closed the door behind me and took a quick look up and down the block to see if the coast was clear. There was a game of mah jongg in front of Gertie's building with a card table set up on the pavement, thermoses of iced tea on the stoop, and a box of graham crackers close by on the ground. Gertie leaned forward with her playing tile as I hurried to Jeffrey's car, climbing in before he could even get there to open the door for me, shielding my face with my hand. "Hey, what's the hurry?" he laughed as he closed the door and started the engine, turning on the air conditioner. I held my breath until the Cadillac pulled away from the curb. The women at the card table wouldn't hesitate for a minute to tell Selma what they saw with their own two eyes in broad daylight in front of the building of her future daughter-in-law.

We turned the corner toward the Expressway. "Where are we

going?" I asked, wondering what tickets were tucked into the pocket of his shirt this time. "If we're on our way to the Opera I can run back and change my clothes." Jeffrey laughed and I smiled along with him. I was actually starting to feel comfortable with him, especially now that we were out of range of the mah jongg group. A peaceful happiness was settling over me, the likes of which I had never known.

"I thought we'd visit my friend Josh. He and his girlfriend just got back from the Cape." I tensed. I might be growing comfortable with Jeffrey, but nobody said anything about meeting his friends. He was upbeat. "You'll really like him. We've been best friends since junior high."

"What about his girlfriend?"

"Tracey? He met her at school this year so I barely know her."

"They don't go to Washington?"

"New Haven."

"The University of?" I asked, proud of my ability to talk college talk.

"Yale, actually."

"Of course. I knew that."

His eyes smiled at mine. He thought I was being funny again and he obviously liked it. We rode in silence as the Cadillac glided away from Queens and entered the forbidden and lush land of Great Neck, a place I knew nothing about. It seemed odd to be surrounded by old majestic trees when we were just a few short miles from the concrete jungle of Walnut. "Hey, it's Friday the thirteenth," I said as we turned a corner onto Oak Street.

"Our lucky night," he winked.

The car stopped in front of a large brick Tudor home, three stories high and impossibly beautiful. I had never seen a house like it other than in the movies. "Is this Josh's house?"

Jeffrey sighed. "Actually, it's mine."

"*Yours?*"

"Maybe it's stupid but I thought we could say hello to my mother. If it's too weird, I completely understand."

"No, I'd like that." *He wants me to meet his family after only one date*. I figured I must've really impressed him, talking about van Gogh so intelligently.

Jeffrey hopped out of the car and opened the passenger door. I stood up and tugged on my short-shorts, wishing I had gone with a pair of long pants and a bra and maybe even a sweater, even though it was over ninety degrees with a hundred per cent humidity. "You look terrific," he said softly. "Let's get out of the heat."

We started up the brick walkway but I stopped suddenly, Jeffrey nearly tripping over my feet. "I just realized — what am I supposed to call her? I don't even know your last name."

"It's Stewart," he said.

I laughed nervously. "For a minute I thought you said your name was Stewart."

"I did. Why?"

"Oh, nothing." *Of course it's Stewart.* It was God's reminder that my fiancée was, at that very moment, being denied his thrice-weekly creampuff from the woman he was about to marry.

I followed Jeffrey toward the immense maple door with its oversized brass knocker, and held onto the wrought iron railing. "Just be yourself," he said with a little smile, putting the key into the hole and turning the brass knob. I gasped at the grandeur that lay before me, but who could blame me? Even Jay Gatsby, another Great Neck resident whom I'd read about in twelfth grade English, would've gasped at the interior of the Stewarts' enormous estate.

Straight ahead in the overly air-conditioned entranceway was a grand hallway with marble floors, behind which stood a curved oak staircase the color of honey. The house opened to rolling lawns, a swimming pool and a tennis court. There was room after room of fancy furniture with enough couches to fill the showroom at Sears.

"Come wait in the library," Jeffrey said. "I'll tell them you're here."

"Them?" My voice rose two octaves.

"My mom's uncle John is visiting from Philadelphia. He's my favorite relative in the whole family."

I followed Jeffrey gamely to a room that smelled of wood and leather and had all sorts of knickknacks far too valuable to touch, much as I was tempted. While Jeffrey rounded up his family, I was left to peruse a most extraordinary piece of art above the massive fireplace. I found myself drawn to the painting, lost in the dark image of tortured, anguished figures, hoping Jeffrey and I could talk about it later and figure out what the artist was trying to say. I was startled by a genteel man's voice behind me.

"Do you like Bacon?"

"I do but I'm not allowed to eat it."

The sound of laughter made me turn at once to a gray-haired gentleman who wore a brown suit and a large burgundy bow tie. "I told you she's hilarious," Jeffrey said with a laugh. "Ro, say hello to my Uncle John."

"I'm delighted to meet you," Uncle John said, kissing my hand with rubbery lips. "Anyone who jokes about a Francis Bacon earns my respect." The older man stood back and gazed at me with pleasure. If only I had dressed more appropriately for the occasion. The full-length gown I had rented for my cousin Artie's Bar Mitzvah in Yonkers would have done nicely. "Have a seat," Uncle John said. "What are you drinking?"

"I'll have a Coke," I said stupidly as I lowered myself onto a frosty leather couch, the hide cold against the bare skin of my thighs.

"Nonsense. You'll have a brandy." Uncle John gave me a sly wink as he moved to the bar, pouring some sticky brown liquid into three over-sized stemmed glasses and carrying them across the room. I leaned forward and accepted the glass gingerly. I was the only kid at Walnut Gardens who hated alcohol, who had never downed a gallon of Gallo and spent the night praying to the Porcelain God, and I had gotten plenty of flak for it, too. It wasn't that I objected to drinking for moral reasons - I just couldn't get used to the bitter taste.

I held the glass of brandy as if it contained arsenic and turned to Jeffrey who raised an eyebrow at me, signaling for me to drink. I took the tiniest sip possible, squeezing my eyes shut against the horrible wooden flavor. Uncle John, meanwhile, had already drained his glass, and looked ready for more. "Delicious," he said. "So tell me about yourself, Ro."

"I...well...There's not a whole lot to tell."

"Where do you live?" Uncle John asked jovially. "Let's start there."

"The Walnut Garden Apartment complex. You can see it off the Expressway at exit twen..."

"I know exactly where that is," Uncle John said, holding up a hand to stop me from continuing, his smile thinning just a tiny bit. "I used to buy my cigars from a little smoke shop not far from there, years ago when I lived in New York. I wonder if it's still there."

"I wouldn't know because I don't smoke cigars."

"Or drink brandy, by the looks of your glass."

I glanced at the barely touched brandy in the fancy glass, winced and took another tiny sip. "It's very tasty," I smiled, feeling sick to my stomach.

Jeffrey tried to offer some relief, but only managed to worsen an already unfortunate situation. "Uncle John's retired from the Philadelphia Philharmonic. He was the second principal cellist."

Uncle John waved a dismissive hand. "It's nothing like it used to be, thanks to the new musical director..."

I nodded. I couldn't think of an appropriate response, and I worried I was disappointing Jeffrey with my inability to carry on a simple conversation with a member of his family. The silence hung in the cool air. "My uncle traveled everywhere when he was with the symphony," Jeffrey said. I couldn't tell if he was trying to be helpful or waiting to see what I would do with the information.

"We were at the Guggenheim last night," I offered hopefully. "We saw the Post-Impressionists. Did you know they painted what they saw in their everyday lives?"

Uncle John glanced at Jeffrey briefly before turning back to me. "Yes, I did know that," he said tentatively. "How was the exhibit?"

"Oh, it was wonderful. I just love the Guggenheim. It was designed by Frank Lloyd White." I smiled sweetly and let myself exhale, happy to have redeemed myself in Jeffrey's eyes.

"So where do you go to college, Ro?"

"Actually, I just graduated high school in June."

"Nothing wrong with that. Where are you headed in the fall?" I placed the glass of brandy on the coffee table in front of me. "Something wrong with the brandy?" Uncle John asked.

"No, not at all, it's delicious," I said, hugging my arms which by now had developed low-grade frostbite, my teeth chattering. Jeffrey moved to the arm of my couch and sat down, holding me close and stroking my neck gently. I was amazed how his hand stayed so warm in the sub-arctic room.

The moment was interrupted by a beautiful woman who breezed into the library. It was obvious she was Jeffrey's mother even though she looked nothing like any mother I'd ever seen. For one thing, she wasn't wearing hair curlers or a seersucker housecoat. She was tall and thin with manicured nails and lots of thick gold bracelets and a wispy apricot-colored dress that ended just above her pointy gold flats. She had incredibly thin ankles and I wondered if this was a privilege of the very rich. It was difficult to picture her with nylon stockings rolled above her bedroom slippers, the way my mother wore her stockings at the end of a long day at work.

"Don't get up," she said as she moved to the bar to pour herself a brandy. I thought of my father taking a nip from the Jim Beam he kept hidden behind the dish towels in the narrow linen closet near the bathroom and tried to imagine him drinking from one of these fancy glasses instead of slogging it straight from the bottle.

"Mom, this is Rhona Lipshitz," Jeffrey said. "She lives at the Walnut Garden Apartments in Queens. You know where that is, don't you?"

Mrs. Stewart looked at her son, the bottle poised in her hand. "I believe I've passed it in the car." From the disdain in her voice it seemed she had more than just passed it in the car, but I couldn't be sure.

Jeffrey was animated. "Ro just graduated high school. Uncle John was asking about her college plans."

"Yes, I heard part of the conversation on my way in."

Mrs. Stewart walked across the room and settled into a beige chair, crossing her delicate, pointy feet on the ottoman in front of her. She had the grace of a ballerina and I could tell she was looking at me with a disapproving eye, as if I were a fan dancer in a Vegas lounge act here to seduce her precious son.

They looked at me with anticipation, including Jeffrey, who didn't know what I was doing come September, either, since we hadn't gotten around to discussing my upcoming plans. Now Jeffrey and his mother and Uncle John were waiting for an answer, and telling them I was getting married to Stuie Weiner a week from Sunday was definitely out of the question. It was time to pull a harmless white lie out of the air, the survival tool I was beginning to rely on. "I haven't quite decided yet," I said. "But I've narrowed it down to one college in the United States and one in Europe."

Jeffrey seemed surprised. "Europe? Which one?"

I crossed my legs and glanced at the bottom of my sandal. "The University of Taiwan."

Jeffrey coughed, covering his mouth with his hand. Mrs. Stewart seemed confused. "But I'm leaning toward Albany, at least right now. We'll see." Albany was the school Marsha would be attending, starting two days after my wedding. "That's in upstate New York," I added. "I believe it's the capital."

"Surely you've made your decision by now," Mrs. Stewart said. "It's practically the middle of August."

"I told them I needed more time. It's a big decision, picking the right college. You can't just rush into these things."

"But deposits were due the first of May."

I looked at Jeffrey for help, but he seemed as baffled as his mother. I sighed, defeated. "Okay. I'm not going to Albany, or anywhere else for that matter. I graduated high school with a commercial diploma and I'm hoping to get a job as an assistant bookkeeper or a stenographer."

All breathing stopped in the room. Mrs. Stewart arched an eyebrow in his direction, then turned back to face me. "A commercial diploma," she repeated frostily.

"How about another brandy?" Uncle John asked affably, rubbing his hands together, probably to keep warm. Between the air conditioner in overdrive and the chill in Mrs. Stewart's voice, the room had become suitable for hanging meat.

That's when a white standard poodle bounded in, groomed and

prim and freshly bathed, nails clacking on the wood floor, a sweet aroma emanating from his fur unlike anything I had smelled on the scruffy dogs in my neighborhood. He immediately came to the couch to investigate the stranger, poking his long snout directly between my legs and liking what he had discovered. I gently guided his face away, but the dog was not only young and strong, he was also relentless.

"Matisse, no," Jeffrey admonished, but Matisse, with all his breeding, ignored him. "Matisse!" Jeffrey said more firmly, tugging at the animal's collar.

"Come here, darling," Mrs. Stewart offered, snapping her long fingers. Finally, with great reluctance, the dog scampered over to Mrs. Stewart's chair where she stroked his head and cooed her appreciation. "What's wrong, sweetheart? Is there a stranger in the room?" I looked at Matisse with loathing. Even the dog was held in higher esteem than me, but then the poodle hadn't graduated high school with a commercial diploma.

"We're going over to Josh's," Jeffrey announced.

"Give him my best," Mrs. Stewart replied, forcing me to envy Josh as much as I envied the dog.

Without warning Jeffrey rose and I found myself following suit. My outer layer of skin, which had been stuck to the sofa, separated from the leather with an unsavory whoosh. I followed Jeffrey through the library, pulling on my shorts in an attempt to lengthen them, trying to hide the backs of my thighs that must have been beet red from the assault of the cool leather.

"I'll be in Queens at Ro's apartment till pretty late tonight," Jeffrey said flatly. "So don't set the alarm before you go to bed."

Mrs. Stewart stared at her fingers and examined a pesky cuticle as we headed for the door. "Enjoy the evening," she said without looking up.

"It was nice to meet you," I said.

Jeffrey and I walked to the Cadillac. He didn't say a word until the doors were closed and the engine was turned on. "Are you really going to be a stenographer?" he asked. He said it as if I were joining the Foreign Legion.

"Probably. I hope I didn't embarrass you in front of your family."

"I wasn't embarrassed. But I shouldn't have brought you here."

"Then why did you?" Maybe showing off a girl from Queens was Jeffrey's vengeful trick to hurt his mother. He adjusted the air conditioning and put on his seat belt.

"I'm sorry, Ro. My mother treats everyone that way."

"Not everyone. She seems to really like your dog."

"Only because he listens to her." Jeffrey smiled at me weakly. We pulled away from the curb and made a left turn from Oak onto Maple while I sat quietly, staring out the window at the magnificent homes with their shuttered windows and brick walkways, each one perched proudly atop a grassy knoll.

"Did you always live in Great Neck?" I asked.

"We lived in the Bronx until I was two. It was my mother's dream, to move here." Jeffrey turned from Maple Street onto Cedar. I liked how they named the streets after trees, as if each house had deep, strong roots of its own.

"Are you Jewish?" I asked with such urgency that I even startled myself. "I mean, I just assumed you were, but now that I've met your mother, I'm not so sure."

"It's complicated," he said.

"Why? Either you are or you aren't."

"My parents were raised Jewish but they've been atheists for more than twenty years." I gasped at the word, which, in my family, was synonymous with blasphemy. Who walks away from Judaism? Jeffrey noticed my reaction. "What?"

"Does that mean you're an atheist, too?" I asked.

"I'm piecing together my own religious philosophy. I'll probably end up a little bit of a lot of things." As we continued on our way, I hoped that whatever Jeffrey was going to be, the biggest piece would be Jewish. I looked out the window at the lush and pristine lawns, the grand and imposing homes, some of which were behind iron gates. I wondered if those gates protected the secrets of the people who lived behind them more than the people themselves.

We parked in front of a sprawling two-story Cape Cod with a

wraparound porch and a four-car garage. Jeffrey turned to me and stroked my cheek. "Hey," he said softly, turning my face toward his. "Don't let my mother upset you." I wasn't sure if he was referring to her rejection of me or of God, but before I could ask he was kissing me. "We'd better go in," he whispered, reluctantly breaking the kiss and straightening my blouse. "Josh and Tracey are waiting for us." And he hopped out of the car to open the passenger door for me.

• • •

Josh turned out to be a nice guy if a little eccentric, a theater major with a habit of running his hand through his hair when he spoke, which gave everything he said an air of drama. His words spilled out quickly, falling over each other, and it was obvious how much he enjoyed the sound of his own voice and his ability to dominate the conversation. During the long monologues about himself he would jump up from his chair without warning, pace for a while and then plop down somewhere else, only to rise again a few minutes later. I learned quite a lot about him in the few hours we spent in his lushly landscaped backyard. He wanted to go to the Yale School of Drama after graduation but since every serious actor on the planet was applying he was considering other alternatives, although he preferred to remain at Yale. He regaled us with richly detailed stories of the theater productions where he was invariably the lead, and by some stroke of luck Josh never found out I had no idea what the hell he was talking about.

Tracey, his girlfriend, was wafer thin with a dark, thick braid down her back. She seemed lost in her baggy overalls and she wore a delicate strand of Indian beads around her neck and her wrist. Josh would occasionally sit next to her but he never touched her, not once, not even by accident, his hands everywhere when he spoke except in the vicinity of her skinny body. Tracey was from New Jersey and was majoring in Anthropology, which gave her and Jeffrey a lot in common since she, too, had spent part of her junior year abroad. Luckily nobody asked me anything about myself or any trips to Europe I might've recently taken so I was able to just nod along and laugh when everyone else laughed.

Jeffrey kept his hand on my thigh the whole time and I felt protected and cared for. I hoped Tracey wasn't envious of his public display of affection since her own boyfriend barely noticed she was there. By the end of the evening Josh was sprawled on a chaise lounge, tired and spent from his performance, while Tracey sat alone on a teak bench, her long, delicate fingers folded neatly in her lap. Jeffrey started to yawn, saying he was tired and had better get me back home. We wished Josh and Tracey a good night and got into the car. Before Jeffrey even turned on the ignition he was kissing me again, his hands and mouth everywhere. "Let's go to your house," he murmured. "Are your parents home?"

"They're asleep."

"Do they wake up easily?"

"Never," I assured him. "Once we had a fire in the kitchen and they slept right through it."

"That's great news." He was kissing my shoulders.

"Not really. We almost died thanks to a bunch of bananas. They fell on top of the toaster oven, which had a plastic cover on it, and the cover got so hot it burst into flames and the whole kitchen went up. My neighbor Leon had to repaper the entire room, even the ceiling."

"Mmmm." He was licking my ears.

"If the smoke hadn't woken me up it would've been all over. The entire Lipshitz family killed by a bunch of bananas..."

Jeffrey was kissing my lips and I assumed he had heard enough of the story. After a few minutes he started the car and drove us back to my building. That's when the kissing started all over again, even more ferociously than before. His fingers crept beneath the top of my panties, moving all the way down, his arm leaning against my belly. "Let's go inside," he said.

We closed the car doors quietly and I instinctively looked around for any signs of Stuie or Buffa or Larry or some other kid who might be heading home after an evening at the schoolyard, but the street was deserted. I fumbled in the pocket of my shorts and found my key and its leather strap. I swung the strap Mae West-style and said in a voice dripping with seduction, "Ready for action, big boy?"

"You're silly," Jeffrey said, touching my butt. We entered the living room and I was so nervous about what was to come that I completely forgot to be embarrassed by the modesty of the apartment, most of which was obscured by the darkness anyway. Jeffrey said nothing about the unimpressive decor as we tiptoed past the open door of my parents' room. I could see my mother in her curlers and housecoat asleep in the double bed, my father lying prone in his summer pajamas beside her, snoring and snorting and pushing the air out of his mouth with every breath. The apartment smelled of stuffed cabbage as most apartments in Walnut did on Friday night, but neither Jeffrey nor I paid much attention as we went into my bedroom and shut the door. I turned on the overhead light. Jeffrey flinched at the harsh intrusion. "You have anything a little less glaring?" he asked.

"No, this is it."

"Not even a lamp?"

"Uh uh."

"What about a candle?" The only candles we had were the memorial ones we lit on Yom Kippur. I went into the kitchen and returned with the glass of smoky-white wax and a book of matches from Sy's Bagels on Northern Blvd. Jeffrey lit the yortseit candle and turned off the overhead light. It was strange to have that eerie glow emanate from my bedroom, and I was just about to recite Yizkor for my dead grandparents when Jeffrey came up behind me and lifted my shirt over my head.

This was the moment I had been dreaming about for days; indeed, it was the moment I'd been dreaming about all my life. I just never expected it to happen right there in my room with my parents snoring on the other side of the wall and my engagement ring rolled up in a Kleenex behind my radio. All my obsessional fears since last night came rushing back, but this time I couldn't rationalize them away. It didn't matter that I had been starved for real love and desperately wanted it now. It didn't matter that a mere creampuff, perhaps titillating in junior high, was no longer enough to satisfy me. What mattered was that I promised Stuie to be his lawfully wedded wife, to abide by the sacred principles of holy matrimony according to the laws of Israel and the Torah, and here I was, half-naked in my bedroom with a gorgeous man who was unzipping my short-shorts and nibbling my shoulders.

"Let's take these off," he said, sliding his hands deep into my panties and pushing them to the floor. As I stepped out of them and into his arms I felt ashamed of the person I was about to become, a jaded woman who had left her little white lies in the dust on the way to bigger and more dangerous deceptions. Jeffrey ran his fingers up and down my back and I imagined us on the cover of Marsha's latest romance novel, but with one major difference: instead of being the sultry vixen who exulted in her body, my body was shaking uncontrollably and I could feel my guilt breaking out in a prickly rash across my chest.

"Are you okay?" Jeffrey whispered. I nodded and he guided me through the shadows to my bed, pulling back the bedspread, covering us both and easing his body next to mine, his clothes scratchy against my skin. I pictured my engagement ring hurling itself onto the floor, exposing me for the corrupt and sinister woman I now was. I closed my eyes against the lightning bolt that was bound to crash through my bedroom window, followed by Moses himself in flowing robes, arms outstretched, a long mane of gray hair blowing in the wind. He'd be holding the Ten Commandments in his arms as a reminder of my sins, pointing to one in particular, *Thou Shalt Not Covet College Boys From Great Neck While About To Be Married To Stuie.*

"You're shaking all over," Jeffrey said softly.

"It's nothing." He kissed me with an open mouth and I helped him take off his shirt, then his pants, then his briefs, and soon we were skin to skin in my bed, touching and tasting and learning about each other in the glow of the yortseit candle. "Oh, God," I whispered urgently when his lips moved to my ears. He moaned, happy to know he was satisfying me, not realizing I was actually praying for absolution.

Jeffrey moved his face close to mine, grazing the tip of my nose. "I want so much to make love to you, Ro," he whispered, kissing my eyes. "But only if you want me to."

"Oh, I want you to, but I don't think we should."

"It's your first time, isn't it?" *He knows me so well. He can see right through me like no one ever has before.* I leaned in to kiss him, savoring the softness of his mouth and the tender kisses he gave me back, trusting him more than I'd ever trusted anyone in my life. I got lost in the kiss as he moved on top of me, our arms and legs wrapped around each other, mouths locked together once again, and suddenly I felt no guilt.

"I love you," I said breathlessly, gazing at his beautiful face in the glow of the candle. I had never said those words to anyone other than my parents and that was only on special holidays like Chanukah when gifts were exchanged around the electric Menorah. I had never told Stuie I loved him and he'd never said it either, even though I suspected he felt it in his own way. Saying those three extraordinary words to Jeffrey made me realize what I had been missing and I repeated them slowly and breathlessly, enjoying how they made me feel, like a real woman in the throes of real lovemaking.

"I love you, Jeffrey. I love you so much." It was too dark in the room to see the expression on his face but I sensed he was as pleased to hear the words as I would have been had they been said back to me. He put a finger to my lips and I assumed it was time to stop talking. We kissed for a while longer and before I knew it we were actually making love. It was infinitely more wonderful and far less painful than I expected it to be, and it lasted so long I wasn't even sure if morning had arrived.

Afterwards I lay in Jeffrey's arms, warm and wet and so deliciously sleepy, wanting to stay tangled in his warmth all night. He slowly extricated himself from my body, saying it was almost daylight and he'd better get home. "I'll call you tomorrow," he said softly. He slipped out of my bed and put on his jeans. He started to close the bedroom door behind him, then opened it again and walked over to see if I had fallen asleep. "Ro?"

"Mmm?"

"I don't have your phone number."

I yawned. "It's Bayside 2-4046. Can you remember it?"

FRIDAY, AUGUST 13, 1971

"Yeah." He blew out the candle and kissed my cheek before closing the door behind him again. Soon I heard the Coupe de Ville turn over and disappear down the street. I hugged my pillow that smelled like Jeffrey and rubbed my bare legs against the warm sheet, loving my nakedness and luxuriating in my quasi-dream state, when the sound of a pebble hitting the window sent me zooming into reality. I sat bolt upright in bed, heart racing, covering myself with the bedspread. I peered out the Venetian blind, expecting to see Stuie with his nose pressed against the window, waiting impatiently for an explanation about the guy in the Cadillac who just drove away, but the street was empty.

I exhaled, relieved, but my relief was short-lived. Stuie would be knocking on the door for real in just a few hours like he did every Saturday morning, except this time he would be greeted by a woman who was hopelessly in love with another man.

Saturday, August 14, 1971

On Saturday I lingered in bed until ten, cooing like Scarlett O'Hara the morning after Rhett Butler swept her off those dainty little feet and up the stairs for a night of pure, unbridled passion. I was a new woman and my body felt wonderfully different. I was feminine and alive and completely in love with a man more perfect than any I could have possibly envisioned. I breathed in the sweet summer air that wafted through the open window of my bedroom, feeling light and breezy and free of remorse. I had *definitely* been touched in that place where I was woman!

Stuie knocked on the door at a quarter to eleven, just as I was getting out of the shower. I opened the door, clad only in a phony smile, a short bathrobe and the engagement ring I had hurriedly put back on my finger. He headed into the kitchen, returning with a bag of Hershey's kisses, and plopped down in front of the TV, the plastic slipcovers squishing beneath his weight. Peeling back the foil wrapper of the kiss, he focused his attention on a baseball game being played at Shea Stadium, a few miles west of Walnut. "Sit next to me," he said, eyes on the screen. "I feel like I haven't seen you in ten years."

"Come on, it hasn't been that long."

"Feels like it." He reached out to me and pulled me beside him. Stuie liked when I sat on the couch while he watched the game. It didn't matter that I hated baseball and couldn't talk about players and scores and statistics; according to him, baseball was a team effort and he didn't like to experience it alone. "Life is good," he announced, his breath reeking of chocolate. "I've got a dime bag of weed for the week-end, the Mets are on TV and my almost-wife has no clothes on under her bathrobe."

"Almost doesn't count," I said, shifting my body away from his. I wanted to tell him about the aborted wedding plans but the moment had to be right. Words must be carefully chosen lest Stuie fly into a rage or fall into a black abyss, neither of which I was quite ready to handle on this wonderful morning. *I'll tell him later.* Or Sunday morning, at the latest, which would give him a full week's notice.

"Did you hear what happened to Howie last night?" he asked.

"No." I didn't really care what happened to Howie last night. I was too busy reliving what had happened to me.

"He was behind the swings with Roberta Friedman and when he opened her bra a bunch of tissues flew out all over the place." Stuie started to laugh. "So he blows his nose into one of the tissues, puts it back in her bra and says, what else you got in there? Like she was hiding a container of milk and a bunch of Oreos." He looked at me for a response. "Don't you think that's funny?"

"Actually, I think it's sad." Knowing Howie and his big mouth, Roberta's otherwise nice reputation was about to end; this was one of those stories that would follow her deep into the future, getting bigger and crazier all the time until Roberta Friedman would eventually be known as the girl who wore falsies and a variety of prosthetic devices, including a false leg and a rubber nose. But that was Roberta's problem. Right now I had my own future to think about. I would be moving to St. Louis in a week and I hadn't even made flight reservations.

"How come everybody heard about it except you? Where were you last night, anyway?"

"In bed," I said quietly.

"Well, I'm glad *you* don't stuff your bra," Stuie said, idling closer and fumbling to untie my robe. "Go get the cream."

"Not right now, thanks."

"Please? Get it quick before it's too late." That's when the phone rang, making my heart leap into my throat. "Don't answer it," Stuie begged. "Not now."

"I have to. I'm sorry, Stuie. I'll be right back." He continued to rub against me but I slid away from his grasp, not interested in adolescent shenanigans, retying the robe and hurrying to my bedroom. Jeffrey sounded serious on the other end of the line.

"How are you today?" he asked, his voice full of concern.

"I've never been better," I whispered into the receiver to my true love, enjoying my newfound femininity and the feel of the terrycloth robe against my naked body, trying to ignore the fact that my soon-to-be-ex-fiancee was in the living room in desperate physical pain. I lay down on my bed and caressed the smoothness of my own calves, eyes closed, toes pointed toward the ceiling as Jeffrey spoke.

"Feel like taking a walk this afternoon?"

"That depends."

"On what?"

"On whether you'll be there, too." I was born to seduce. It came even more naturally to me than Gregg shorthand.

He laughed. "How about I pick you up at your house in an hour?"

"Mmmm, I'll be waiting for you," I cooed. Suddenly I remembered that Stuie would be hanging out on the block all day, sitting on the stoop with his moronic friends, smoking pot and cigarettes and listening to his transistor radio. These weren't the ideal conditions for him to learn about my romance with Jeffrey. "On second thought let's meet at Sunny's Laundromat on Horace Harding. My parents aren't crazy about my going off in cars with guys they've never met."

I kissed the phone and went back to the living room, suppressing a happy grin, finding Stuie still on the couch, a dozen little foil wrappers in tight bundles surrounding him on the sofa. He reached a hand out to me and I took it, allowing him to pull me beside him on the couch. "Where were we?" he asked.

"Bases were loaded, I think."

"You were just about to get the cream," he said, his eyes on the television screen.

"Stuie? I have to ask you a favor."

"No favors when I've got blue balls, Ro. I can't concentrate."

"Please. It's an easy one."

"What is it?"

"That was Rochelle. She wants me to go with her to Flushing but we sort of have to leave in ten minutes."

"No problem. I'll be done in twenty seconds, maybe less if you take off the bathrobe."

"Can I get a rain check?"

"What do I look like, the car wash?" Just then the Mets scored an unexpected run. Stuie threw his arms up in the air, whild I slid off the couch and into the bathroom to get ready for my date. It's not a sin to fall in love, I told myself sternly as I applied a double dose of mascara. Stuie knocked on the bathroom door. "Come on, Ro, I'm dying here. Just give me twenty seconds." I opened the door and looked into that goofy face, my first boyfriend whom I'd known all my life. I shook my head, realizing the news must be broken gently. Despite how rough he was around the edges and everywhere else, Stuie was a sensitive boy with feelings I'd never want to hurt, and I felt somewhat responsible to help make his life happy and comfortable in my absence. As I opened the medicine cabinet a brilliant thought hit me like a lightning bolt: Ilene Grossman. She would be perfect for Stuie. She not only loved baseball but her parents owned a Kosher deli, which meant there'd be all kinds of tasty noshes to sample while she and Stuie whooped and hollered and cheered together in front of the television. Ilene's refrigerator was always crammed with sliced roast beef and cole slaw

SATURDAY, AUGUST 14, 1971

and macaroni salad and blackout cake, and she knew how to slice a seeded rye bread extra thin without amputating her fingers. Ilene would be the perfect wife for Stuie, talking about RBIs while fixing him a chocolate egg cream with equal parts milk, syrup and seltzer, the way an egg cream was supposed to be made. *If only he could love Ilene instead of me.* I brought down the industrial-size tub of Pond's and unscrewed the lid for the last time.

"That's my girl," Stuie said rapturously, pulling down his pants and untying my bathrobe while I expertly performed the familiar task, my mind a million miles away. Twenty-seven seconds later I carried a wad of tissues to the kitchen garbage bag, feeling a bit nostalgic about giving Stuie his final creampuff, a bittersweet goodbye before sending him on his way.

Stuie went back to the living room, content now and ready to leave my apartment, taking the remaining Hershey's kisses with him. I waited for him to disappear down the block, then tried on seven outfits before deciding on a little orange sundress and a pair of strappy high sandals. Not exactly sensible walking shoes, but they did wonders for my legs, which weren't too bad to begin with. Happy with the final result, I swung a cute yellow purse over my shoulder and headed off to Sunny's Laundromat on Horace Harding Boulevard.

When I got there, the Coupe de Ville was already waiting at the curb. I ran to the passenger side and climbed in. Jeffrey smiled at my ensemble and pulled me into an astonishing kiss that left us both breathless. He looked at me for what seemed like a long time.

"What?" I asked playfully.

"You're a special girl, Ro."

"You really think so?"

"Yes, I do."

"What makes me so special?" I asked as I nestled closer, wrapping my arms around him and toying with the button on his shirt.

"You're cute. And you're fun to be with." I nibbled on his ear, loving my new persona as a woman in love who wasn't afraid to show it.

"That tickles," Jeffrey said as he pulled away. I sat back in the leather seat, happier than I'd ever been. Now that we'd actually made love, Jeffrey and I were connected in a deeply profound way, a way that Stuie and I had never known. We belonged to each other now, I had given Jeffrey a part of myself I could only share with my one true soul mate. Today, I was quite sure, Jeffrey would ask me to marry him, and I would leap into his arms, cover his handsome face with kisses, and tell him yes, I wanted nothing more than to become his devoted and doting wife. Today, or perhaps tomorrow, I would tell him I'd be leaving my former fiance so we could board that St. Louis-bound plane together on Sunday, August twenty-second, the date formerly earmarked as my wedding day to Stuart Martin Weiner at Temple Beth Shalom.

The Cadillac moved onto the Expressway and headed west, passing Great Neck, Manhasset, even Roslyn, with me sitting so close I was practically in his lap. "I thought we were going for a walk."

"We are."

"This is a drive."

"We're driving to the walk. There's a park out past Huntington that nobody knows about."

"So you want to get me alone, do you?" I asked in my best Greta Garbo voice.

"That's exactly what I want. I've been thinking about being alone with you all morning."

The park was as idyllic as Jeffrey implied – nothing like Flushing Meadow, site of the old World's Fair. Jeffrey's park had enormous trees lining a narrow dirt path with wildflowers everywhere. The air smelled sweet and there was a delightful silence that was broken only by the swishing of the trees. What a romantic setting for a marriage proposal, I thought as Jeffrey and I walked along the path, a rolled-up blanket under his arm, my strappy shoes dangling from my index finger. I slipped my other hand into the back pocket of his jeans and felt the bulging leather wallet within. Playfully, I pulled it out and flipped it open as we walked. "Hey, what're you doing?" he asked, not minding the intrusion at all.

"I want to know more about you," I said, rifling through the leather compartments. Maybe his wallet would fill in some of the gaps, some of the pieces of information he hadn't yet had a chance

SATURDAY, AUGUST 14, 1971

to share with me. I bypassed the wad of bills and found a driver's license, a library card, and a laminated student ID. *He's a student, he's got lots of money, he knows how to drive and he likes to read. So far, nothing new.* I removed the ID and looked at the tiny picture of Jeffrey's smiling face, those incredible dimples on each side of his mouth. "Can I keep this?" I asked. He glanced over, not breaking his stride.

"What's that, my ID from junior year?"

"Do you still need it?"

"Probably not. We get new ones every year."

"Thanks," I said, slipping the card into the pocket of my sundress and handing him back his wallet. He put an arm around my neck, pulled me closer, and led me further down the path that smelled of summer flowers and cut grass. "I'm going to remember these smells forever," I said, feeling intoxicated by the pungent air.

We moved to a mature shade tree that was quite a distance from the path. The grass was wet and I enjoyed the moisture between my toes while Jeffrey spread the blanket under the tree and motioned for me to join him on it. Maneuvering awkwardly in my short dress, I reclined in the warmth of his arms, both of us flat on our backs under the wispy clouds and the brilliant blue sky. "How'd you find this place?"

"I've been coming here for years and it's always deserted. I keep waiting for people to discover it but so far it still belongs to me."

"What if you showed up one day and there was a carnival going on with rides and hamburger stands?" Jeffrey smiled and stroked my hair, both of us lost in the soft breeze that rustled the huge tree overhead. We were comfortable with the quiet, comfortable with each other, as we rested on the blanket for what seemed like hours. "Is your Uncle John still Jewish?" I asked.

"Yes." He paused. "He's leaving next week, unfortunately."

"You'll miss him, huh?"

"We understand each other. When he was my age he played his cello at a burlesque house, which of course his parents hated, but that didn't stop him." Jeffrey opened his eyes to the blazing sun, shielding his face with his hand. "Even after he joined the symphony they couldn't understand why he picked music over accounting."

"Accounting's a good field. My Uncle Henry was an accountant, he should rest in peace."

"You're missing the point, Ro. My Uncle John lived his life without having to please anyone but himself. He knew what he wanted and he went after it. That's exactly what I want to do." Jeffrey squinted into the dappled sunlight. "Sometimes I wonder who I'll be when I'm forty. Do you ever think about that?"

"Forty? I haven't even gone as far as twenty."

"Try to picture yourself. What do you see?"

"Somebody who's alive and healthy, kinehora poo poo." I knocked on my head three times. Jeffrey looked at me puzzled. "That's to keep away the evil eye," I explained. "You're not supposed to talk about good things happening unless you knock three times and say poo poo, like you're spitting on the ground. Otherwise you might lose everything. You could even die."

"Says who?"

"My parents."

"They think spitting will keep them alive?"

"It hasn't failed them yet. Kinehora poo poo."

Jeffrey was silent for a minute. I assumed that living amongst the privileged and atheistic, he had never been taught that having too much might deprive others of their piece of the pie. My parents had confused faith with fear; their God would punish them if they took too much. I didn't necessarily agree with those ancient ideas, but I wasn't willing to tempt fate by rejecting them, either. So if spitting and knocking on my head three times protected me from retribution, that's what I would do. As far as I was concerned, it was a small price to pay. "Anyway, to answer your question," I said, "If I'm still alive at forty I hope I'm not living in Walnut Gardens."

"I don't mean the easy stuff like where we'll be living or how many kids we'll have." I looked into his face, trying to contain my excitement. He was talking about our children, where they'd be raised, and how many of them we'd have. *Here comes the proposal of marriage I've been waiting for.* "I'm talking about something bigger than external things, Ro. I want to know if the people we are right now will disappear and some new person, some adult like our parents, will take over."

"I don't want to be anything like my parents, that's for sure."

"Nobody does. That's not what I mean." He seemed frustrated and I felt stupid for not catching on. "I want to know if after we're thirty or forty we'll have any memory of who we are today."

"I'll always have memories of today," I replied dreamily. I tried to picture Stuie lying on the blanket with us, Jeffrey asking him what he thought about being forty. Stuie would light a Marlboro, take a drag and say, "How the fuck should I know, man? What do I look like, Mr. Wizard?"

Jeffrey's mind was racing again, faster than a speeding bullet. "Have you read much Aristotle?" he asked.

Oh Jeez, don't do this to me when I'm on a roll. What normal person earning a commercial diploma reads Aristotle? No fair. "A little," I lied.

"He says every time something changes, part of it stays the same. If you put a fur coat over your dress right now it might change the way you look but you'd still be the same person."

"Just a lot sweatier."

Jeffrey smiled and traced my lips with his index finger. "Let's make love," he said. "I've been wanting to do it all day."

"Here?"

"Why not? We're completely alone." *And practically engaged.* He didn't have to say it — I could feel him thinking it. He leaned toward my mouth and kissed it gently, then he took me into his arms, moving his body on top of mine on the blanket.

"Jeffrey," I whispered breathlessly.

"Yeah?" I could feel his warm breath on my neck as he opened the buttons on my sundress.

"We can't do it here. We're in the middle of a public park. We'll get arrested." He ignored me, planting little baby kisses on my chest, grinding his pelvis against mine. "Jeffrey? It's against the law to do it in public. You'll end up in jail."

He rolled onto his back, gently pulling me into his arms. "So

I'll go to jail. Once they find out who my father is they'll boot me right out."

"Who's your father?"

"He's a judge. The Honorable George William Stewart."

"Wow. I've never met a judge before."

"Let's not talk about my father," he said, resting his chin on top of my head. I wanted to lie in his arms with the sun beating down on us forever, when he suddenly whispered, "Ro?"

"Yes, Jeffrey?"

"I don't even know you."

I felt a sinking feeling in my stomach. "What are you talking about? You know me better than anyone, even..."

Luckily, I stopped myself in time. "Even who?"

"Even my best friends," I said quickly, impressed by my own save.

"Not really. I have a feeling there's a lot of stuff you haven't told me."

"I'm not that complex. You already know everything there is to know."

"What about the diamond ring you were wearing when I met you?"

I held my breath. "What about it?"

"Does it have some kind of meaning?"

"If it did I'd still be wearing it, wouldn't I?"

Jeffery sighed. "Well, I don't know anything about your family. What does your father do?"

"Mostly he watches television. We're saving up for a color set."

"I mean when he goes to work."

"Oh." I hesitated. "He's not a judge, that's for sure. He dropped out of school when he was fourteen. He works in a factory on Seventh Avenue cutting dresses." I looked into Jeffrey's face, searching for a reaction, but he was quiet.

"He must hate it," he said softly.

"He never talks about work. My mother does most of the talking. What about your father? Does he like being a judge?"

"He enjoys bullying people around, so yeah, I guess he likes it."

"I bet he doesn't bully your mother." I looked at Jeffrey quickly, hoping I hadn't said too much. Luckily, he didn't seem mad at me.

"Not anymore." He paused. "I didn't tell you why I had to come home for the summer. My dad moved into an apartment in the city while I was in Spain. They're getting divorced."

I felt a chill race up my insides. "Oh, no. Are you sure?" I tried to picture my own father packing his bags and moving away. The apartment would be so eerie, so empty without the sounds of cursing and fighting.

"It was supposed to be a trial separation but so far he hasn't said a word about coming back. He seems to be in love with some other woman." Suddenly I realized why Jeffrey's mother had been so unfriendly. She obviously had a lot on her mind, a lot of pain and uncertainty to sift through. "This isn't the first time he's fooled around," Jeffrey continued. "But I think it's the first time he's really serious."

"I feel sorry for your mother."

"Feel sorry for *me*. She's got this brilliant idea I'll move back to New York so she can control my life."

"What if you don't?"

"She's already threatened to cut off my trust fund. She dangles it in front of me, then snatches it away if I don't do what she wants." This was a problem I'd never heard of before. Nobody at Walnut had funds to dangle or snatch. Most of the time it was a struggle just to pay the rent. "I feel like a slave to that damned fund," Jeffrey said. He looked at me sadly. "Do you hate me for admitting that?"

"Of course not." *How can I hate you when I don't know what you're talking about?*

"I have no idea what their problem is. Aren't European history majors supposed to travel? I mean, what's so wrong with that?" He looked at me imploringly, as if I understood his parents better than he did.

"There's nothing's wrong with it," I said softly.

"You know, you're really easy to talk to, Ro. I like that."

I smiled happily. "Tell me some of the countries you plan to see."

Jeffrey stared at the branches overhead, and I could actually feel his longing for adventure. "I thought I'd start off in Ireland. I want to sleep in medieval castles and climb round towers from the ninth century. I want to stand on the Hill of Tara and imagine battling the Vikings."

"It sounds so romantic."

"It's magical. Have you ever been there?"

"Are you kidding? I've never even been on an airplane. The furthest I've gone in my whole life is Baltimore for my cousin's wedding." I snuggled closer, lost in the image of Jeffrey and me traveling from city to city, Polaroid cameras around our necks. As he stroked my cheek, I could feel the sadness in his touch. "Do you really want to be a stenographer?" he asked.

"It pays well," I said.

"But if you could do anything at all," he said, "what would it be?"

"Well. I don't have a whole lot of talent but I guess there are a couple of things I can do." I gave him a gentle poke. "I'm pretty good at kissing." His smile was thin, forcing me to be serious. "I think I'll be a good mother, and I know I'll be a great wife." I waited for him to respond, but he didn't. "Sometimes I dream about being a poet. That's the job I would really love." I covered my face with my hand. "I can't believe I told you that. You're the only person who knows."

"Why does that embarrass you?" Jeffrey asked.

"Are you kidding? Who am I to write poetry?"

"Who is anybody to write poetry?"

"I'm not even going to college."

"Do you want to?"

"Maybe some day, but right now I can't. My parents think it's a waste of time and they won't pay for it. Besides, I have an interview as a junior secretary at my mother's hospital next Tuesday, right after the w…" I stopped with a gasp.

"After the what?"

"After the weekend. My mother loves the hospital," I said quickly. "She always says she should have married a doctor."

SATURDAY, AUGUST 14, 1971

"Why?"

"She says doctors are as good as they get. If she had married one she'd sit at the front desk making appointments and she'd wear beautiful clothes so everyone could envy her for being the doctor's wife."

Jeffrey was quiet for a minute. "My mother's a doctor."

"Your *mother's* a doctor?" I was shocked. I pictured Mrs. Stewart browsing through fancy stores all day or walking Matisse leisurely down beautiful Oak Street, her long apricot dress billowing around her as she praised the poodle for relieving himself on somebody else's lawn.

"She's a pediatric cardiologist downtown. Now that my dad's moved out she wants to sell the house and get a co-op in the city with a separate suite for me."

"But you would never do that."

"Not if my life depended on it. Of course she wouldn't even bother to ask my sister to move back because she knows what the answer would be."

"I didn't know you had a sister."

"We hardly ever see her. She's getting her third master's degree."

"Wow. She must be really smart."

"No, she's just scared she won't find a job and that will displease my parents. She's been hiding out in Boston."

"And she won't come home, even with the divorce?"

"Debra's way of dealing with our parents is to avoid them completely, unless she needs money. Then she finds them real fast." We fell into a silence, having done plenty of talking. I could feel our relationship moving closer and closer to the ultimate commitment, the one that brings a man and a woman together for the rest of their lives. It was clear Jeffrey longed to leave Great Neck as much as I longed to leave Walnut. How much we would have in common, I thought, traveling the world, finding just the right tiny corner to call our home, living each day with joy and wonder and gratitude. I was about to point all this out to him, thereby speeding up the inevitable proposal, but he was glancing at his watch. "I guess we should take off pretty soon," he said. "I've got a family dinner to go to." He sat up, the curve of his back so strong and inviting I had to stop myself from sliding my hand beneath his shirt.

"Want me to come along?"

He seemed uncomfortable. "Next time."

"That would be great. I'd love to meet your relatives. Are they Jewish?"

"Some of them." The sun was beginning to drift toward the tall leafy trees in the distance, casting beautiful pink shadows on the park grounds. "Isn't the sky so beautiful this time of day?" I asked.

"It is," Jeffrey said without looking up. He helped me to my feet and I straightened my hair and buttoned my dress while he rolled up the blanket. I cuddled up beside him on the ride home, watching the sky grow pinker still as we traveled west on the Expressway, the radio tuned to my favorite station. "Should I drop you off at the laundromat?" he asked.

"Thanks, but not necessary," I said. When we arrived at Walnut I threw my arms around him for a hot kiss right in front of my building. "What are you doing tomorrow?" I cooed.

"Working. It's my last day."

"Let's go to the movies to celebrate," I said, my fingers boldly inching up his leg. "No one'll see us up there in the balcony. I can give you a little congratulations present in the dark."

"Mmm. Don't stop."

"So I'll see you tomorrow around seven?" I gently moved my hand to the inseam of his jeans. He moaned softly and pulled me toward him, sliding his hands under my short dress, pushing my panties down toward my knees. "Tomorrow," I whispered, reluctantly pulling away. Tomorrow would be a big day for sure, the day Jeffrey would ask me to be his bride, the day I would tell him, at last, about Stuie and the enormous mistake I almost made. I gave Jeffrey three little kisses and jumped out of the car, completely unaware that Iris Sinitsky was peeking through the gauzy curtains of her living room window.

Sunday,
August 15, 1971

"Marsh? We have to talk. You're gonna die." I wanted to shout it from the rooftops of Walnut Gardens that I, Rhona Gail Lipshitz, was utterly in love with the smartest, sweetest, sexiest man on Long Island, the man who would whisk me off to St. Louis in exactly one week. Soon I would be on a jet plane soaring high above the clouds, waving good-bye to all those I held dear, blowing kisses and wishing them well. But until Stuie had been told, only my two best friends would be privy to the secret. After all, it wasn't fair for Stuie to receive such potentially devastating news second-hand.

"Can I come over later?"

"Marsha, this is the most important thing that's ever happened to me."

"Okay. Give me fifteen minutes. I'm on the last chapter of my book and it's a good one."

"Read fast." I smiled at my own joke. Marsha was the fastest reader I'd ever seen, her eyes moving back and forth on the page so quickly it was a wonder she didn't hypnotize herself and start barking like a dog. Marsha carried a book wherever she went, and I wasn't surprised when she came over with a paperback novel in her hand. "You'll love this one," she said as she placed it on my dresser. "So tell me, what's going on?" I wiggled my bare ring finger and smiled. "Oh my God, you and Skully broke up. What about the bridesmaid dresses? I just had mine altered."

"We didn't break up. Not yet, anyway. But I have something to show you." I reached into my sock drawer and pulled Jeffrey's ID card from beneath the pile. I handed it to her and she looked at it, then turned it around as if searching for a clue.

"Who is he?"

"My boyfriend," I said proudly. "Pretty cute, don't you think?"

"I don't understand."

"Sit down. You want anything?"

"Yeah, I want you to tell me what you're talking about."

"Wait here and don't move." I raced into the kitchen which was only steps away as everything was in my parents' apartment and grabbed a large bottle of black cherry soda, a box of chocolate covered donuts and a large bag of peanut M&Ms. Arms full, I opened the bedroom door with a pinkie and closed it with my hip. Marsha was sitting on the bed in the same position I had left her in, staring at Jeffrey's picture. I dropped the goodies in front of her, took the laminated card out of her hand and returned it to the safety of the drawer, then tore into our snacks as we sat together on the bedspread. "You see this bed?" I asked her solemnly.

"Of course I see it. We're sitting on it."

I ignored the sarcasm and popped a handful of M&Ms into my mouth. "We made love on this bed. On Friday the thirteenth."

"Get out of here."

"He said it would be a lucky day and it was."

"You can't be serious."

"Marsha. Would I lie about something this important?"

"Who is he?" she asked again.

"His name's Jeffrey Stewart."

"I saw that on the card. He's a junior at Washington University in St. Louis, Missouri."

"Very observant. He'll be a senior in September."

"Where'd you meet him?"

I sighed. "He drives the ice cream truck." She started to interrupt but I held up a hand. "Just listen to me. He's the most amazing guy I've ever met and he's completely in love with me so don't even think about talking me out of it."

"When did you meet him?"

"Wednesday. But we've already been out three times since then, and each time was incredible. I feel like I've known him my whole life. We're both so open and honest with each other. I can tell him anything."

"Did you tell him about Skully?"

"That's not the point. The point is, we've already fallen in love and we actually did it on this bed, after he introduced me to his mother and his uncle. Not to mention his body." I stroked the pillow softly, remembering the evening in its full splendor. Marsha was counting her fingers.

"You did it with him two days after you met?"

"I just told you, it's like I've known him forever. If it weren't the absolute right and natural thing to do I wouldn't have done it."

"But you're engaged to Skully, and you've never even done it with *him*."

"Listen, Marsha, I didn't ask you to come over so you could give me a lecture."

"Ro, this is insane. You're marrying Skully a week from today and you made love with some ice cream man from Great Neck?"

"Pretty crazy, huh?"

"I thought you were saving it until you got married."

"And I did. I saved it for Jeffrey, and he's going to marry me. So technically I haven't broken any rules."

"When are you going to tell Skully?"

"Tomorrow morning."

"He's going to have a fit, you know that."

"I'll be gentle. It's not like I'm some horrible person who goes around hurting people on purpose."

"Why do I feel like I just entered the Twilight Zone?"

"Doo-doo-doo-doo, doo-doo-doo-doo," I sang, tickling her sides. She moved away. "It's not a game, Ro."

"I'm so happy today, Marsh, there's nothing you can do to put me in a bad mood."

"I just can't believe you've been seeing another guy and lying to both of them about the other." This wasn't what I had in mind. I had invited Marsha over to eat chocolate and look at Jeffrey's picture and hear about my future as Jeffrey's wife, not to give me a sermon about virtue as if she were Rabbi Marks on the eve of Yom Kippur. "The whole thing is just plain wrong."

"Excuse me, Eleanor Roosevelt. I'm sorry I can't live up to your code of ethics." I looked at her with annoyance. "I better get ready for tonight. Jeffrey and I have all kinds of plans to make."

"What kind of plans? You met him Wednesday. Today's Sunday."

"He's a serious guy, Marsh. He's older than us. He's graduating college in less than a year and then he wants to travel around the whole world."

"So what's that got to do with you?"

"Everything. His mother wants him to move back to New York but I'm going to help him follow his own dream, just like he's going to help me follow mine."

"He wants you to go with him?"

"He told me I'd love Europe, and he's already talking about our future. We were out at this park in Huntington yesterday and we talked for like six hours and he started saying when we're thirty or forty, what's it going to be like...as if we'd be married or something."

"Are you positive about this?"

"I'm not a moron, Marsh. I don't imagine things. He even talked about our children."

"Your children."

"That's right. Here, look at these." I pulled the love beads, hiding beneath my collar, toward her so she could get a closer look. "He bought them for me in the Village on Thursday night." She leaned in toward my neck and ran an index finger along them.

"Nice. But it's not exactly an engagement ring. Where's the one you're supposed to be wearing, by the way?"

I rubbed my bare finger self-consciously. "It's behind my radio. Don't worry, it's safe." Marsha shook her head disapprovingly. I preferred the sympathetic Marsha to this parental figure who was reaching into the box of donuts and breaking one in half. "Take the whole thing," I offered.

"I only want half," she said.

"I'm not a terrible person," I said quietly.

"So you're definitely not going to marry Skully."

"I can't marry him," I said, aware of the finality of the words leaving my mouth. "How can I marry Stuie when I'm moving to St. Louis with Jeffrey on the same day?"

There was a sad moment of silence, broken by the crisp sound of cellophane as Marsha reached for the other donut half. "Your parents are gonna die," she said softly. "And I don't even want to picture what Skully's parents are going to say."

I watched her pop the donut half into her mouth, looking me right in the eye as she chewed. We didn't say anything for a few minutes. "So don't you want to know what it's like to actually do it? That's one of the main reasons I wanted you to come over, you know."

"Okay. What's it like?" I couldn't tell if she really wanted to know or not. Marsha was funny that way. There was only one boy she'd been with in her whole life, a guy from Canarsie named Stanley Liebowitz who had gone to third base with her and never called her again. Between the rejection from Stanley and the persistent taunting by the Walnut boys, Marsha had had it with the opposite sex. If she weren't Jewish I would have suggested she join a nunnery instead of going to Albany in the fall, but then again, she probably wouldn't be allowed to bring her sexy novels to the nunnery.

"You really want to know?" I prodded, deciding I'd only tell her if she begged for it.

"Yeah. Go ahead." She brought the bottle of soda to her lips.

"Well, it's..." I sighed and grabbed the bottle from her hand, taking a mouthful for myself. "Thanks a lot, Marsha. I couldn't wait to tell you and now you're not even listening."

"I'm listening, Ro. Tell me."

I took a deep breath. "It's the most amazing thing in the whole world, especially when you really love the person you're doing it with. First he took all my clothes off one piece at a time, and th..."

"Poor Skully."

"What do you mean, 'poor Skully'? I thought you hated him?"

"I do, but that doesn't mean I can't feel sorry for him. He's going to be really upset, Ro. This is a huge big deal, breaking up with him a couple of days before the wedding."

"First of all, it's not a couple of days, it's almost a week, and second, it's not like he's going to die or anything. People get hurt all the time and then they get over it."

Marsha poured herself a huge handful of M&Ms and ate them one color at a time, starting with brown and ending with red. Although I respected her, I questioned the wisdom of choosing her as my confidante for this particular secret. I should've just gone to Rochelle who would've savored every sordid detail. "What time is he coming over?"

"Seven. Do you want to meet him?"

Marsha took one last swig of soda and stood up, brushed off her shorts and said she'd better get going, that her parents wanted her home to take care of her little brother. I thanked her for being there for me even though I was sort of mad at her, and walked her to the door. "I guess I'll see you later," she said.

"Seven-thirty, okay?"

"Fine." I hugged Marsha and she patted me lightly on the shoulder instead of giving me a real squeeze. I watched through the window as she walked down the stoop and cut across the playground to her building. It wasn't until I turned back toward my bed that I realized I had peeled the label from the soda bottle into a million tiny, sticky shreds that were now deeply imbedded in the crevices of the chenille bedspread.

SUNDAY, AUGUST 15, 1971

• • •

"Chelle?"

"Yeah?"

"It's me. I was wondering...you still have that lavender flowered dress? The sleeveless one with the scoop neck?"

"I think so. Why, you and Skully going out tonight?"

"Not exactly."

"Then what's it for?" At Walnut Gardens, privacy was unheard of.

"Can you keep a secret? I mean a really, really big secret."

"No one does it better than me," she said with growing interest.

"I'm coming over." I threw on a pair of Keds, grabbed Jeffrey's ID and ran all the way to Rochelle's apartment, the second building on the left around the corner across from the laundry room. I loved going to Rochelle's apartment. When she was twelve she installed a deadbolt on her bedroom door and no one in her family had seen the inside of her room ever since. She had magazines with naked men and all kinds of forbidden books and even a vibrating massager right in plain sight. Rochelle answered the front door with the lavender flowered dress in her hand.

"Look what I found in the back of my closet." She sniffed it briefly. "I think it needs to be washed. It smells like strawberry oil."

Rochelle's mother Shirley was in the kitchen making a chicken, a rarity for her. The radio was on and she was singing along with Perry Como, "Catch a falling star and put it in your pocket..." Shirley ignored me as I walked past the kitchen, following her daughter and the lavender dress into the bedroom.

"Can I try it on?" I asked.

She held the dress over her head and smiled mischievously. "Only if you tell me why you need it." Rochelle was the girl I'd always wanted to be. She knew how to get a boy excited in a way that seemed effortless. Perhaps it was her trademark burgundy Mary Quant lipstick or the fringed suede Indian jacket or the red platform wedgies but whatever it was, Rochelle had style like no one else and the guys went crazy for it, especially her gorgeous boyfriend Sal.

Shopping was Rochelle's favorite pastime and she was never afraid to take the subway all by herself to Fifth Avenue and browse through the junior department at Lord and Taylor or B. Altman or Bergdorf's. It was pretty obvious she stole most of her wardrobe because there was no way her father could've afforded so much great stuff on a truck driver's salary. Even with her penchant for kleptomania I envied her, and I looked forward to knocking Jeffrey dead in Rochelle's slinky little dress that smelled just like her.

She dead bolted the door while I stripped down to my underwear. I playfully grabbed the dress from her outstretched hand and slipped it over my head. It was short and tight just the way I wanted, and the slight trace of strawberry oil made it even sexier. "It looks great on you," she said. "So tell me everything."

"You have to swear on your mother's life you'll never tell a soul."

"I swear."

"And on your grandfather's grave."

"I swear. Come on, Ro..."

"Not even Sal."

"Why would I tell Sal? He doesn't care about this kind of stuff."

"Swear to me you won't tell him."

She sighed. "I swear I won't tell Sal."

"Okay." I sat on the bed in her short dress, milking the moment for all its dramatic effect, while Rochelle watched me with wide brown eyes.

I picked up my shorts that were lying on the floor and pulled the ID card from the pocket. Without saying a word I handed it to her, and she took it greedily, her brown eyes all over it. "He's adorable. Who is he?"

"The man I'm going to marry. I'm completely in love with him, Chelle."

She swooped me up in a tight hug. "Thank God you're finally getting rid of that asshole. I'm so happy for you."

"Yeah, but Stuie's gonna freak when he finds out." I couldn't believe it. I was turning into Marsha Kotner.

"Screw Stuie. I always knew you'd do a lot better than that little schmuck." She looked at the card again. "Jeffrey Stewart. He lives in St. Louis?"

"Only during school. Otherwise he lives in Great Neck."

"So he's adorable *and* rich. Nice combination."

"But even more important, he's sweet and he's brilliant. Seriously, he's like no one we've ever known. He wants to live in Europe, and he wants it so much he's willing to go up against his parents who want him to be a la..."

"...Let's get to the important stuff. Have you guys done it yet?"

God, I love her. "Yeah. Friday night. In my room. Chelle, you can't tell anybody. Not even Sal. At least not until I break the news to Stuie. I have a feeling he's going to have a total fit."

But Rochelle didn't hear a word I was saying. She was screaming and clapping her hands so loudly her mother called from the kitchen, "Rochelle? Everything okay in there?"

"Fine, ma," Rochelle called back. She turned to me, her eyes glowing. "Welcome to the club."

"Thanks."

"I want every single detail. Don't leave out one thing or you're dead meat, Rhona."

"Rhona? All of a sudden I'm Rhona?"

She plopped on the bed and I spilled the story, down to the way he undressed me and kissed me and pulled me on top of him under the bedspread. "How big was it?" Rochelle asked, and I smiled, adoring her for her delicious candor and predictability.

"Bigger than Stuie's," I said, and we broke into giggles, stifling the sound with a pillow.

"I'm proud of you, Ro."

"For what?"

"For breaking up with Stuie. Most people wouldn't be brave enough to call off their wedding a week in advance."

I sobered. "Do you think I'm a terrible person, hurting Stuie like this so close to the wedding?"

"He'll get over it."

"Not necessarily. Sometimes when people get really hurt they carry it around with them for the rest of their lives."

"Do you love Jeffrey?"

"Of course I do. But that doesn't mean I have the right to hurt Stuie. What if he ends up lonely and depressed or even suicidal because of me?"

"If you really love Jeffrey there's only one thing to do." She jumped up and rooted through the second drawer of her dresser. "I have a little mazel tov present for you," she said as she pulled out a pair of crotchless black lace panties and waved them near my face. "You like?"

"You don't actually *wear* those things?"

"Oh, yes I do. They drive Sal absolutely crazy." She put her hand through the open middle. "See? You don't even have to take them off. They're perfect when your boyfriend's so hot he can't wait even one more minute."

"I don't know, Chelle. They're not exactly me."

"Sure they are. Just make sure I get them back by the weekend."

"I don't think Jeffrey's that kind of guy."

"He's a guy, isn't he?"

"Yeah, but he goes to college."

"So? People in college don't like sex as much as we do?"

"It just seems wrong, wearing those things before I even tell Stuie."

"If you're in love with Jeffrey you owe it to him to wear sexy underwear every single time. At least that's how it works in *my* book, honey." She pressed the panties into my hand. "Stop worrying already and have a little fun. Where are you going tonight, by the way?"

"The movies."

"Perfect place to fool around. Make sure you sit off to the side in the last two seats, way in the back. Get a big thing of popcorn so you can hide behind it just in case the ushers come by with those flashlights. If there's anything else you need to know, call me from the lobby. I'll come over and give a demonstration."

"Very funny." I bent down to grab the clothes I had been wearing earlier, making sure the ID was in the pocket of my shorts. "I'd better get home and take a shower before Jeffrey comes over."

"I seriously have to meet him," Rochelle said as we walked to the door, her mother peeling carrots at the sink, singing, "Or would you like to swing on a star, carry moonbeams home in a jar..."

I hesitated. "Maybe tomorrow."

"What's wrong with tonight?"

"I don't want to bombard the poor guy with all my friends at one time and Marsha's meeting him tonight."

"Why'd you invite *her*?"

"I didn't. She asked."

"So why can't we both meet him?" I hesitated again, wondering why I'd confided in Rochelle when I knew she couldn't be trusted. She had a mouth the size of the Tri-state area and would tell anyone who cared to listen about my personal business. "Come on, Ro," she pleaded. "Don't keep such a cutie all to yourself. Share the wealth, honey." I turned away so she wouldn't see my ambivalence. Not only was Rochelle liable to spill the beans all over Walnut, she was also a bit of a predator and went after what she liked without hesitation. What if Jeffrey liked her better? I couldn't take that chance, not when everything was going so smoothly and I was this close to a marriage proposal. I had to be careful about exposing him to potential competition, at least until our engagement was secured. No, I decided, she definitely shouldn't meet him tonight. "What time should I come over?" Rochelle asked.

"Seven-thirty," I sighed.

"I'll be there." She looked pensive. "I wonder what I should wear. Something fun and revealing, don't you think?"

She raised an eyebrow and closed the front door. As I turned the corner and walked toward my building I saw Iris leading her almost-blind dog to the fire hydrant. I tried to sneak past but it was too late. She looked up with narrowed eyes as I approached in the short, tight dress. "Nice dress," she said.

"It's Rochelle Davis's," I answered as calmly as I could.

"I thought so. Where are you and Skully going, out to eat?"

"That's exactly where we're going," I said as I ran up the stoop to my apartment. "See ya later." I closed the door and let out a long breath to cleanse myself from the close call. It was five-forty, allowing me just over an hour to get ready before Jeffrey would arrive to meet Marsha and Rochelle, the prude and the slut, each one, I decided, representing a different side of me.

I carefully pulled the dress over my head and realized Rochelle was right, I should just stop worrying and get on with my life. In the morning I would find the right words to tell Stuie before introducing Jeffrey to my parents. A formal engagement would be necessary in order for them to accept my going off to Missouri with a man they hardly knew. The wedding could take place over Christmas vacation, or maybe spring break, allowing us a full week in New York without Jeffrey missing class. I would even consider a summer wedding if that made things easier, as long as the plans got underway immediately and both families understood it was a done deal.

As I climbed into the shower I wondered if Rochelle and Marsha would be able to use their just-altered bridesmaid dresses at Jeffrey's and my wedding. Probably not. Knowing how intrusive Dr. Stewart was, she'd want a say in the color scheme, which was just fine with me, and she'd no doubt want to go with a more expensive bridesmaid's gown, maybe a peach-colored silk with a little more lace at the throat and a bow in the back. I wondered if she would allow Rabbi Marks to perform the ceremony. Hopefully she would understand his importance to my family. Or maybe we could just elope near the University, thus avoiding the subject of religion altogether. I made a mental note to suggest it to Jeffrey after the movie. I toweled off, shaved my legs right up to my thighs and covered my entire body in Yardley lilac lotion to go with the lavender dress. I admired myself in the mirror, pleased with the outcome. It was the best I'd ever looked and I couldn't wait for Jeffrey to take me in his arms and revel in the scent of my dress and my skin and my hair. At six-thirty my mother knocked on my door. "We're going for Italian in Flushing," she said. "You want to come?"

"No thanks, ma."

"You sure? This is the place with that special spaghetti sauce and the warm bread."

SUNDAY, AUGUST 15, 1971

"I'm not hungry, ma. I'll get something at the deli later with Rochelle."

"You sure?"

"Yes, positive." I lay down on the bed and waited for seven o'clock, picturing Jeffrey and me on a California beach on a moonlit night. There'd be a soft breeze and we'd be dressed in white. We'd laugh and kiss and listen to the sound of the pounding surf. I closed my eyes and drifted away on the luscious fantasy, thousands of miles from the Walnut Garden Apartments. I was floating with Jeffrey on a gossamer blanket high above the ocean, floating so peacefully, cushioned by pungent sea air. I glanced at the clock radio near my bed and jumped up suddenly, realizing I had been lulled into a gentle sleep. It was just after seven, with dusk looming large. I looked nervously through the Venetian blinds but the Coupe de Ville was nowhere to be seen. It wasn't like Jeffrey to be late, but I didn't make too much of it as I went into the bathroom and brushed my teeth for the fifth time that day and re-applied my lip-gloss.

Seven-twenty. No sign of Jeffrey. I paced the empty apartment, stopping in front of the air conditioner in my parents' bedroom for a blast of cold air. Missing the movie wasn't the worst thing in the world. It would give us time to talk, and we had plenty to talk about. We had to make reservations right away for my trip to St. Louis on Sunday. Having never flown before, I'd ask Jeffrey if I could sit by the window just in case I got a little queasy, which sometimes happened to me on long car trips and could easily occur on the plane, too. After the travel details were out of the way Jeffrey would probably propose, and knowing Jeffrey as well as I did, he'd follow it with some special alone time in my bedroom. It would be a big night, followed by an equally big day on Monday. My mother and I would need to call the caterer and the Rabbi and the photographer and all our guests to let them know the wedding was off. Selma would be furious but I wouldn't care, I'd be packing my bags and whistling a happy tune.

At seven-thirty-two the doorbell rang. I flung the door wide open to Marsha Kotner, who had put on some lip-gloss herself and was standing there with an expectant smile. "Sorry I'm late. Is he here yet?" she whispered, looking around the living room from the front door.

"Any minute," I said as she made herself comfortable on the plastic-covered velveteen couch. "It's his last day of work."

"You look really pretty," she said.

"Thanks, Marsh."

Within seconds there was another knock. I held my breath and opened the door to Rochelle, who looked luscious and voluptuous in a hot pink tube top with short-shorts and four-inch platform wedgies, her toenails painted the same neon shade as her top. She glanced around the room and joined Marsha on the couch. "He's not here yet, huh?" she asked as the plastic slipcovers sighed beneath her.

"Not yet," I said. They sat quietly on the couch like two ladies in waiting, these two friends of mine with nothing in common, having said less than five words to each other their whole lives. Marsha saw Rochelle as an ignorant tramp; Rochelle saw Marsha as a bookworm who wouldn't know a good time if it came up and slapped her in the face. Still, they were cordial to each other, and tonight they had a lot in common. Both of them were dying of curiosity, wanting to meet the boy from Great Neck who was going to provide me with a life of happiness as Mrs. Dr. Jeffrey Stewart, educator of European History.

I moved nervously from one mirror to the other while they assured me I looked wonderful. I smiled and laughed and thanked them for wanting to meet my true love. "If he ever shows up," Rochelle snorted.

At seven-forty five a wave of panic rushed through me. "Where is he?" I asked fearfully. "He's never late. If anything, he's always early."

"Maybe the ice cream truck broke down," Marsha offered.

"What ice cream truck?" Rochelle asked. "You never said anything about ice cream."

"His summer job," I said. "Never mind. It's not important."

"Why don't you call him?" Rochelle asked.

"I don't know his number."

"Are you kidding? You're planning to marry the guy and you don't even have his phone number?"

"I didn't need it, Chelle. He had mine."

"Call information," Marsha suggested, always the practical one.

"Do you think I should? What if he's still working?"

"Call him," they said at the same time, smiling at each other. I went to the kitchen phone and dialed information. There was a pause. "In Great Neck," I said to the operator. "The name is Stewart. George William Stewart. He's a judge." Marsha raised an eyebrow. I waited, tapping a pencil against the kitchen wall while the operator looked for the number. Marsha and Rochelle never took their eyes off me. Finally, the operator came back on the line. "That's it, on Oak Street." I wrote quickly, thanked her profusely, and hung up.

I looked at the scrawled number with trepidation. "Maybe we should give him another five minutes," I said. "You never know with traffic."

Rochelle jumped up from the couch and went to the living room window. "Call him right now," she ordered. "He's almost an hour late."

"I think Rochelle's right. You should call him," Marsha said. I couldn't tell if they were hungry for drama or if they actually had my best interests in mind.

"Are you sure?" I asked.

"Yes," they said together and this time started to giggle.

Rochelle looked out the Venetian blinds in both directions. "I don't see anybody," she said. "Pick up the phone already. What if he's lying somewhere in a ditch?"

"God forbid, Chelle." I took a breath and dialed the area code, 516, then the prefix, Hunter 7. Exhaling slowly, I dialed the last four digits and waited while the phone connected. One ring. I was starting to sweat. Two rings. My mouth was dry. Three rings, and a woman's voice answered.

"Hello?"

"Dr. Stewart?"

"Yes?"

"This is Rhona Lipshitz. I'm a friend of Jeffrey's? I met you Friday night...?"

"Oh, yes." Her tone was steely.

"Um...is Jeffrey home?"

"Yes, he's right here."

"Oh." I paused. "Can I talk to him?"

"Just a minute."

There was another pause under which I could hear muffled, angry voices, and then Jeffrey came to the phone. "Hello?"

"Jeffrey? It's me. Ro."

"Hi." His voice was cold and distant, like the alien who took over human bodies in The Day Mars Invaded The Earth.

"It's eight o'clock. I thought we were going to the movies tonight. I mean, that's what you said."

"Listen, Ro, I can't come over. I'm really sorry."

"That's okay. We can do it tomorrow. Just make sure you get here early so we can go over all the plans for next wee..."

"...You don't understand. I can't come over at all." There was a brief silence. "I leave for school on Sunday and I have all kinds of stuff to do."

I struggled to remain upbeat. "Would you rather just meet me on campus?"

"What?"

"I'll come down in a couple of weeks, once you're settled in. I know I've never flown before but I'm a big girl, I can do it."

"What are you talking about?"

My head began to spin. "I'm going back to St. Louis with you, aren't I?"

He laughed briefly out of embarrassment. "You're joking, right?" A whoosh of blood rushed to my brain, making the kitchen spin in crazy circles. "Hang on a second." There were more muffled, impatient voices and then he was back. "Listen, I have to hang up."

"Wait. When am I going to see you, Jeffrey?"

"Come on, Ro. Don't do this." He sounded anxious. "You're a nice girl and we had a fun couple of days, but that's all it was. You knew that."

"No." My voice was hoarse, barely audible.

"Take care of yourself, okay? And good luck with whatever you do next year." And then he was gone.

"No," I said softly, staring at the receiver.

"What happened?" Marsha asked.

I put a hand to my stomach and breathed deeply, desperate for oxygen. Rochelle was in the kitchen now, an arm around me. Marsha jumped up to join her and together we leaned against the refrigerator, all of us holding onto each other. I began to cry, then to sob, then to heave, mascara dripping down my cheeks. Marsha ran to the bathroom and grabbed some toilet paper, dabbing at my face with gentle fingers.

"Shhh," she said comfortingly. "It's okay."

"No, it's not," I sobbed. "Don't tell me it's okay when it's not. Okay?"

"Let's sit down," Rochelle said. We moved in unison to the couch and sat down as one, me in the middle, holding tight to Rochelle's hand as Marsha continued to dry my tears. "I'm so glad we came over."

"She never could have handled this without us," Marsha agreed.

I continued to cry, the pain gnawing into every part of my body with sharp teeth. "You want to tell us what happened?" Rochelle finally asked. I closed my eyes, hoping the nightmare would disappear. But the nightmare was here to stay.

"First his mother got on," I sobbed, my chest heaving.

"What'd she say?" Marsha asked softly, like a nurse in a tuberculosis ward trying to comfort a dying patient.

"She covered the receiver and talked to him and then Jeffrey got on the phone and said he's really sorry but he can't see me anymore because he's going back to school."

"What an asshole," Rochelle said.

"Oh God," Marsha said, covering her eyes with her hand.

"It gets worse."

"Worse? How can it get worse than that?" Marsha was no stranger to rejection, and I was grateful for her empathy.

"He laughed at me. He actually *laughed* at me."

"Oh, God," Marsha said again.

"Then his mother started talking to him and he wished me luck next year, after we spent the whole day yesterday planning our future."

"You want to go out for a while?" Rochelle asked. "We can go over to the bowling alley or something."

The tears were coming fast. "...He's leaving without me after I had sex with him and everything." I looked at them with terror in my eyes. "I let him go all the way. What if Stuie finds out?"

"Let's get you into bed," Marsha said soothingly.

"He'll kill me. So will his father. So will *my* father. The whole neighborhood will know what I did. I'll be like Hester Prynne, walking around with a big 'A' on my forehead."

"It was her chest," Marsha said gently.

"Who cares?" I shot back. I looked into their faces. "Guys, don't leave me. Please."

"We're staying right here, all night," Rochelle said.

"I've got to be home by ten," Marsha apologized. "But Rochelle will sleep over. Right?"

"You know I will." They walked me to my room, leading me as if I were a zombie, easily pulling the tight dress over my head. Marsha gasped when she saw the crotchless panties. "They're on loan, like a library book," Rochelle said, opening my dresser and removing a soft cotton nightgown.

Marsha pulled back the bedspread and helped me get under the covers. "Do you want some water?" she asked.

"Yes, please."

She went into the kitchen and came back with a tumbler while Rochelle tucked me in. I grasped the love beads around my neck, proof that Jeffrey had actually existed. "You need to sleep," Marsha said. "You've had a major shock."

"Where are you going?" I asked.

"We're right here," Rochelle said, sitting on the edge of the bed near my feet. "Nobody's leaving you." She stroked my calves over the covers and looked helplessly at Marsha, not quite sure how to comfort me. I sat up suddenly.

SUNDAY, AUGUST 15, 1971

"The ID," I said. "I need it. It's in the second drawer under my socks." Marsha rushed to the dresser, found the laminated card and placed it in my trembling hand. Jeffrey's face was still smiling, the dimples evident even in the tiny picture way off in the corner. I began to weep softly as I held it to my breast. We sat in silence, the three of us and the picture, until the sound of a pebble hitting the window made us jump.

"Oh, no, it's Stuie," I whispered, squeezing my eyes shut.

"Let me handle this," Rochelle said. She peered through a slat in the Venetian blind and came face to face with Stuie and Buffa.

"Where's Ro?" Stuie asked.

"Sleeping."

"It's not even eight-thirty."

"She's not well."

"What's the matter with her? This is the second time this week. Lemme see her."

I shook my head furiously to Rochelle, who got the message loud and clear. "Can't do it," she said through the slat. "She's in bed and she's really sick."

"Tell him it's the summer flu," I coached.

"It's the summer flu, the worst case they've ever seen."

Buffa pulled Stuie by the tee shirt. "Come on, Skully, we gotta go."

Stuie reluctantly complied. "Tell her to feel better and I'll see her tomorrow."

"Gotcha," Rochelle said, replacing the slat to its original position. My face was buried in the pillow and I was breathing deeply. "Don't smother yourself," she said with alarm.

"I'm checking for Jeffrey's smell," I said into the pillowcase. I looked up, terror in my eyes. "I can't smell him anymore, Chelle. It's gone."

She stroked my hair with gentle fingers and my puffy eyes began to close. When I woke up she and Marsha were sitting cross-legged on the shag carpet playing gin rummy. It was pitch dark outside. "What time is it?" I yawned.

"Nine forty-five," Marsha said. "I've got to leave in a couple of minutes."

"Are my parents home?"

"Yeah, they watched TV for a while, then your mother came in and said they were going to bed."

"Didn't she want to know why I was sleeping?"

"I told her you had the worst menstrual cramps in the history of menstruation," Rochelle said. I sat up and drank some water, then remembered why I was in bed in the first place and started to cry all over again. Never had I known such profound sadness, my dreams shattered by one miserable phone call.

"Poor Ro," Marsha said sympathetically, leaning over to kiss my forehead. "I'll call you first thing in the morning." She walked toward the bedroom door. "You'll stay with her, won't you, Rochelle?"

"All night," Rochelle assured her with a smile. Marsha nodded.

"Good night," she said softly, closing the door behind her. When she was gone, Rochelle looked at me and sighed.

"Sure you don't want to go out? We can have Sal pick us up."

"I don't want to see anybody."

She sat on the bed and draped an arm across my legs. "Then what do you want to do?"

"I want to talk about Jeffrey."

"Go ahead, if it makes you feel better." So I relived every moment of the past three days, van Gogh and Matisse, the Guggenheim and Lombardo's Italian Cafe, the head shop in the Village, the intense make-out sessions in the front seat of the Cadillac, Jeffrey and his uncle and the leather couches in the air-conditioned library, Josh with all his affectations and his skinny girlfriend Tracey and the deserted park and how we talked about Aristotle and Debra and his father the Judge and his mother the Cardiologist, who would surely cut my heart right out of my body just as quickly as she'd cut off her son's finances. It was pretty clear Jeffrey wasn't about to let go of that precious inheritance for anybody, not even me.

"How much you want to bet he doesn't become an educator?" I asked bitterly. "I'll bet you five bucks he goes to law school."

Rochelle glanced at her watch. "Can I use your phone?"

"Yeah, sure."

SUNDAY, AUGUST 15, 1971

She lifted the receiver, dialed a number and waited. A seductive smile came to her full lips. "Hi baby," she said. There was a pause. She giggled. "Me, too." Another pause, and then, "I wish. But I have to sleep over Ro's tonight." She listened for a minute and then said softly, "Tomorrow, baby, all day. I promise." Covering the receiver with her hand, she asked, "Ro? Can Sal call here later?"

I nodded. "You can call anytime," she said into the receiver, then giggled again. "Stop it, Sal. You're making me horny." She kissed the phone and hung up, finally noticing my anguished face. "I had to call him, Ro. He was waiting for me." She patted my foot. "I'm sorry, honey."

"I can't believe I went all the way with him. Why was I so stupid?"

"Love is never stupid."

"What's it like?" I asked her.

"What?"

"Loving a guy who loves you back."

She thought about it. "With Sal I never really know if he loves me or not."

"What do you mean? You've been together since tenth grade."

"Yeah, meanwhile he took Denise Silver behind the electrical towers last week."

I sat up quickly. "No. How come you didn't tell me?"

"It's not exactly something I wanted to advertise."

"But I tell you everything."

"So?"

"So how could you keep it from me that Sal took the world's biggest prude behind the towers?" Compared to Denise Silver, Marsha was a streetwalker on Seventh Avenue.

"Do you want to hear what happened or fight about why I didn't tell you?"

"I'm sorry. What happened?"

"You sure you're up to this?"

"I really want to know, Chelle."

She sighed. "On Tuesday we made love three times and Sal was so turned on he wanted to do it again so we took a bath."

"Why's that? To cool off?"

Rochelle smiled at the memory. "He loves to do it in the water. He thinks it's exotic."

"Wow." One thing about Rochelle Davis, she was always a fascinating source of important information.

"So we're in the tub with tons of bubbles, having a really great time when he says he's going home for band practice but first he has to stop by the schoolyard."

"Without you?" Sal DiMatelli would never lower himself to hang out at the schoolyard unless Rochelle was at his side.

"He said he wanted to cop a few joints for the ride, but it turns out he'd seen Denise last time we were there and he wanted to put the moves on her. So he buys a couple of joints just to make it look good, then he asks her to take a walk."

"And she went?"

"Yep."

"But she's never been touched by human hands."

"She said yes to Sal."

"How do you know all this?"

"I'll get to that in a second. So he gets her behind the towers and he starts making out with her and she's so upset...you're not going to believe this."

"What?"

"She throws up all over the place."

"Get out of here."

"Swear to God."

"He told you this?"

"No, she did."

"Denise told you she was making out with your boyfriend?"

"Would you believe it? She called me the next day crying hysterically and saying she was sorry, she never expected him to put the moves on her like that."

"What did she think was gonna happen?"

"Exactly. She's so stupid. She thought they were just going for a walk. Or so she says."

"Why Denise? I don't get it."

SUNDAY, AUGUST 15, 1971

"She's a *virgin*." She said the word with bitterness. "I guess that appeals to him. Who the hell knows?" We sat quietly for a moment, her anger hanging in the air. "When I saw him on Thursday I asked him about it."

"And what'd he say?"

"He started crying and he told me he loved me and he'd never let anyone come on to him again."

"But Denise never came on to anyone in her life."

"What are you saying, that Sal lied to me?"

"It kind of sounds that way, Chelle."

"Look. Sal and I are back and everything's fine and that's all that matters. Jeez, it's like you want me and Sal to break up just because *you* got dumped."

I gasped, wounded by her sudden meanness. "Thanks a lot, Chelle. I really needed that tonight."

"I'm sorry, Ro, but you're getting on Sal's case just because misery loves company."

"That's not true."

"Yes, it is."

"No, it's not."

We sat in uncomfortable silence for a long time. I yawned, emotionally drained from the highs and lows of the day. Rochelle caught my yawn and curled up next to me in the twin bed, pulling the bedspread up to her ears. "I'm wiped out," she said.

"Me, too."

"What are you doing tomorrow?" she asked quietly as she moved toward sleep.

"Pretending today never happened. What about you?"

"I'm going to spend the whole day in bed." I could hear the smile in her voice.

"Alone?"

"Uh uh." She yawned and drifted off to sleep, her arms wrapped around my waist. I tried not to hate her for loving a man who loved her back, when all I had I had was a fiancé I didn't want and a wedding that was six days away.

97

Monday,
August 16, 1971

An urgent pounding on the door sent me springing from my bed with a racing heart. *Jeffrey, you came back.* I ran to the living room, swung open the door and nearly leapt into the arms of a sweaty deliveryman.

"Sign here," he said, handing me a clipboard, before reaching down for the large cardboard box at his feet.

"Thank you," I said glumly, not even trying to hide my despair. I carried the carton to the couch and tore it open. When I saw a smaller box wrapped in shiny white paper with a bright yellow ribbon, I grew hopeful. *Jeffrey, my darling, you do want me.* Unwrapping the box carefully with trembling fingers, I wondered what kind of present Jeffrey had sent to make up for his uncharacteristic behavior the night before. Perhaps it was another necklace, this one made of diamonds, or a ring or a watch or a pin. I tore open the tissue paper and uncovered some kind of crystal *thing* with a silver lid and a tiny spoon. I opened the card that was tucked inside. 'Congratulations Mr. and Mrs. Weiner, from everyone at Bridger's

Petites.' Mr. and Mrs. Weiner! I looked at the words as if they were my own obituary. Perhaps my father would be pleased that the secretaries at the factory had sent a gift, but for me it was nothing more than a cruel joke. "I am *not* Mrs. Weiner," I said, throwing the unidentifiable thing onto the couch.

I shuffled back to the bedroom and shook the immobile body hidden under my blanket. "I'm sleeping," it moaned.

"Come on, Chelle, wake up."

"Ow. Leave me alone."

"I made a decision. I need you."

"What time is it?"

I strained to look at the clock. "Nine thirty. Almost. It's five after nine."

"It's too early to need me. Need me at twelve."

"But I need you *now*." I pulled the covers from her face. Even in the morning she was pretty, the faint traces of lipstick still on her mouth.

"Okay, I'm here. I'm awake," she yawned, a little more sympathetic now that her eyes were opening. "What's the big decision?"

"I'm seeing Jeffrey today."

"Where?"

"His house."

"He called?"

"No. But I'm going over there, anyway."

Rochelle rubbed her eyes with both hands. "I'm starving. What's there to eat?"

"We've got powdered donuts. You think I'm making a mistake?"

"You know I do."

"Can I wear your purple dress?" I scanned the room and found it crumpled on the floor, under the leg of my desk chair. "Uh oh," I said as I dislodged it. "Maybe I should take it down to Sunny's and wash it." I paused. "Should I be doing this, Chelle?"

"You know you shouldn't."

MONDAY, AUGUST 16, 1971

• • •

Mondays were always hectic at Sunny's Laundromat. It was nearly one o'clock by the time I wiggled into the tight purple dress, still warm from the dryer, in the tiny bathroom at the back of the storefront. You're doing the right thing, I told myself firmly as I threw my old sundress into my shoulder bag and set out for the bus stop. My pink high-heeled pumps were already beginning to chafe my bare ankles and pinch my toes. *Nice going, moron. Why couldn't you have picked a pair of flat sandals?*

Finally, after half an hour in the hot sun, the MTA bus pulled to a noisy stop. "Do you go to Great Neck?" I called from the curb, squinting up into the driver's dour face.

"Not all the way. I'll give you a transfer for Little Neck Parkway, then you gotta switch to the Long Island bus at Northern."

"Three buses?" I asked in disbelief. "Isn't there a faster way?"

"Call a cab," he said without the trace of a smile.

I paid the fare, received a transfer, and lowered myself into a seat up front, trying not to expose my underpants beneath Rochelle's short dress. The bus smelled of days-old sweat, despite the humid breeze blowing through the open windows. I could see rings of moisture under the driver's armpits as he grasped the large horizontal wheel in his hands. We lurched forward and began our trek eastward, stopping at almost every corner along the way.

Playing with the love beads around my neck, I closed my eyes and pictured myself on Jeffrey's doorstep. I would ring the brass bell and he'd open the door. "What are you doing here?" he'd ask, not quite sure what to make of my unexpected visit. "Looking for you, big boy," I'd say with a sexy pout. "Can I come in?" Without waiting for a response, I'd playfully push him out of my way and sashay into the air-conditioned entranceway. "It's nice and cool in here," I'd say, slipping off my shoes. With a mysterious grin, I'd beckon him upstairs, and he'd follow obediently. Inside his room, I'd close the door and lean against it, smiling wickedly, my arms folded across my chest. I'd nod toward the bed and he'd comply. We'd look at each other wordlessly for a minute, then he'd smile that gorgeous, big smile and pull me down beside him. "Jesus, Ro, what was I thinking," he'd gush into my hair. "I must've been crazy to let you go."

And then we'd make love all afternoon in his warm bed that would smell clean and boyish, just like him. We'd be like Rochelle and Sal, napping, waking, napping and waking some more. He'd sneak away to the kitchen and come back minutes later with a couple of sandwiches, rare roast beef with plenty of mustard on rye, maybe a little potato salad or a knish on the side. I'd ask him everything I needed to know while we ate our sandwiches, and he'd thank me for being bold enough to knock on his door, he'd praise me for being woman enough to make the first move. And he'd tell me how much he loved me.

After twenty minutes of lurching and stopping, the bus driver pulled open the door. "Over there," he said, pointing to the stop across the street. "You'll want to get off at Northern Blvd."

I thanked him and descended the steps with care. It was after two, with the sun as strong as ever. The freshly washed dress was sticking to my back, and I'd lost all feeling in my toes. When the northbound bus pulled in, I handed the driver my transfer and took a seat up front. *I hope we have time for that sandwich.* I loved rare roast beef on rye with mustard.

When we arrived at my stop at two fifty-one, I was queasy from the heat and the jerky motion of the bus. I crossed the street and waited for the eastbound bus, which was nowhere in sight. By now I, too, had rings of sweat under my arms. It must have been in the high nineties with even higher humidity, the dreaded dog days of August in New York. At three-fourteen the Long Island bus crawled down the street. Weary, I deposited my coins and plopped into a seat. When the bus pulled to a stop on Middle Neck Road in Great Neck, it was three forty-six. I wondered if it would be polite to take a shower before going upstairs to Jeffrey's room.

I staggered off the bus and glanced at the unfamiliar surroundings as I walked toward the residential area where Jeffrey lived, my shoulder bag heavy, my feet on fire. I walked block after block in search of Oak Street, passing Redwood, Pine and Ash. A twinge of panic began to form in my stomach as I looked for a pedestrian who might help me out. Finally, a woman with large round sunglasses opened the door of the Oldsmobile in her driveway. "Excuse me," I said in my most un-Queens-like voice, "I'm looking for Oak Street, please."

"Three blocks east, then make a right," she said, glancing at my outfit with disdain.

I thanked her and waited until she drove away, then I leaned against a tree to remove my pumps. Hampered by the prickly concrete beneath my bare feet, I plodded along, gazing into bay windows and shaded courtyards and open porticos, wondering about the people who lived in each enormous house. Why wasn't anybody hanging their wash out the window or playing mah jongg on their front lawn? Why do rich people behave so differently, I wanted to know. Who taught them to speak quietly instead of shouting from room to room? How did they know to pour milk into a glass, and not drink it straight from the container? I tried to picture Sadie or Millie or Gertie or my own parents living in one of those fine homes. I tried to imagine them playing the piano or reading a book. But instead of the strains of lovely music, all I could imagine were the blare of game shows at the highest volume, and the characteristic sounds of never-ending chaos.

I gasped slightly as I turned the corner and recognized the impossibly beautiful Tudor estate on its little grassy knoll halfway down the block on the other side of the street. I put my shoes back on, although my feet screamed in protest, and began my trek toward the Stewart home, one painful step at a time.

As I crept up the brick walkway toward the front door, I could swear I heard the music from *Psycho*, those distinctive eerie strings forshadowing inevitable doom. I stopped suddenly, unable to take another step. Somehow Jeffrey's house didn't seem so beautiful anymore. It was beginning to look like that awful old mansion up on the hill, the place where Norman Bates kept the skeleton of his beloved mother. You're being stupid, I thought as I walked up to the porch and reached for the doorbell.

I closed my eyes and whispered the only prayer I could think of at the moment, the Hermotzie, which my father recited over the bread before slicing it. "Amen," I said as I hit the doorbell. I held my breath and waited. Nothing, no footsteps on the polished hardwood floors within, no voice calling, "I'm coming." I pushed the bell again, harder this time, holding my finger so fiercely on the button that the skin around the nail turned white. Still no answer. I tried a third time, an even longer ring. Again, nothing. I banged on the big mahogany door with the brass knocker. "Jeffrey! Jeffrey!" I was using my loudest voice. Finally, I heard the clacking of Matisse's manicured nails, and then an angry-looking Dr. Stewart turned the deadbolt and opened the door. I wondered if she had had a bad day.

"What is go…?" She stopped mid-word. *Maybe she doesn't recognize me.*

"Hi, Dr. Stewart, I'm Rhona Lipshitz."

"I know who you are. What do you want?" She was wearing the same apricot dressing gown that she wore Friday night. Funny, I expected her to be in a different ensemble.

"Is Jeffrey home?" I tried to look beyond her into the grand foyer, but she intentionally held the door against her back. Even Matisse was having a difficult time poking his long snout through the narrow space.

"No, he's not. He's out with friends."

My heart dropped down to my squished toes. How could he not be there, after I'd taken three buses to see him? "Do you know when he's coming back?"

Dr. Stewart flared her nostrils, looking like an emaciated hippopotamus, if there were such a thing. "He'll be gone all night," she said. "In fact, he won't be home until tomorrow. *If* then." Without another word the door closed in my face. I felt a fine trickle of sweat run from my neck into my bra. I'm not leaving, I thought. I'll wait till tomorrow morning if I have to, but I'm not going anywhere until I see him. I sat down on the top step and rested my head against the wrought iron railing. It was a hot day all right, and I was mighty thirsty and practically starving. I tried not to think of that roast beef sandwich with mustard and cole slaw. At five thirty-six a white Mercedes pulled slowly into the driveway. Uncle John climbed out of the car, a brown paper bag in his arms. He looked baffled.

"Ro?" he said as he approached the front steps.

"Hi," I smoothed out my dress as I stood. I wasn't sure what to call him. 'Uncle John' seemed a bit inappropriate, under the circumstances.

"What are you doing?"

"Waiting for Jeffrey."

"Is he expecting you?"

"Sort of."

"That's strange. He didn't mention you'd be joining us for dinner."

"He's eating dinner here? Tonight?"

"I'm making a special dish," Uncle John said. "A little bon-voyage meal before he goes back to school on Sunday." Uncle John seemed ill at ease. He transferred the grocery bag to his other arm and fumbled with his keys. "I'd better bring these in before they melt in the heat."

I nodded, disappointed. "What are you making?" I asked to cover the hurt.

"Sambhar. It's a lentil curry. I found the recipe in Delhi."

"I had a feeling you were Kosher."

"*Delhi.* In India."

I didn't even know they *had* delis in India. "It sounds delicious," I said, hoping he'd get the hint.

"Actually, it's very spicy."

"I love spicy." There was long pause. "Spicy is my favorite. Nothing is too spicy for me."

Uncle John smiled uncomfortably and moved toward the door. "It's good to see you, Ro," he said as he slid the key into the keyhole.

"You, too."

He turned to face me. "I'm sorry I can't invite you in. Are you sure you want to wait out here like this?"

"I'm sure."

He closed the door softly, leaving me alone on the front porch.

I sat down on the top step and leaned my head against the railing once again. The air was beginning to grow cooler as the sun moved west behind a big leafy tree. At six oh-four the Coupe de Ville swung around the corner and pulled to the curb. My heart moved into overdrive as I watched Jeffrey bound up the walkway. The look on his face was a blend of pity and curiosity. "What are you doing here?" he asked. Those were his opening words from my fantasy, but "looking for you, big boy," somehow didn't seem like the best response.

"Waiting," I said in a small, shaky voice.

"What for?" Only three days earlier we held hands on this very walkway. Had he forgotten everything?

"There's something important I have to ask you," I said. I paused, my voice catching in my throat. "Sorry. This is a little harder than I thought." I closed my eyes, filling my lungs with the sweet summer air. "Remember when we were in my room on Friday night, and you told me how much you wanted to make love to me?"

"Yeah, I remember," he said.

"And then we started kissing, and it was all so perfect, and I felt so close to you?" He looked past me toward the front windows of his house, the early-evening sunlight playing off his blonde hair. "Never mind. I shouldn't have bothered you."

"No. Go ahead."

I picked up my bag and slung it across my shoulder. "Forget it. It was really stupid of me to come here."

"Just say it." His voice was firm, but not unkind.

"When I told you I loved you, I...just want to know if you loved me back, even for that one minute. Did you love me at all, Jeffrey?"

He let out a deep breath. "Actually, I didn't," he said. "But I liked you, Ro. I still do."

I stood absolutely still, absorbing the words. Then, without looking into his face, I walked down the brick steps to the sidewalk. He didn't call me to come back, but I could feel his eyes on me as I hurried past the Coupe de Ville. Suddenly I became aware of a blonde girl in the front passenger seat applying lipstick to her pretty mouth,

MONDAY, AUGUST 16, 1971

pouting into the visor mirror. She glanced at me briefly before turning her attention back to her lips. I walked faster and faster, until I was running, all the way to Middle Neck Road, the pain from my feet shooting straight into my heart. I pulled a dime from my bag and pushed it into the pay phone on the corner.

"Chelle? Can you pick me up?" I was so breathless I could barely speak. I leaned my head against the metal phone, hot tears coming hard.

• • •

It took Rochelle half an hour to buck her way through eastbound rush hour traffic in her parents' Plymouth Duster. When she screeched to the curb at seven-fifteen, I was an absolute mess.

"I knew it," she said as I climbed in beside her. "Tell me everything." And I did, down to the tiniest detail, the words spilling out so fast that she had to stop me several times and ask me to say it again. "Well, at least he likes you," she said when I was finished.

"So what he likes me? He doesn't love me, Chelle, and he never did." I kicked the dashboard with my bare foot.

"Hey, watch the car."

We rode in silence for a few minutes while I regained some kind of equilibrium. "So you think the blonde girl in the car is his girlfriend?" I asked.

"Who cares? You'll never see either one of them again."

"I have to know if he's in love with her."

"It sounds to me like Jeffrey's in love with one person only, and that's Jeffrey."

The Duster crossed the Long Island border into Queens. "I can't believe how close I came to telling Stuie everything. I was going to tell him *today*. This morning. And then I was going to tell my parents."

Rochelle shrugged. "Maybe you should've."

"Are you crazy?"

"At least the wedding would've been called off." She waited for a response and when I didn't answer, she glanced at me. "Don't tell me you're going through with the wedding?"

"I don't have much choice, do I?"

"Jesus, Ro."

"At least somebody wants to marry me. He might not be the person I want, but he's *somebody*."

"If you ask me, Stuie Weiner is a nobody."

"He's never hurt me, Chelle, not once since third grade. He's safe and reliable."

"So is this car, but you don't see me marrying it."

"That's because you're going to marry Sal."

"Says who? He's only the eighth guy I've ever slept with. There's a whole world of men out there."

"But you love him."

"I love him today," she answered, matter-of-factly. "That doesn't mean I'll love him tomorrow."

"Remember that poem we read in English? 'And if I loved you Wednesday, then what is that to you. I do not love you Thursday, so much is true.' That was such a great poem. Who wrote it again?"

"I don't know. Elizabeth Barrett Browning?"

"No, it definitely wasn't her. It was someone else with a lot of names. Edith...Elsie...something."

"Elsie the Cow," she said definitively.

"That's it."

There was a pause. "I think you should cancel the wedding," Rochelle said flatly.

"I can't do that."

"Why not? You were willing to cancel it yesterday afternoon."

"That's different. Yesterday afternoon I thought Jeffrey loved me."

"What does *that* have to do with anything?"

"I'm not taking a chance being alone my whole life. What if no one else comes along and I end up an old maid like my mother's cousin Elise?"

"You're not her."

"And I don't want her life, either. She lived with my Tanta Ceil and my Uncle Al until they died, in the same bed she grew up in.

MONDAY, AUGUST 16, 1971

They never even bought her new sheets. I think they still have pictures of baby chickens on them and she's forty-three years old."

"That's pathetic."

"Well, it could happen to me. If I don't marry Stuie I might live with my parents forever."

"That's still not a good enough reason to marry him."

"There are other reasons."

"Name one."

"It won't make any sense to you."

"Try me."

I paused, not wanting to do this. "We've already booked the Temple."

"Now *there's* a great reason to get married," Rochelle said sarcastically as she flew through a yellow light.

"I told you you wouldn't understand."

"Give me another one."

"I can't hurt Stuie. I know how much he loves me, even though he never actually said it."

"But you don't love him back."

"Not like that."

Rochelle frowned. "You don't want to be alone, the Temple's booked, and you can't hurt Skully. That's three dumb reasons. Any more?"

I let out a breath, knowing reason number four was just as bad as the first three and Rochelle would have no problem telling me so. "The whole neighborhood knows about the wedding. They'll never stop talking about me if I call it off now and it'll embarrass my parents."

"Therefore you're willing to spend your whole life with the wrong person."

"Maybe he's not the wrong person. Maybe he's the right person and I just don't know it yet."

"Do you really believe that?" I turned away. "That's what I thought."

"There are more reasons." I suppressed a smile. "I really like those matchbooks with my name on them."

Rochelle shook her head. "Yeah, and what about reason number six? You're a total masochist, moving into Skully's house when you hate his parents and they hate you back."

"Not both of them. Just Selma."

"That's bad enough."

I was beginning to enjoy the game. "Want to hear reason number seven? I love chicken and rice and if I don't have it at the wedding, I don't know when I'll have it again."

Rochelle slapped my leg good-naturedly. "Number eight. Weiner is a better name than Lipshitz. But then again, anything is better than Lipshitz."

"Reason number nine. I don't want to enjoy sex for the rest of my life." I stopped smiling, the horror of my own words changing the mood so fast there was a wind behind it. Rochelle stopped smiling, too.

"I'm so sorry," she said.

There was a long pause. "Edna St. Vincent Millay."

"Huh?"

"She wrote the poem."

"Right."

"You know something, Chelle? Guys like Jeffrey don't marry girls like me."

"And that's why you're marrying Skully."

"Yeah. It's reason number ten, but it's really number one." There was another pause, a longer one this time as Rochelle parked the Duster in front of my house. "Can you come in for a couple of minutes?" I asked. "I'll make you something to eat."

"Just a couple. Sal's coming over at nine."

We climbed the front stoop and walked through the living room. Rochelle stopped to pick up the unidentifiable gift I'd left on the couch that morning. "What's this?" she asked.

"I have no idea," I called as I grabbed a bag of potato chips and a fresh package of bologna from the kitchen. "Leave it alone."

"Wait a second, let me see it." She turned it over and over, examining it with great concentration. "It's a wedding present, isn't it?"

MONDAY, AUGUST 16, 1971

"Put it down, Chelle."

"I know what it is. You're supposed to put fancy baby food in there when company comes. See?" She tapped the tiny spoon against the glass. "That's why the spoon's so small, to fit in the little stinker's mouth."

She followed me into the bedroom. I turned on the radio, plopped down on the bed and stuffed three pieces of bologna into my mouth. Ziggy was playing four songs in a row from the Jefferson Airplane. Rochelle picked up a note lying on the bedspread. It was in my mother's illegible scrawl. "Went for Clu-ee-uu-eese," she read.

I grabbed the note from her hand. "Went for Chinese. Can't you read?" I crumpled it and threw it on the floor.

"What are you going to do with those?" Rochelle asked, pointing to the love beads around my neck.

"Wear them forever. They'll be buried with me in my grave."

"What if Skully asks where you got them?" She reached into the bag and placed one large potato chip on her tongue.

"He won't. He doesn't notice anything about me."

"He'll notice you're not wearing the diamond ring. Make sure you put it on."

"Good thinking," I said, getting off the bed to retrieve the balled-up tissue behind the radio. Suddenly my heart stopped.

"Oh my God, Chelle! It's gone!"

"What are you talking about?"

"The tissue's gone. I put my ring in the tissue and now it's gone."

"Let me see." Rochelle jumped off the bed. "Move over." She elbowed past me and poked around, turning the radio over, looking between the dresser and the wall, knowing as well as I did it was a lost cause. "Look in the drawer," she said.

I rooted through eighteen years of miscellaneous stuff, certain the ring wasn't going to be there, and it wasn't.

"What am I going to tell Stuie?" I asked weakly. I was on trauma overload, fighting to hold it together. Twenty-four hours earlier my life was full of promise. Now it was a disaster.

"We don't know for sure that it's lost," she said.

"Oh, yeah? Then where is it?"

"Call your mother. Maybe she saw it when she cleaned your room."

"Call her where? At the Chinese restaurant?"

Rochelle ran to the kitchen and came back with the local telephone book. "You think they're at Hong Joy?"

"Yeah, it's the only Chinese restaurant they trust enough to go to."

She leafed through the white pages. "Here it is. Two two three, seven four eight six."

I picked up the phone and dialed. "Hello, I'm looking for my parents who are having dinner at your restaurant. What? My parents. Mother and father?" I looked at Rochelle helplessly. "I don't think they speak English very well."

"Give it to me." Rochelle grabbed the receiver and spoke slowly, in a voice so loud they could've heard her in Shanghai. "Hello? I need woman. Yes. Woman. Short. Fat."

"Hey, my mother's not fat."

Rochelle waved at me to be quiet. "Red hair. Her name Sylvia. Yes. Sylvia. She eat now. With tall man. His name Mel. This is emergency. Yes. E*mer*gency." I stared at Rochelle in awe. Boy, she was good at everything. She waited a minute before giving me the thumbs-up. "Hey, Sylvia, it's Rochelle. No, she's fine. She's fine. She's right here. Hold on." I grabbed the phone from her hand.

"Ma? Have you seen a tissue on my dresser behind the radio? A white tissue, all crumbled up?" I listened to my mother's ranting voice and put a hand to my forehead. "Shit," I said as I hung up.

"What'd she say?"

"She said she was so sick of the soda cans and the Hershey wrappers that she threw everything in the garbage yesterday before she went to work. And from now on I should leave her alone when she's eating unless it's a real emergency."

"Shit."

"I'm dead, Chelle."

"You're right."

"Wait a second. If she threw it out yesterday it means it's still in the garbage room."

"Are you kidding? You're gonna find a crumpled tissue in the garbage room? There are probably a million tissues in the garbage room, probably all of them covered with snot."

"Yeah, but only one of them has my ring."

"Forget it. Whatever you're thinking I'm not going to do it. No way."

"Chelle, come on, it's a matter of life or death. I think Stuie's parents love that ring more than they love their own children."

"I'd do anything for you, hon, but you're aski..."

"Then let's go. If you really want to help me, this is the way."

"You're going to wear my beautiful dress to look through the garbage?"

"Let's *go*," I said more forcefully, slipping into a pair of flat sandals before heading to the door. "It's getting really dark."

"Take a flashlight," Rochelle said. I ran back and grabbed one from the broom closet, then took Rochelle's hand and dragged her to the garbage room, where flies swarmed overhead and metal cans overflowed.

"We're never going to find anything," she said, taking her hand back. She looked around helplessly. "Where does your mother usually throw everything?"

"Whichever can is the least full."

"It reeks in here, Ro. I'm not sticking my hand in garbage."

"This is my only chance of getting the ring," I said. "The garbage men will be coming."

"You're crazy, you know that?"

"Keep your voice down. The last thing we need is Stuie poking his big head out the window, asking what we're doing."

"Tell him we're jewelry shopping," Rochelle said.

"Very funny," I answered, gingerly lifting the lid of a metal can and shining the flashlight inside. I was greeted by leftover spaghetti, an empty carton of milk, a sliver of soap, coffee grinds and orange peels. It was more than disgusting. Peeking out from under an empty jar of grape jelly was a crumpled tissue. "Do you think this whole thing is a symbol for something?" I asked as I pulled the tissue out with two fingertips, using them like a pair of tweezers.

"A symbol, like your life has turned into garbage?"

"That too, but I meant maybe I lost the ring on purpose."

"I'm just glad you didn't flush it down the toilet or we'd be swimming in the cesspool by now." I shook out the tissue, holding it as far from my body as I could, but it was empty. Rochelle, meanwhile, had moved on to another can, a distorted grimace on her face. "I don't think I can do this, Ro."

"Look for the white crumpled tissues," I said. "Don't be such a wuzz."

"Oh God, there're bugs all over these chicken bones!" she screamed, slamming the lid shut. She walked to another can, afraid to lift the lid.

"White crumpled tissue," I reminded her.

"How about a pink one?"

"White."

"I can barely see but I think there's a white tissue in here," she called triumphantly. "Come here, Ro. It looks like something's in it."

"Can't you do it?" I shouted back, opening another can on the other side of the room.

"You do it. I'm not touching it."

I put the lid down and walked over to her. She pointed. "Right there. See it? Behind the tuna fish sandwich."

"I don't think that's tuna fish," I said.

"Then what is it?"

I shone the flashlight directly into the can. "A boogie and pus sandwich," I said menacingly, turning the light to my own face for effect. She screamed in horror. "Quiet or Stuie's going to hear us," I scolded, reaching into the can to grab the tissue. I shook it open and a piece of gum flew across the room. Rochelle shrieked and grabbed me so hard we both nearly fell down. I got my balance back and we started laughing until we cried, the hot tears on my cheeks a welcome relief from the tears of sadness I had previously been crying. I didn't realize how loud we were until we heard Stuie's voice at the window.

"Ro? That you?"

MONDAY, AUGUST 16, 1971

"Stuie?" I looked at Rochelle with a new wave of panic, the laughter gone. "Oh, no, what am I going to do now?" I whispered.

"I'm out of here," Rochelle said, wiping her hands on her shorts. "I gotta get ready for Sal."

"What do you mean? You can't leave me now."

"Oh, yeah? Just watch."

And she started to leave for real. I looked up and saw Stuie's big head in the window. "Come up here," he said. "I haven't seen you all day."

I ran to catch up with Rochelle. "I can't be alone with him," I said. "He'll kill me for sure."

"I hate the sight of blood even more than the smell of garbage. Call me tomorrow when it's all over."

"Don't do this to me." I aimed the flashlight at her body.

"First I drive to Great Neck in horrible, miserable traffic, then I stick my hands in disgusting garbage. I think that qualifies me as Friend of the Year, don't you?"

"Please, Chelle, I'm begging you."

"I have to take a shower and shave my legs."

And she crossed the street toward her building, leaving me with no other choice than to tell Stuie not only that the coveted ring was lost, but why it had been removed from my finger in the first place. What a day it had been. I could barely remember washing Rochelle's purple dress down at Sunny's Laundromat that morning.

Rehearsing my apologies in a frantic whisper, I rang Stuie's doorbell at eight-fifteen. Selma opened the door, teasing the top of her hair with a small round brush, a couple of plastic curlers already in place along the sides of her head.

"Stu-ee!" she screamed, annoyed when he didn't respond. "He's watching TV in his room. Go ahead in."

I walked past her quickly, hiding my left hand from her view. The Weiner apartment was similar to mine, with plastic-covered velveteen couches, faded gold shag carpeting and the faint, lingering smell of stuffed cabbage. Selma loved to needle point and there were needle pointed rabbis, needle pointed Torahs and needle pointed Stars of David all over the living room walls. I knocked once on Stuie's bedroom door and walked in. He was lying on his bed watching cartoons, content with the world.

"Come here," he said as he leaned up. I sat on the edge, my heart pounding hard, wondering how to tell him the bad news without setting off an atomic bomb. He unzipped the back of the dress, sending a cold chill up my spine. The top hook of my bra came undone. "So you're not sick anymore?"

"Not really, but I'm still pretty fragile." I forced a nervous laugh. "I hope nobody tries to beat me up tonight because I'm just too weak to defend myself."

"You want to eat something? We got chicken left over that tastes like shit but if you drown it in ketchup it's not so bad."

"No thanks."

Stuie fumbled with the second hook and my bra fell open.

"You want to lie down for a few minutes?" he asked, making room for me on the twin bed.

"Where's Nola?"

"She's at a slumber party." He pulled me toward him and reached into the dress, cupping my breast in his hand and squeezing it just a little too hard. "Let's take all our clothes off," he said hopefully.

"Come on Stuie, not now. Your mother's in the other room."

"She hasn't come in here in ten years."

"Who washes the sheets?"

"Nobody."

"We have to talk. That's why I came over."

"You always want to talk."

"There's something important I have to tell you."

"Let me guess. You found the perfect shoes to match your wedding dress."

"I've had my shoes for weeks. This is *really* important."

Ignoring me, he pulled his tee shirt over his head, revealing a chest as smooth as a baby's, the flesh loose and undefined. He started to tug on my bra but I pulled away, adjusting the straps with trembling fingers. "Something bad happened today, Stuie. Something really bad."

"Don't tell me. Your radio broke."

"I'm serous. This is huge." I had his attention now. I looked at him but I couldn't get the words out. My body was hot and cold and my teeth were starting to chatter.

"Stop it, Ro, and tell me already."

"Okay. I was taking a bath last night and I took off my diamond ri..."

"You lost the ring," he said incredulously, his voice barely audible.

"Let me just tell you what happened."

He put a hand to his head. "You lost the ring."

"It was an accident."

"I don't believe it."

"Me, neither."

His voice began to rise as the weight of the news set in. "How the fuck could that happen, Ro? That ring's been in my family..."

"Since the war," I said along with him. "I know. I'm sick over it."

"Shit!" He sat up suddenly and slammed his hand into the wall, then picked up a comic book and flung it across the room. The cover flew off and landed near the closet. I cowered on the bed, holding onto my bare arms.

"Stuie, please."

He was pacing around the tiny room, both hands deep in his curly brown hair. "My father's going to kill me, do you realize that?"

"I'll tell him I was the one who lost it and it had nothing to do with you."

Stuie's face was white as paste. "I'm dead. That's all there is to it. My ass is grass and I'm fuckin' dead meat."

"Tell him it was my fault. He wouldn't kill *me*...would he?"

"He'll kill us both. Damn it!" Stuie picked up a hockey trophy and threw it against the wall, breaking the stick right off and sending the whole thing flying in all directions.

"Stuie? Is everything all right?" Selma called.

"Yeah, fine," he shouted back.

"What if *I* tell him?"

"It won't matter. All he'll care about is the fuckin' ring going down the drain."

"It didn't go down the drain," I said. "I wrapped it in a tissue and my mother threw it out. That's why Rochelle and I were in the garbage room. We were trying to find it."

Stuie's nostrils flared, his voice loud and booming. "How're you gonna find a tissue in the garbage room? You think it's Waldbaum's, used tissues on aisle five?"

I don't know what came over me but the image struck me as funny and I started to laugh and I couldn't stop. I was a lunatic, a crazy person sitting on Stuie's bed, my body wracked with uncontrollable laughter. "What's the matter with you?" Stuie shouted without a trace of amusement. "You think this is funny? You think this is a fuckin' joke? Get hold of yourself, Ro, you're out of control."

He was right, I was out of control, and losing control was my darkest nightmare, the reason I never sampled the assorted narcotics that made their way around the schoolyard. While other kids feared getting busted, I feared getting high, picturing myself crouched in a urine-soaked cell at Creedmore State Hospital, hallucinating, my arms strapped across my body in a dirty strait jacket, my mouth foaming as I shouted unintelligibly into the darkness. *Get it together*, I told myself firmly as I sat on Stuie's bed cackling like a hyena, my face drenched with tears, my heart racing.

"You got a real problem, Ro, you know that?" Stuie said angrily. My laughter faded into a mournful silence. There was nothing funny about the situation. He had no idea what I'd been through all day, losing Jeffrey, losing the ring – I was losing my sanity and it was taking its toll. I took a deep breath and sat quietly on the bed, hands folded in my lap, trying not to look at my shirtless fiance who stood over me, a band of extra fat around his middle. I wondered if I could learn to be attracted to his body over time, or would it become increasingly repulsive as we got older?

"I don't think you realize what my father's gonna do," he said.

I started to cry for real, so heavily I could barely speak. "I feel terrible and I'm sorry," I wept. "It was my ring, too, you know."

"No, it wasn't. It was my *father's* ring. He's the one who risked his life to get it. He didn't even want to give it to you but I promised

MONDAY, AUGUST 16, 1971

him you'd never lose it." Stuie whirled around and kicked the closet door. "Now look what you did. He's gonna blame the whole damn thing on me."

"I didn't lose it on purpose, Stuie..."

"Don't say anything, Ro. Just stop talking. Stuie glared at me with narrowed eyes and a fiery wave of terror welled up inside me, starting in my stomach and moving up toward my chest. I could feel my skin get hot and damp, I could feel my face flush, and it was suddenly difficult to breathe. The lost ring was nothing compared to having sex with Jeffrey. What if he found out Jeffrey and I did everything Stuie begged for? I'd be in for it all right. It was just a matter of time until someone, Iris or Marsha or Rochelle accidentally on purpose blew the whistle. I stood up and tried to regulate my breathing, deep inhalations through my nose, forceful exhalations through my open mouth.

"Why are you doing that?" he asked with annoyance.

"Why do you think?" I asked between breaths. "I'm upset."

"You've been all weird lately, laughing one minute and crying the next, having the flu and then not having it..."

"I've been trying to figure out a way to tell you about the ring."

He looked into my face for clues. "What else haven't you told me?"

I turned away with a mouth so dry I could barely open it. "Nothing. I don't know what you're talking about."

"I'm talking about you hiding something from me. What is it, another guy? You been doin' stuff to some other guy?"

"Of course not."

"Swear it."

"I...swear." I squeezed my eyes shut. *Please God, don't punish me.* I really was a good person, despite all the lying and cheating.

"Go home, Ro, and let me figure out what to say to my father when he comes home. He's gonna have a conniption when he finds out."

"When will he be back?"

"Late. It's his poker night."

"Should I wait here and tell him myself?"

"No. I want you to leave now."

I walked through the empty apartment on trembling legs and as I opened the front door I could hear a loud and deliberate thud from Stuie's bedroom, like a piece of furniture thrown in anger across the room.

Tuesday, August 17, 1971

Worn out by the harrowing events of the day, I passed out on top of my chenille bedspread, still wearing Rochelle's purple dress, a bag of crushed potato chips beneath my exhausted body, and didn't wake up until two-thirty Tuesday afternoon. I forced myself into a sitting position, my feet dangling off the side of the bed, horrible memories of Monday rushing back with crystal clarity: Jeffrey's parting words, the blonde girl in the Coupe de Ville, my failed mission in the garbage room, and Stuie's tantrum. I hate my life, I thought, as I padded into the kitchen and took a package of bologna, a jar of whole Kosher dills and a container of brown mustard off the shelf. I peeled off a couple of slices of meat, wrapped them around a big, juicy pickle, and spread mustard over the top. It was exactly the breakfast I needed. I ate one pickle roll-up after another until the jar was nearly empty. Feeling bloated and a little nauseated, I went back to my room and picked up the phone.

"Ziggy? It's Rhona Lipshitz." It had only been a few days since my last call. I hoped he didn't see me as a pest.

"Hello Rhona Lipshitz from Queens. How's everything on the other side of the midtown tunnel? At least the heat wave is breaking."

"I guess."

You don't sound like your usual chipper self today."

"Everything is terrible," I said glumly. It was the first time I'd spoken to him about myself. Usually we talked about my favorite records, the latest cover story of Rolling Stone, or upcoming concerts at the Fillmore.

"What's making you so unhappy?" he asked.

"Did you ever love someone and they didn't love you back?"

"There's not a person alive who doesn't know how that feels."

"I doubt it, Ziggy. Not like this."

"Should I play a couple of sad songs for you tonight?"

"Actually, I just wanted to hear your voice." It was difficult to tell who was more surprised by this, me or Ziggy.

"That's very nice," he said. "I hope it helped."

"It did."

"Be good to yourself, Rhona from Queens. Let me know what happens."

"I will. I promise." I hung up the phone and shredded one tissue after another, tissues damp from my own tears. At five o'clock I heard the carnival music signaling the arrival of the Good Humor truck. I peeked through the Venetians and watched as Billy hopped out of the driver's seat to fetch an éclair pop for Iris. But instead of his homely face with its sadistic sneer, I was sure I saw Jeffrey's green eyes glinting in the early evening sun, and that beautiful smile with a dimple at each end.

How could so much have happened in a week, I wondered. How could I have gone from unconscious to euphoric to miserable in a mere five days? The range of emotions was of epic proportion, something Rabbi Marks might talk about during High Holy Day services.

I took a notebook from my dresser drawer and made a list of my most precious possessions, along with the name of the person who'd get them upon my death, just in case that were to happen

TUESDAY, AUGUST 17, 1971

later that night. Rochelle would receive all my clothes plus everything I'd borrowed but had neglected to return, like her crotchless panties. Marsha would receive my phonograph records and all my books, even though most of the books were hers. My mother would receive the crystal thing still on the couch, my father the FM radio on my dresser. To Stuie I would leave my notebooks filled with poetry. Perhaps they would give him insight into the woman he only thought he knew since grade school, the woman even *I* didn't know until now.

The love beads, still around my neck, would be mailed back to Jeffrey along with an appropriate letter, maybe even a poem. I wanted him to know I respected his honesty, but did he really need to be *that* honest? I'd tell him how it felt to see a girl in his car, sitting in *my* seat, the one where he kissed me so sweetly on Thursday, Friday and Saturday. I tore a piece of paper from my notebook. A few minutes later my poem was complete. Taking a deep breath, I read it out loud in a soft, slow voice, liking the way I rhymed 'aesthetic' with 'pathetic,' and 'devastation' with 'isolation.'

I sat without moving for an entire hour, wanting Jeffrey so badly I could barely take in a breath without feeling a sharp pain in my chest. My whole body ached with sorrow as I tucked the poem behind my folded socks in the second drawer of my dresser, right next to the ID card. Maybe someone would find them after my tragic and most untimely murder once Sam found out about the ring, and deliver them along with the beads.

But I didn't want to die. I wanted to live, to feel the way I had felt during those three perfect days. I wanted to taste the meat of life in a world beyond Walnut Gardens, I wanted to fill my senses with the vibrant colors of the rainbow. I lifted the telephone off its cradle and dialed. One ring. Two rings. "Help me," I said sadly. "I'm desperate for human companionship."

"I'd love to come over but we're going to my grandparents' for dinner."

"I need you, Marsh. I need you to sit with me and mourn."

"My parents are waiting in the car. I just came back in to get my book."

"Call me when you get home and if I'm not here call the police." I hung up and skimmed through my notebook, reading the silly things I'd written a few weeks earlier, before meeting Jeffrey. How young and carefree I was then, not yet feeling the weight of the world on my shoulders. The phone rang, and thinking it was Marsha I said into the receiver, "I'm begging you to come over right now," when Stuie's voice interrupted with, "It's me." My body stiffened. At least he was still alive, which bode well for my own safety.

"Oh. Hi."

"Who were you expecting, another guy?"

"Don't be ridiculous. I thought you were Marsha Kotner."

"Why would you beg her to come over?"

"I miss her. She's one of my best friends and I haven't seen her all day."

"My parents want to talk to you."

"Now?"

"Yeah."

"On the phone?"

"No. Here. Can you come over?"

"I'm about to have dinner. In fact I can hear my mother in the kitchen banging pots and pans all over the place."

"It won't take long. Just come over now."

"Stuie?"

"Yeah?"

"How mad is he?"

"Just get here as soon as you can." And he was gone. I wanted to hide. I wanted to run into my mother's arms and confess everything, but she'd repeat every last detail to my father, and he'd never forgive me for having sex with a person other than my husband, especially a week before the wedding. No, there was no way I could tell her about the lost ring or how Jeffrey had made love to me Friday night in my twin bed.

I walked past the kitchen where she was making flank steak with boiled potatoes. "I'll be back in a minute," I said.

"Make sure you don't get lost somewhere. We'll be eating as soon as your father gets here."

TUESDAY, AUGUST 17, 1971

I walked toward the door, the crystal present taunting me from the couch. "Hey, ma, did you see what I got from dad's work?"

"Yeah, I saw it."

"What's it supposed to be?" Whatever it was, I hated it already, this *thing* intended for Mr. and Mrs. Weiner.

She shrugged as she held a saucepan under the running faucet. "It's just a little chatchkela to put on a shelf for display. Are you coming with us to bingo on Thursday or are you too busy so close to the wedding?"

"I'll be busy, ma," I said, closing the door behind me and heading out into the warm evening air. Iris was still outside with Scampy who must've been constipated, poor thing, because he was squatting in front of the hydrant with a strained look on his pointy face, his matted tail quivering from the effort.

"Going to Skully's?" she asked, the empty popsicle stick in her mouth.

"That's right," I said as I headed off toward his building. "I'm going to Skully's."

"Hey, Ro," Iris called, almost as an afterthought. I stopped and turned around. "I saw the ice cream man last night."

"Where?" I tried to sound casual but it wasn't working.

She took the stick from her mouth. "I was coming out of the movies in Great Neck with my parents and he was on line waiting to go in."

"All alone?" I kicked myself for taking the bait from a thirteen year old, but I needed to know.

Iris snorted. "Not exactly. He was making out with some girl with long blonde hair."

"Was she pretty?"

"Yeah. She was. *Really* pretty."

I nodded and took off fast, trying not to cry but losing the battle. When I got to Stuie's front door I stood there quietly, breathing deeply before knocking. But the horrible picture was as real as if Jeffrey and his girlfriend were standing in front of me, arms wrapped around each other, her glossy lips reaching out to his.

"It's open," Sam called. He and Selma were sitting in front of the television watching a game show with an impossibly loud laugh track that belied their somber mood. Stuie frowned at me just to show his parents whose side he was on. He joined them on the plastic-covered couch, leaving me to sit by myself across the room, waiting for the interrogation to begin.

Sam switched off the TV while Selma picked up her sewing and draped it over her knee. Her new project was a companion piece to the framed Rabbi above her head. This new Rabbi had his eyes closed as he reverently touched the Torah. The face was somber, invoking the authority of the Temple, filling me with fear.

"Skully told us you lost the ring," Sam said. *Here it comes.* I waited for him to reach beneath the pillow cushion and pull out a revolver. "We know you feel bad," Sam continued, "but you also have to understand the position we're in. That ring has been in my family since the war and this was the first time we let it out of the safe deposit box."

Selma frowned and dipped her needle into the canvas. She was working on the Rabbi's ample white beard, which had bits of gray around his lips. "I'll be honest with you, Rhona, we're all sick over your carelessness. You *knew* how reluctant we were to let you wear it." She peered at me over her reading glasses and I started to cry, maybe for the millionth time since Sunday. I was an emotional wreck and Selma's words, sharp as arrows with poisoned tips, reached their target.

"Please forgive me," I wept pathetically. "I would never lose your ring on purpose."

Selma wasn't backing down. She was going to milk the moment for all it was worth. "It was incredibly irresponsible of you. It shows you have no respect for this family and no respect for tradition."

"That's not true," I said between sobs, wiping my face with the back of my hand. "Stuie can tell you how much respect I have. I've been miserable since it happened."

Stuie didn't move a muscle, not wanting to displease his parents. And yet I could see the sympathy in his eyes. Selma, meanwhile, ignored my tears, building an even fuller head of steam. "Take a good hard look in the mirror and think about what you've done.

TUESDAY, AUGUST 17, 1971

You'll see you've hurt every one of us with your selfishness."

I slumped forward in my chair, defeated, accepting the punishment I rightfully deserved, not just for losing the ring, but also for behaving so irresponsibly with another man. Selma stopped sewing and glared at me over the rim of her glasses, her jaw set in an angry scowl, allowing me to cry quietly into my hands without so much as a word of comfort. Just then Nola walked into the living room, regarding me with puzzlement, happy it wasn't *her* in the hot seat.

"What's going on in here?" she asked, trying to suppress a smug little smile.

"None of your business," Stuie answered angrily.

"How come Ro's crying?"

"She's not crying," Stuie said.

"Yes, she is. Look at her."

"Nola, get in your room," Sam said.

"But I don't want to."

"Cookie, go watch some TV in my bed," Selma cooed to her daughter. It was an extraordinary feat, shifting her tone like that. I was momentarily stunned by the smoothness with which she did it.

"Can I sleep in your bed all night?"

Selma started to answer but Sam said, "Get in your room now, Nola," in a firm voice that was not to be reckoned with. Nola frowned and walked out, leaving the four of us in the same miserable silence in which she'd found us.

"You okay?" Stuie finally asked, his voice softening. I nodded, not trusting myself to speak.

"There's a tissue in the bathroom," Sam said, "if you want to blow your nose."

"I'm okay." I wiped my eyes and looked down at the shag carpet.

"So this is what we decided," Selma said. "Obviously the ring can never be replaced but we want you to buy a new one with your own money and you need to do it before Sunday. It'll teach you a good lesson, to think before you hurt people." I looked at her blankly but she kept going. "We know a good jeweler in Bay Terrace. He'll make sure you get the most for your money. Why don't you go home now and tell your parents what you did."

I rose from the chair, grateful to be alive, and walked to the door. Stuie watched from the couch with a blank expression on his face. I tried to make eye contact with him but he looked away as I shut the front door behind me and ran all the way home.

My parents were in the middle of eating and there was no way I was going to tell them anything, at least not then.

"What's going on over at Stuie's?" my mother asked.

"Not much. We were talking about the flavor of the wedding cake." Lying had become a way of life.

"It's not up to them. I'm paying for the damn cake," my father said through a mouthful of flank steak.

"Hey dad, did you see the present in the living room?"

"Your mother showed it to me. It's from the girls at work." He seemed pleased with himself and the fact that the secretaries at Bridger's Petites had acknowledged him.

"What is it?"

"How do I know? But whatever it is, it's expensive, that much I can tell you."

"Explain to me about the cake," my mother said. "I've already ordered a white cake with a layer of butter cream. Is that no good?"

"I'm not a big fan of butter cream. I'd rather have a layer of fudge."

"Syl, bring out some more soda." My mother jumped up from the table and opened the refrigerator, grabbing a large bottle of black cherry.

"What about *them*?" she asked when she sat back down.

"They agree with me. White cake with a layer of fudge."

"Then it's settled. White cake with a layer of butter cream," my father said firmly as he opened the bottle and poured himself a glassful. I was impressed with his priorities. Displeasing the Weiners was a lot more important to him than pleasing me.

After dinner I excused myself and went to my room, curling up on my bed with Jeffrey's ID card, gazing at the handsome face way off in the corner. On Sunday he would soar above the clouds while I would descend into the gates of hell. I looked at the clock on my

TUESDAY, AUGUST 17, 1971

FM radio, watching the second hand tick away, each tick bringing me closer to my terrible fate. If only I were to become Rhona Gail Stewart on Sunday, everything would be perfect. Rhona Gail Stewart. I repeated the name over and over in my mind, oblivious to the persistent knocking on my door. My mother poked her head in. "Ro?"

"You're supposed to knock." I slipped the ID under my pillow.

"I did. Can I sit down?" I couldn't remember the last time she'd sat on my bed. It must have been years. "You want to tell me what's bothering you?"

"It's nothing."

"Your face is all bloated. You look terrible."

"Thanks, ma."

"Why were you crying? Tell me."

I leaned against the pillow and looked into the familiar face that had grown older since the last time I'd really examined it. The skin around the neck was starting to resemble a turkey's, the lines around the gray eyes were deeper now and the shape of the face was rounder than it used to be. Still, she was sort of pretty and still had a few good years left in her before she turned into one of the old bubbas who shuffled up and down the block in black lace-up shoes with swollen ankles, a copy of the Jewish Daily Forward grasped by arthritic hands. I sighed with fatigue. "Selma hates me and I don't know why."

My mother stiffened. "Who is she to hate my daughter?"

"She's someone I'm going to have to live with, probably for the rest of my life." I closed my eyes at the horror of it.

"Maybe she's afraid you're taking her son away."

"Taking him where? I'm moving into his room, into the same bed he's had since he's three years old, for God's sake."

"To a mother he's still being taken away by another woman."

"Well, if she wants him that badly she can have him."

"*Sha.*"

"She can't hear me, ma. She's all the way up the block."

"*I* can hear you."

"Maybe if I bought her a present she'd like me." It was too bad

I couldn't afford anything as nice as a brooch or a blouse. I had exactly two hundred four dollars in my private stash, saved in dribs and drabs from birthdays, Chanukahs and baby-sitting. Every penny of it would go to my new diamond ring. "Do you think I can do something special for her that doesn't cost money?"

My mother frowned, hating the notion of my doing anything special for Selma Weiner at all. "Why don't you write her a poem?"

"I have nothing poetic to say to her. What else?"

"Maybe you can take her to a movie or a show downtown."

"Just me and her? I don't think so. What else?"

"You can cook all of them a special meal."

"If only I could cook."

"After work tomorrow I'll show you how to make a brisket. You can bring it over there as a nice surprise."

"You'd really do that for the Weiners?"

"I'm not doing it for them. I'm doing it for you."

"And you think it'll help?"

"It's a start. At least it'll show her - and I spit on her, by the way - that you want to get along."

My mother was a genius. Cooking a meal for the entire family would solve all my problems: Selma and Sam would realize I wanted them to like me, and Stuie and I would get back on track. He was, after all, my future, my only option, and it was important to make him happy. "What time are you working till?"

"I've got the early shift, seven in the morning to three. There'll be plenty of time when I get home."

"Thanks, ma. I know how hard this must be for you, preparing a meal for Stuie's family."

"I spit on them," she said, rising from my bed and walking out of the room.

Wednesday, August 18, 1971

I ran all the way to Rochelle's apartment, banging loudly and desperately on the door. She answered in a short blue nightgown with satin spaghetti straps and a slit right up to her hip, her hair a mess and traces of lipstick around her mouth. Only one eye was open.

"What time is it?" she asked drowsily.

"Eight-thirty."

"In the morning?"

"Yes, in the morning. I can't believe you're still sleeping."

"Any chance you can come back later?"

"I would, but it's super important. It's an emergency."

"What's so important it can't wait an hour?" I followed her into the kitchen. "There's never anything to eat in this God damn place," she said with some annoyance, removing a can of Coke from the refrigerator and puncturing it with a can opener. I sat down at the kitchenette table while Rochelle leaned back against the counter, drinking her soda from the can. She was the sultriest woman I'd ever seen, even when she wasn't trying to be.

"Stuie's mother freaked when she heard about the ring," I said. "And here I thought Sam would be the one to go crazy."

"She's a lot worse."

"You're not going to believe what she made me do."

"A hundred push-ups?"

"I have to buy a new one with my own money."

"They won't even split it with you?"

"Not one dime."

"That sucks. How much you got?"

"Two hundred four bucks. And it took me five years to save it, too."

"Do you want me to steal a ring for you?"

"No, thanks. But I want you to come with me to Jamaica to get a new one. I never bought a diamond before." I paused as Sal wandered into the kitchen in nothing but a pair of tight jeans, exposing his flat belly and the line of dark hair below it. It always amazed me how Rochelle's parents ignored the sleepovers.

Sal took the open can of Coke out of Rochelle's hand and took a long pull, his tattooed arm draped around her neck. "I told Sal how we went through the garbage room yesterday looking for your ring," she said. "That was the most disgusting thing I've ever done in my life, even more disgusting than when I slept with Tommy McDaniel. Remember that putzhead from the dance at the Y?"

The blood rushed out of my face. "You told him I lost the ring?"

"I tell him everything."

"You told him about Jeffrey?"

"Ro, it's no big deal."

"But that was a secret, Chelle, and you knew it. You even swore on your grandmother's grave."

"No, I didn't."

"Yes, you did."

Sal took another pull from the soda can. "What's the difference? Her grandmother's already dead."

Rochelle giggled and poked her boyfriend playfully. "Don't

WEDNESDAY, AUGUST 18, 1971

worry, hon, you can trust him."

Trust him? What about Denise Silver? "You have to swear and mean it this time that you won't say one word to anybody. If Stuie finds out about Jeffrey, I'm dead."

"Take it easy," Sal said, drawing Rochelle closer. She leaned her head against his bare chest, fingering the silver cross that hung around his neck from a silver chain.

"You don't understand. My life would be over for real."

Rochelle shook her head. "You are *so* dramatic."

"This is serious stuff, Chelle. Which reminds me, there's something I have to ask you later."

"Ask me now. Sal doesn't mind, do you, baby?" Sal shrugged and scratched his flat belly.

"Okay. Is there any way for Stuie to know I'm not a virgin? Like, what if he senses something?"

Sal was quiet, pondering his own experiences, of which there were probably thousands. "A guy can usually tell when he's popped one. It feels tighter. It's really nice." Rochelle turned away.

"So Stuie will know I've done it, even though he's a virgin himself?" I asked.

"How many times have you actually gotten laid?" Sal asked me, looking right into my eyes. I was so flabbergasted I couldn't respond.

"Once," Rochelle said. She looked at me for confirmation and I nodded. "Yeah. Once," she repeated.

"Then you should be okay. He won't know anything."

"Hey, I've got a great idea," Rochelle offered. "When Stuie puts it in, why don't you scream like you're in pain, just to throw him off the track?"

Sal winked at me. "That'll work. Guys love it when their chicks scream." By now Sal was getting turned on by all the sex talk. He pulled Rochelle right into him, sliding his tongue into her open mouth. She held onto his belt loops while he caressed her hips, grinding himself against her at the kitchen counter, the kiss showing no sign of letting up. I tried to look away but I couldn't, staring instead with breathless envy as Sal's hands moved up the flimsy blue nightgown. I watched, spellbound, as he led Rochelle into her parents' bedroom without a word, his hand cupping her full behind. He looked back and caught my eye. Before I could turn away he beckoned with his index finger for me to join them. I shook my head fiercely and he blew me a kiss, then winked and closed the door behind them.

Forty minutes later Rochelle emerged and was ready to go, dressed in her tightest white jeans and a halter top. I turned off the TV in her living room and soon we were on the bus to Jamaica, gazing out the window at the brick apartments along the boulevard.

"How are you holding up?" she asked.

"I wish Jeffrey would kiss me again the way Sal was kissing you."

"I'm sorry, honey." She smiled sadly and I vowed to myself I would never, ever tell her how her boyfriend had propositioned me.

The bus passed a teen-aged couple holding hands in front of a candy store. The boy leaned over and kissed his girl tenderly on the forehead.. *What about me? Where's my chance at happiness?* There was no way I had already used up my fair share, no way I had taken too much. Rochelle leaned over and took my hand. I held onto it and didn't let go.

We spent the morning wandering in and out of half a dozen jewelry stores that were way out of my league until we finally found a little shop off Jamaica Avenue that was going out of business. I picked the cheapest ring on display, a third of a carat, fifty per cent off. It came to a hundred ninety eight dollars. I felt a surge of anger as I handed over my entire life savings and pocketed the change.

"Let's get some Chinese for lunch," I said. "My treat."

I ordered pork chow mein, fully aware that my parents didn't allow pork consumption under any circumstances. I dug into my lunch defiantly, resenting the entire world for the injustices thrown upon me, and praying I wouldn't be punished with botulism for my mutinous behavior.

As we rode the bus home I played with my new ring, turning it around on my finger, liking the fact it carried no emotional or historical baggage and belonged just to me. "Whatever you do, don't take it off, no matter what," Rochelle said as we walked home from the bus stop. "I can't go through this again."

"I know what you mean."

"I hope Skully's bitchy mother is happy now," Rochelle added as we neared my building.

If not, I thought, there's always a homemade brisket to appease her.

• • •

My mother came home early as promised, changing out of her shirtwaist dress and into a floral housecoat and bedroom slippers. "Now I can concentrate on cooking," she said, bending below the sink to retrieve a large metal roasting pan, the one she'd gotten as a wedding gift twenty-something years earlier. "You've never watched me make a brisket before, have you?"

"No. But I'm watching now."

She tied a blue checked apron around her thick waist and opened the refrigerator. "Take down the oil. You're taller than me." I reached up and opened the highest cabinet, retrieving a slippery bottle of vegetable oil while my mother gathered ingredients, announcing them like guests at a party. "Salt. Pepper. Paprika."

"Got it. What next?"

"The first thing is heat the oven to three-twenty five." I looked at her for guidance. "Go ahead and do it," she said. I was embarrassed at how little I knew about the appliances I'd grown up with. The most elaborate dinner I'd ever made was a bologna sandwich on Wonder bread with a Twinkie and a root beer float for dessert. I turned a couple of knobs and finally managed to find the right setting, grateful for the fact I wasn't being criticized for my ignorance. "Now rinse the meat off with water and pat it dry."

"With a paper towel?"

"Dish towel. You don't want little pieces of paper in your brisket, do you?"

I rinsed the huge piece of meat, big enough for five people with enough left over for sandwiches the next day, and patted it with the dishtowel we'd bought on a family vacation in Hershey, Pennsylvania. The towel had a drawing of a smiling Amish couple and a horse that was also smiling. My mother loved buying souvenirs from wherever we'd visit during our annual five-day vacation. She had bought a spoon rest with a picture of President Kennedy while we were in Washington, D.C. but felt it was disrespectful to rest a dirty spoon on the President's face, especially after he'd been killed so tragically. So instead she hung it on the wall near the small window, enjoying how handsome he looked with that big Irish smile, feeling like a good American for not tarnishing the President's image with spaghetti sauce or gravy. There were salt and peppershakers of the Statue of Liberty and the Empire State Building, a napkin holder from Atlantic City and a refrigerator magnet from Grossinger's Hotel in the Catskills. "These beautiful things are from my travels," my mother would tell visitors to her kitchen.

"What now?" I asked, referring to the heavy piece of meat in my hands.

"Lay it on a board," she said, taking a worn cutting board from under the sink. "I talked to Grandpa Morris this morning."

"Grandpa Morris has been dead for eight years, ma."

"I told him you're marrying Stuie Weiner from up the block and I asked for his blessing."

"I don't want his blessing."

"*Sha.* Show some respect."

"You know what I really want, ma?"

"What?" She was taking a knife out of the drawer.

"I want to run away and not get married at all."

"Here, cut up the garlic. Tiny little pieces, as small as you can make them."

"Did you hear what I said?"

"I heard. Every bride feels that way right before her wedding."

"Yeah, but I felt this way even *before* right before my wedding."

"So did I, believe me." This information came as no surprise. My mother had reluctantly married at the advanced age of thirty-four, unheard of in her generation. She had been too involved with her own life to think about a husband, enjoying her job as assistant bookkeeper in a downtown handbag factory, feeling like a desirable single woman in the big city. She lived with her over-bearing immigrant parents in a five-story walk-up in the Flatbush section of Brooklyn and dated a variety of local Jewish boys. Her parents protected her from the fact she was creeping into middle-age, keeping her at home for as long as possible so she could help pay the rent and take care of them. When my mother turned thirty-four she realized for the first time that all her girlfriends were married, which forced her to re-evaluate her choices and consider a more traditional life, one that would include a husband and perhaps even children.

But the idea of spending her life washing someone's dirty socks, tying herself down to one needy and cloying man repulsed her. Perhaps she would have made the sacrifice had her groom been a doctor or a movie star, but there were no men like that on the horizon, only dress cutters and cab drivers, which left her in a terrible bind.

"Here. I can't do this." She handed me the bottle of vegetable oil, which I opened with some difficulty and handed back to her.

"Why'd you marry dad?" I asked, but I already knew the answer. By the time she was ready for marriage, in her mid-thirties, she knew there'd be slim pickings; it behooved her to find herself a mate while she still had the looks to snare one. Even the handsome young men she'd previously flirted with, not just the Jewish boys from Brooklyn but Italian and Irish boys she'd meet on week-end vacations, were disappearing from her life, their wolfish, betraying eyes wandering to bodies more nubile than hers. My mother still kept a secret scrapbook in her bottom drawer filled with faded photographs of herself posing like a starlet in a black bathing suit, surrounded by seven or eight shirtless men with gold crosses around their necks. I was fascinated and scared and repulsed by those photographs. I wished she'd throw them away but she apparently needed to keep them as a reminder of when she was young and pretty.

"What made you marry him, ma?" I asked again, a little more challenging this time.

"He smelled nice when he came to pick me up. He had such white teeth and his fingernails were always groomed. He had the hands of a dentist. Start chopping the garlic." I removed the outside peel, then broke apart the individual cloves with a knife. "Keep the pieces small."

"Like this?"

"That's good." She scooped up the peel and tossed it into the garbage. "Did I ever tell you that you wouldn't be here if it wasn't for Alan Ladd?"

"Yeah, but tell me again." She sighed for dramatic effect, loving the Alan Ladd story as much as I did, happy to tell it one more time. I wondered if one day I would stand in the kitchen with my own daughter and tell a similar story about Jeffrey. "Let's see. I had just gotten my engagement ring from Charlie."

"Charlie Rubin, the guy with the big ears who couldn't have children." I couldn't resist jumping in, knowing every beat of the story by heart.

"Huge ears, like an elephant."

"So he took you out to dinner..."

"He took me out to dinner somewhere on the East Side and then to a love story at the Loew's Delancey starring Alan Ladd."

"Who was the leading lady again?"

"You think I remember? I only had eyes for Alan Ladd. Anyway, I turned to Charlie and I saw that hook nose and the big ears and I knew. I just knew."

"You couldn't possibly love him if your life depended on it."

"And there was nothing I could do."

"Except tell him the truth and give back the ring."

"Two carats with ruby baguettes set in platinum. Everyone thought I was out of my mind."

"But you didn't care. How were you supposed to marry a man you didn't love?"

"He cried for weeks and his sister Rose told me he'd never get over it. She wanted to know why I changed my mind but what could I say? That Charlie couldn't give me chills the way Alan Ladd did? Rose would think I was crazy, too."

"So you married dad, what? A year later? What did you see in him, other than his groomed dentist hands?"

She put two onions in front of me on the counter. "Do these

next."

"You didn't answer my question."

"A movie star in Hollywood marries Alan Ladd. In New York you take what's in front of you."

"So you didn't really love dad."

"Did I say that? He hasn't been such a bad husband."

I thought about that with some sadness, how similar we were and how I had no right to judge her; I would soon accept Stuie because my own Alan Ladd was gone forever. Pushing the chopped garlic off to the side, I reached for an onion and peeled back its brittle brown skin.

"Stick a piece of bread in your mouth," my mother said. "It'll absorb the onion juice so you won't cry."

It wasn't the onion that was causing the tears, it was knowing my situation was even worse than hers. My mother had never actually gone to bed with Alan Ladd. She had never been on the brink of changing her life, she had never met a man who could know her better than she knew herself. Once you experience the sheer intoxication of that, you can't go back to Mel Lipshitz or Stuie Weiner and pretend everything is okay.

"I can't get married on Sunday," I said, wiping a tear from my cheek, then wiping my hands on the Amish dish towel.

"Do yourself a favor and get married now while you have someone who's good to you. Wait for someone better and you could end up like my cousin Elise."

"Cousin Elise is forty-three. I won't be her age for twenty-five more years."

"Exactly my point. When she was eighteen she thought she had all the time in the world but her age crept up and now look at her, a lonely and miserable old maid. That's what sent my Aunt Ceil to an early grave."

"No, it didn't. Tanta Ceil died from brain can..."

"Shh. Don't say the word. Don't *ever* say that word out loud."

"What, cancer?" She made a spitting sound with her tongue. "But it's what killed her, ma."

"Ceil never would have gotten you-know-what if she hadn't been so aggravated over her daughter."

"Is that what you're afraid of? That you'll die of a brain tumor if I don't marry Stuie?"

"There you go again. What did I tell you about that word?"

"I said 'brain tumor.' It's different."

"No, it's not."

"Is that what you're afraid of?"

"At least you'll be married and settled with a nice boy and I won't have to worry about you. Can't you understand that?"

"Wasn't Charlie Rubin a nice boy? How come you gave the ring back and I can't?"

She examined the onions and garlic. "You might not be lucky like me. Who knows where I'd be if I hadn't met your father? Here. Chop the carrots and celery. Small pieces."

"That's the point, ma. Maybe you would've had a better life."

"Or a worse one." She wiped the cutting board, which had a picture of the Liberty Bell on the front. She'd bought it on our trip to Philadelphia for her second cousin Hilda's Bat Mitzvah "I only want good things for you, ketzie, like a husband and children. That's all I want."

I chopped the carrots two at a time, thinking about my mother's revelation at the Loew's Delancey and my own epiphany just blocks away at Lombardo's Italian Cafe when Jeffrey looked right through me for the first time, sending those very same chills that my mother had felt up my own eager spine. Those chills were powerful. Those chills had caused her to change her plans and change her life and she was absolutely right, if it wasn't for Alan Ladd she would have married Charlie Rubin, a man she could never love, a man who couldn't have children and I surely wouldn't be here at all, not in any permutation. In a way my mother was more courageous than me. She gave back the diamond ring and said I'm out of here, while I took the coward's way out, losing my ring and going ahead with the wedding despite the fact I didn't want any part of it. It didn't even matter that she went and married a man who was every bit as dull as Charlie Rubin; what mattered was that unlike me, she listened to her heart and followed through. It was a true act of heroism, an act that deserved every ounce of my respect.

She showed me how to rub the garlic into the meat and I was back in kindergarten, finger painting, making a mess and not getting yelled at for it. "That's enough," she said. "Pour some oil in the pan and brown the meat on both sides. You'll have to turn it over with a spatula."

"But I like this part. Can't I do a little more?"

When the meat was sufficiently browned we transferred it to the big pot and added the onions, celery and carrots. She showed me how to sprinkle an envelope of dried onion soup on the top, then we put the heavy pot into the hot oven for three hours. I patted her on the shoulder. "Thanks, ma. I owe you one."

"Just make your parents proud of you," she said.

I sat at the kitchenette table while the brisket cooked, basting it every three hours the way I was shown, enjoying the fragrance of the onions and garlic and the meat's natural juices. I'm getting married in five days, I thought as I squirted the big plastic bulb. We'd already arranged the table seatings, keeping the Weiner clan as far from the Lipshitz brood as possible; we had chosen witnesses to sign the katuba; confirmed to the caterer we'd need sixty-four chicken and rice dinners. Our wardrobes were in place: I had a white picture hat that hung over my forehead and a pair of white satin pumps to match my dress. My mother's pink gown coordinated with the bridesmaid's dresses, and my father found the gray suit in his closet he'd worn to my Uncle Henry's funeral a couple of years before. Stuie would be wearing his Bar Mitzvah suit, lengthened and let out in the waist and shoulders since it had been hanging in his closet for five years. Of course Selma didn't share with me what she was planning to wear, just as she didn't ask about my dress, either. I wondered if bribing her with a brisket was the key to bringing us closer together, or was I being overly optimistic to think that anything good might come from it?

• • •

My mitted hands ached as I carried the hot brisket and potatoes in the heavy roasting pan up the block to Stuie's building. Golden shadows fell across the red brick buildings of Walnut and I realized the neighborhood was really lovely at certain times of day, all those apartments lined up one after another, each brick slightly different from the one next to it. When I reached Stuie's apartment I banged on the door with the toe of my sneaker. Sam answered, the TV Guide in his hand. "What's this?" he asked.

"Surprise," I said with as much enthusiasm as I could muster. "Can I put this down somewhere? It's really heavy."

He opened the door wider and I scooted to the kitchen, dropping the pan onto the Formica counter just in time, my arms aching. Selma walked into the kitchen from the bathroom.

"What's going on?" she asked with suspicious eyes.

"I cooked you a brisket."

"You cooked *me* a brisket?"

"Not just you, it's for the whole family. I think it came out pretty good." Before she could respond Stuie came in from his bedroom wearing just his dungarees. He looked like he'd been napping.

"Smells good. What's going on?"

"I cooked dinner for everybody as a surprise."

"But my mother was just about to pick up pastrami sandwiches from the deli."

"Well, now you're having brisket," I smiled.

Stuie glanced at Selma's unsmiling face. "Maybe you should've told us first," he said.

"It was a *surprise.*" Selma said the word as if I were some Japanese Kamikaze invading Pearl Harbor. She lifted the foil and peeked in.

"I have a new ring," I said, removing the oven mitts and holding out my left hand. "I bought it myself."

"That reminds me," Selma said icily, letting my hand dangle in mid-air. "Tell your mother my Cousin Shirley's in the hospital again so she won't be there on Sunday. Tell her to cancel one diabetic dinner."

"I will."

"Did you see my jeweler in Bay Terrace?" She took my hand

WEDNESDAY, AUGUST 18, 1971

roughly to examine the ring more closely.

"Actually, I found a different jeweler on Jamaica Avenue."

She made a tsk-ing sound with her tongue. "Mine would've given you a better deal."

"Thanks, but it worked out fine."

"Sam, come see the ring," Selma called to her husband who was watching television in the living room.

"In a minute."

Nola walked in just then. She'd been experimenting with make-up, looking like Cleopatra with gobs of blue eye shadow covering her lids and bright red rouge on her cheeks. "What's that?" she asked, regarding the roasting pan with curiosity.

"Ro cooked us a brisket for dinner," Stuie replied.

"I thought mommy was going to the deli?"

"Not anymore."

"That's not fair."

"Let's sit down and eat," Selma said. "Stuie, take out the bridge table."

"Can't we just sit in front of the TV?"

"Take out the table." She frowned at me and I realized the way to my future mother-in-law's heart was definitely not through her stomach, no matter how fine the cut of beef might be.

Selma took down five Melmac plates, five metallic tumblers and banged them on the countertop. She waited for Stuie to assemble the legs of the table before placing everything on it. Sam walked into the kitchen for his first evening cocktail, chugging it right from the bottle the way my father had his own cocktail every night before supper. But unlike my father who kept his liquor in the linen closet, Sam kept *his* in the cupboard next to the Malomars and the Cheese Doodles, apparently not concerned whether the family monitored his alcohol intake or not.

I sat at the far end of the table, Sam on one side of me, Nola on the other. Sam looked at his daughter's make-up disapprovingly. "Go wipe that crap off your face," he said.

"Leave her," Selma said as she brought out two large bottles of soda, black cherry and vanilla cream. She went back to the kitchen for the roasting pan containing my delicious brisket, the meal I had prepared with the apparently naive expectation of falling into the Weiners' good graces.

When we were all seated Sam sliced the meat and put several pieces on his plate. Selma took her fork and doled out generous portions for herself and Nola. "That's too much," Nola whined, still mad about not getting her pastrami sandwich on rye with French-fried potatoes.

"Eat what's on your plate," Sam said sharply. "Ro cooked this for us."

"Yeah, but nobody asked her to."

Sam's nostrils flared. "Shut up or you're going in your room and that'll be the end of it," he said.

Stuie stuck his fork into the roasting pan and piled his plate with meat and potatoes. I watched as the family ate, the silence broken only by the sound of chewing and swallowing and forks scraping. Nobody noticed that my plate was still empty. After a while I reached over and served myself one slice of brisket and a lone potato.

"The meat's delicious," Sam said, washing it down with a full glass of vanilla cream and helping himself to more.

"Thank you."

"How long did you cook it for?" Selma asked, pulling a piece of fat from her mouth and examining it before wrapping it in her paper napkin.

"Three hours. That's what my mother told me to do."

Selma's body tensed. "It could've used another half hour. Brisket is supposed to fall off the knife when you cut it."

"Leave her alone," Sam said. "She made us a nice meal."

"That's right," Stuie agreed, glancing at his father.

"Who asked you?" Selma asked her son.

"Nobody. But that doesn't mean I can't have an opinion."

Sam glared at Stuie with a look that said keep your mouth shut, and Stuie did just that.

"Next time I'll leave it in longer," I said with an eye on Stuie, concerned he might take his mother's side and deem me unworthy to be his bride. Much as I didn't want him, I needed him. My mother was right, any woman could end up like her cousin Elise if she weren't careful, so I'd better hang on for dear life or Stuie might be snapped up by someone else in the neighborhood, some female viper just itching to get her talons into the skin of an eligible bachelor.

Nola put her fork down. "Can I have my pastrami sandwich from the deli? Please, ma?"

"Are you for real?" Sam bellowed.

"You can't blame her for being hungry, Sam."

"There's plenty to eat right here." He leaned over and began to cut Nola's meat.

"Don't touch my plate," she wailed.

"Then eat."

"I already tried it and I didn't like it. The meat's not cooked enough."

"I said eat it." Sam was shouting now.

"Leave her alone, Sam. If she doesn't like it don't force her." Selma was really getting mad now, too.

"How much you gonna spoil her? What do you think's gonna happen when she's out in the real world? Do you think a boss will put up with that kind of shit?"

"I'm going to be a movie star, I won't have a boss," Nola said.

"Yeah. Okay. Fine."

"She's not the one to blame," Selma said to her husband for my benefit. "You can understand why she's disappointed."

"So what? Isn't everybody disappointed sometimes?"

We sure are. I played with my potato, tossing it from one side of the plate to another like a hockey puck.

"You *know* what it's like when you want something and then you find out you can't have it," Selma said tauntingly to her husband.

Boy, I sure do. There was silence at the table until Sam turned to his daughter with quiet resignation. "Just take one more bite and then you can leave the table."

"I don't want to."

"You can't make her, Sam."

"Don't argue with me in front of the children, Selma."

"We're not children," Stuie said, glancing at his mother. "At least me and Ro aren't." Selma sat up straight in her chair, her shoulders tense.

"You're spoiling her," Sam said harshly. "Pretty soon you'll have a monster on your hands."

"Pretty soon?" Stuie asked with a snort.

"Stay out of this, Skully. I'm talking to your mother, not you."

Selma put down her fork. "What should I do, let my own child go hungry because Rhona made a brisket nobody even asked for? I bet she didn't even cook it herself. I bet her *mother* cooked it for her." She spat out the word as if it were acid on her tongue.

"Enough," Sam said.

"Am I right? Did your mother cook this?"

"Not really, she just..."

"See? I was right."

"Let her finish, Selma."

"I cooked it myself but she showed me how."

"Why's that? Is this supposed to be some kind of peace offering to make us forget everything?"

"That's not why I did it," I stammered, staring at the leg of the metal bridge table.

"No? Then why all of a sudden you're cooking a big meal for us out of nowhere, the day after you lose our ring?"

"Selma, cut it out."

"I have a right to know. She obviously has an ulterior motive."

"Okay, I was trying to make up with you. I'm moving in here next week and I was scared you were mad at me."

"So it *was* about the ring."

"Not just the ring. You've been mad at me my whole life and I don't know why."

"You want to know why?" There was venom in her voice. "You don't show respect. As long as I've known you, Rhona, I've been aware of it. And quite frankly, it sickens me. It's not what I wanted for my son, right from the beginning." She took a drink from her

WEDNESDAY, AUGUST 18, 1971

cup of soda, all the while staring at me with cold eyes. I looked at Stuie for help but he was playing with a piece of onion, twirling it back and forth on his fork, avoiding my eyes at all costs. *Come to my rescue.* But Stuie continued to play with his food, mashing a piece of carrot with the back of his fork.

"I'm sorry, I'm not feeling so good," I said, rising from the table and running for the door.

• • •

I breathed in the evening air as I walked quickly down the block, my pace quickening as I made my way toward the playground, recognizing two figures there, a child in the sandbox and a reed-thin woman swinging on the swing, her red hair flying in the breeze.

Marsha smiled happily when she saw me. "What are you doing here?" she asked. The overhead street lights had already come on, illuminating the playground.

I tried to catch my breath before speaking. "I was at Stuie's house. Is it okay if we talk in front of your brother?"

"Don't worry, he's not listening."

"Still, he's just a kid."

"Hey, Scott," she called. He ignored her, busying himself with his green plastic soldiers, setting them up for battle in the glow of the nearby street lamp.

"Scott," she called more loudly.

"Yeah?"

"Ro and I are gonna talk about grown-up things for a while, so try not to listen."

"Okay."

I sat on the swing next to Marsha, my hands in my lap. "What happened?" she asked, her swing rocking gently next to mine.

"I'm falling apart piece by piece. I know it sounds crazy but it's the truth."

"Tell me everything."

"I would but my brain was the first to go."

"Sounds like you and Stuie had a fight."

"His mother picks on me all the time and he never says anything. What's it going to be like when I'm actually living there?" Marsha blinked, not sure how to respond. She had never had a boyfriend or a boyfriend's mother to deal with, so what was the point in asking her advice? "Let's not talk about it tonight," I said, gripping the rusted chains and soaring higher and higher like we did when we were seven, my hair blowing back in the breeze. "I bet I can go higher than you."

"No way." She pumped the swing as far as it could go, but I beat her by a couple of inches. I slowed it back down, a look of smug victory on my face as I dragged the tips of my white Keds along the ground. Marsha slowed her swing, too, her red hair all wind-blown and falling into her eyes. "That was fun," she said, brushing away a strand.

"Yeah, like the good old days."

"And now I'm going to college," she said. "We're shipping my trunk tomorrow."

"Are you excited?"

"I'm a little more scared than excited." She looked off beyond the clotheslines. "Albany seems so far away."

"Is it too late to change?"

"Are you kidding? It took three months to talk my parents into letting me live in the dorms. They wanted me to stay home and go to Hunter, remember?"

"So tell them you changed your mind."

"I can't. I already made the decision and we gave the deposit and everything. I have to go through with it."

"Please don't go to Albany," I begged, surprised by my own neediness.

"It's not forever."

"Yes, it is. It's four years."

She leaned her slender back against the rusted chain. "Do you think you'll still be in Walnut four years from now?"

"Either here," I said sadly, "or buried six feet under at Forest Hills Cemetery."

"Don't talk like that. It gives me the creeps."

"But it's true."

"What, you're going to kill yourself?"

"I might just die of loneliness. And a broken heart." We sat in silence, listening to the happy sounds of her brother playing with his soldiers. I was about to tell Marsha about my trip to Great Neck, but quickly decided not to revisit the experience. "You know something, Marsh?" I said. "I'm getting married this weekend and it's supposed to be the best day of my life and instead I want to run away and never come back."

Marsha nodded, absorbing the depth of my plight. "I'm glad I don't have a boyfriend. It seems like it's more trouble than it's worth." She glanced at me quickly. "I shouldn't have said that. I didn't mean to make you feel worse."

"That's okay. I don't think I could feel any worse if I tried." I got off the swing and sat at the bottom of the slide, my head in my hands. Marsha's brother continued to play, making war sounds as his soldiers dove into the sand, ignoring his sister and me and our boring, grown-up conversation. *Just you wait, Scott.* In ten years his life would be a lot more complicated and he would surely long for the days of playing in the sandbox.

Marsha rose from the swing and came over to where I was sitting at the bottom of the slide. She knelt beside me and put her arms around me. We hugged tightly, hot tears rolling down my cheek, drenching the sleeve of her white cotton blouse. "Don't look now," she whispered into my neck. "But here comes Skully."

"Oh, no." I pulled away from Marsha and turned around to see Stuie making his way toward the playground entrance.

"Scott, it's time to go home," Marsha called sharply.

"I'm playing. Leave me alone."

"Then I'm going without you." Marsha stood up and made her way toward the chain link gate of the playground. Scott threw down his pail angrily, but Marsha remained patient. "Put your soldiers away. We'll come back tomorrow."

Scott did as he was told, not liking it but not protesting, either. Stuie walked in the gate just as Scott and Marsha were leaving. She smiled briefly, then hurried along the path toward her building, a protective hand on her brother's back. I wiped my face quickly on my shirt while Stuie walked over to the swing Marsha had vacated and sat down.

"I'm sorry about what happened," he said. "My mother can really suck sometimes." I didn't know how to respond. It was one thing to say your own mother sucks but it was a whole different thing to say someone else's did, even if it were true. "It was nice you made that brisket for us."

"Thanks." I got up from the slide and sat on the swing beside him.

"But it probably could've used another half hour in the oven." He smiled and took a pack of cigarettes from his pocket and lit one up, cupping his hands around his chrome lighter, snapping it shut when he was finished. "My father and I were just talking out on the stoop." He leaned his head back and made a perfect smoke ring. "He asked me how I felt about getting married on Sunday."

"And?" I held my breath, expecting Stuie to call it off right then and there. I was surprised by my own nervous reaction. Although I didn't particularly want to be his wife, I was getting a little excited about the reception on Sunday afternoon, having always loved parties since I was a little kid. *Maybe we can just have the party and not get married.*

"I told him I'm scared. I mean, I've known about it for a long time but you never think the day's actually gonna come, you know?"

"You're...scared?" Why hadn't it ever occurred to me that Stuie might be scared, too?

"Well, yeah. I mean none of my friends even has a girlfriend. What's going to happen when I suddenly have a wife? Are you gonna let me hang out at the schoolyard or tell me to clean out the garage?"

"Stuie, we don't *have* a garage."

"You know what I mean."

"To tell you the truth, I hadn't thought about it."

"Well, think about it now. What's going to happen if I want to get high with Buffa and Larry? Are you going to stop me?"

"That's what you're scared of? That I'll tell you what to do?"

"Well, yeah. And other stuff, too."

"Like what?"

"I'm worried about money. My father said they'd pay the rent but we have to split everything else, like food and the phone bill."

"But you'll have a job."

"I hope so." He paused. "What part of being married scares *you*?"

"I'm scared about living with your mother. She hates me, Stuie. Everybody knows that."

"She doesn't hate you, that's just the way she is. She's like that to everyone except my sister."

"Did you see how she treated me tonight?" The anger was returning.

"Yeah, and I said I'm sorry."

"You didn't say it in front of her."

"Next time I will."

"You better, Stuie. Because starting Monday we all have to live there together and I don't want to be treated like I'm the same age as Nola."

"Look, we won't be there forever. One day we'll move out."

"To where? Another apartment in Walnut?"

"I guess. My father said he'd go with us to the rental office and see if they have any one bedrooms after we have some money saved." We sat in silence for a minute. Stuie took a deep drag of his cigarette and put it out on the concrete, crushing it with the heel of his Converse high-top. "My father was telling me tonight about him and my mother."

"What'd he say?"

"He was saying how she's been a friend to him all these years and how she stuck by him and stuff."

"Wow."

"I know. It's kind of sick to think about them like that. But he was trying to say that you and me have been friends, too, and that it's important to do that when you're married. Be friends, that is."

"They don't really seem like friends. They yell at each other all the time."

"Underneath they're friends. I guess. That's what he said, anyway."

"Stuie, do you ever wonder what we'll be like when we're thirty or forty?"

"Forty? I haven't even thought about twenty."

I smiled. "Just try it. Do you think we'll have the same voice in our heads, or will it change?"

"I'm not sure what you mean."

"Close your eyes."

"I don't feel like it."

"Please."

He lit another cigarette and closed his eyes, breathing the smoke through his nose, his large head bobbing. I gave him a minute before I spoke. "You hear that voice?" He shrugged. "What's it saying?"

"It's saying why the fuck are you sitting on a swing with your eyes closed, asshole?"

"Perfect. Now try to picture yourself being really old, like forty. Is the voice going to sound like the one tonight, or will it be different, like some adult we don't know yet?"

"How should I know?"

"I'm just asking you to think about it. Part of us has to change, but another part is going to stay the same. Aristotle said that."

"That's wonderful, Ro," he said sarcastically. "What does he want, a medal?"

"I'm just saying he was pretty smart."

"I'm smart, too. But that doesn't mean I go around acting like King Shit."

"He said you can get old but still be young inside. Look at my Tanta Ida, for example."

"No, thank you. She's got mold growing between her teeth."

"Seriously, she sees herself as a teen-ager even though she's in her eighties."

"That's only 'cause she's senile."

"No, it's because part of her hasn't changed. Get it? Every time something changes, part of it stays the same. That's what Aristotle said."

"You already told me that."

"I just want to know if you agree with it."

"I'm still thinking about how I'm gonna have enough money for a nickel bag of weed when I have to pay for groceries." I rocked absently back and forth in my swing. "I'm going to the schoolyard," Stuie said. "You want to come?"

"Maybe later. I'd like to hang out alone for a while." I started to get up but Stuie reached for my hand. There was no way I'd give him a creampuff in the playground, not now, not tonight, so he'd better not even ask.

"My father said it's important to tell you I love you," he said tentatively. He got up from the swing and pulled me to my feet, dropping the cigarette to the ground. He stood close and we looked right into each other's eyes, possibly for the first time ever. I had no idea there were green flecks around his irises. "I...love you, Ro." I stared at his face, not able to speak. "It's okay. You don't have to say anything." He leaned forward and kissed me on the lips. I held my breath the whole time and when the kiss broke we looked at each other awkwardly. "That was nice," he said. I smiled, and the sadness in my chest was so fierce I had difficulty breathing.

"I'll call you later," I whispered with a thin smile as I headed back to my apartment. I closed my bedroom door and lay down on my bed, the chenille bedspread soft and welcoming beneath me. I stared at the orange walls, tears streaming down my cheeks and into my ears. Stuie really *did* want to be a good friend and a responsible husband and I actually respected him in a way I didn't think I was capable of. But I would never look forward to his coming home at the end of a long day, I wouldn't find my heart pounding with eager anticipation when we got into bed at night. Maybe we'd become friends over time, but we'd never have sweet memories of a passionate beginning. I closed my eyes tight, tears running into my mouth, realizing with great sadness that this coming Sunday marked the beginning of the end.

Thursday, August 19, 1971

When I woke up Thursday at one in the afternoon there was a note lying at my feet in my mother's illegible scrawl. 'Dear Ro: Got called in under fire.' A second glance revealed she 'got called in until five.' On the back of the note was a carefully printed list of wedding-related people to call and errands to run in her absence. When I got to the last demand, 'pick up shoes from shoe man, make sure pumps match mother-of-the-bride dress exactly,' I burst into tears. I was surprised that a pair of dyed-to-match shoes could leave me such an emotional wreck, but I was admittedly unstable and unnaturally emotional in these final hours before the countdown to purgatory.

At four o'clock I trudged back into the apartment, my arms filled with dry cleaned clothes, a box of shoes, two packages of nylon stockings, a 46-D support bra for my mother and a travel tube of Gleem toothpaste for my overnight bag. I dumped everything on my parents' bed and stopped in the kitchen for a huge slab of peanut brittle before locking myself in my room. I turned on the radio, plopped onto my bed, and allowed songs of love to wash over me. I always found it weird that lyricists depicted love as a matter of life and death: 'I can't live without you,' 'I'll die if you leave me,' – it was as if the songwriters out there were all a bunch of suicidal maniacs, unable to cope with the realities of life, choosing death over rejection. Real life couldn't possibly be that dramatic although now, suddenly, my own situation seemed so tragic and hopeless that I was beginning to wonder.

If Jeffrey hadn't come into my life so serendipitously, I realized, I would marry Stuie on Sunday and be none the wiser, surviving each day in blissful ignorance. But Jeffrey *did* come into my life, offering me a taste of the delicious world beyond Walnut Gardens, showing me how hungry I was for possibility, how much I needed it for my steady diet, how reluctant I was to accept an empty plate. Or an empty roll. I was reminded of my Grandma Pearl who spoke only Yiddish and never bothered to learn a language as worthless as English. She used to say, "Alts drait zich arum broit un toit." Everything revolves around bread and death. According to Grandma Pearl and Millie Rosenblatt and my parents and everyone else at Walnut, basic sustenance is all one needs and all one deserves until the inevitable end. No wonder they wanted me to marry Stuie. As long as he put rolls on the table, empty or otherwise, what more could we want?

There was so much to ponder that I put all my questions into a poem and called it 'Ode to a Bread Basket.' I was reading it for the tenth or fifteenth time when my mother knocked on my closed bedroom door, still breathless after rushing home from the hospital. "Do you want to come to bingo with us?"

"I can't. I'm writing."

"Forget writing already and play some bingo. It'll be good for you."

"I don't want to."

"Can I come in?" Without waiting for a response she opened the door, one arm hidden behind her back. "How'd it go with the brisket last night? We must've been sleeping when you came home."

"They liked it."

"And?"

"And nothing. They liked it."

"Did they say anything about me?"

"Not a word. Oh, their Cousin Shirley can't come to the wedding so they have to cancel one diabetic dinner."

"Oh my God, we have to call the caterer right now."

"I already did."

"And you told him to cancel her meal?"

"Yes."

She seemed pleased. "Come to bingo. You need to get out."

I sighed. "Fine."

"I have something for you." Hiding behind her back had been a white box with a silver bow.

"What is it?"

"A little mother-daughter present."

"Can I open it?" Without waiting for a response I untied the bow and removed the lid. Beneath the tissue paper was a brightly flowered apron with the words 'Rhona's Kitchen' embroidered across the chest. I lifted it from the box, hiding my disappointment as best I could.

"That's for making a perfect brisket," she said.

"Thanks, ma, but it could've used another half hour in the oven."

Her eyebrow shot up. "Is that what she said?"

"Of course not. I was kidding. I love the apron, ma. I'll wear it every night."

"Good." She walked toward the door. "Let me get you a steak sandwich for the car. You want a little cole slaw and mustard on it?"

Moments later I was in the front passenger seat of the old Chevy, wolfing down my overstuffed sandwich while Gertie and Sadie and Millie sat shoulder to shoulder in the back seat. They chattered endlessly about the wedding, how excited they were, how Gertie was getting her hair set and her nails polished at the beauty parlor on Saturday morning.

"Tell me, mamala, how are you going to wear your hair?" she asked.

"Like it is now," I said between bites, licking cole slaw juice off my wrist.

"Just like that? You're kidding."

"What's wrong with my hair?"

"It's just so...plain," she said with a shrug.

"Gertie, leave her," Millie said, coming to my rescue with a nudge to Gertie's bare arm. "Kids don't wear their hair up anymore. That's for old women like us."

"Speak for yourself, I'm not an old woman," Gertie said.

"You're not Rhona's age either," Sadie chimed in.

"Who wants to be Rhona's age?" Gertie asked. "You think I want to do that all over again?"

"Yes."

"Well, you're wrong. Not on your life."

We rode in silence for a few minutes until out of the blue my mother started singing in her horrible, off-key soprano that could set a person's teeth on edge. "I'm always chasing rainbows, watching clouds drifting by..."

She sounded dreadful but nobody dared tell her. Instead, we gazed out the window until we arrived at the Temple parking lot. "Just think, in three days we'll be here again," Sadie said. I turned around and looked at those ubiquitous curlers beneath her mesh hairnet underneath the floral kerchief.

"Are you going to take out your curlers for the wedding?" I asked.

"What kind of a question is that? Of course I'm going to take out my curlers. This is your wedding we're talking about." She turned to Millie, uncomprehending. "What's the matter with her?"

Millie and I shared a secret smile. I was on the verge of becoming a married woman, no longer Sylvia's teen-age daughter. It gave me a sense of confidence, it was a passage into womanhood, and it allowed me to press the issue. "So Sadie, do you wear your curlers when Lou makes love to you?"

"What's got into her?" she asked with outrage. "What kind of a question is that?"

"She's a little nervous about Sunday," my mother said, trying

THURSDAY, AUGUST 19, 1971

not to laugh.

"I'm not nervous, I'm curious," I said. "Is that so wrong?"

"It's none of your business what I wear or don't wear when Lou makes love to me," Sadie shot back.

"I don't think Lou's made love to you since Gary was conceived thirty years ago," Millie said with a laugh.

"Listen to how you talk in front of the kinde," Gertie said with annoyance.

"She's not kinde anymore, in three days she'll be married." Millie turned toward my mother, who was making a wide right turn into oncoming traffic. Horns blared. "So have you talked to your daughter about you-know-what? Watch out for that car."

"Go shit in your hat and squeeze it," my mother yelled to the offending horn-blower. "What are you asking me, Millie?" Have I talked to her about the S-word?"

"*Sha*," Gertie snapped.

"Which S-word do you mean?" I asked. "Stuie? Or Selma?"

"I'm talking about *sex*," Millie said. "The act of having a man breathe down your neck three minutes a week." She leaned over and whispered conspiratorially, "That's what your mother wants you to think, but don't you believe it." She paused. "It's actually three minutes *twice* a week."

"Millie, stop it already," Gertie said.

"Don't shut her up," Sadie laughed. "Ro needs to know the truth before it's too late."

"Make sure Skully doesn't force you to do things you don't want to do," Millie said with a wink.

"What kind of things?" I asked.

"Things only animals do," Sadie replied as my mother swerved into a parking space, jolting us forward in our seats. "You'll know soon enough. They're all a bunch of animals, every last one of them."

We entered the sanctuary where long wooden tables were set for the upcoming game. I followed my mother to the corner of the room to buy our bingo cards. "Give me fourteen," she said, holding out a twenty dollar bill, "and my daughter wants...?" She turned to me and waited.

"Four," I answered.

"She'll take eight cards," my mother said.

"No, I won't, ma. I can't follow that many. It gives me a headache."

"Take them and I'll play whatever's too much for you."

The woman behind the table waited for me to protest, and when I didn't, she counted out twenty-two disposable bingo cards and handed them to my mother.

"How much I owe you?"

"Twenty-two dollars."

I reached into my pocket and came up with two crumpled bills. "Thank you, dolly," the woman said as she put the money in a metal box. We found a table with enough room for all five of us. My mother began the ritual of unpacking her bingo bag, a gingham-checked vinyl tote that housed her flat-topped marking pens, rabbit's foot and whistle which she blew for good luck whenever Morty called O-69.

I set up my eight cards neatly before me, end to end, wondering how I would manage to work them all without spinning into a frenzy. She leaned over and said, "Don't worry, ketzie, if it's too much for you I'll take over."

"Thanks, ma."

"You okay? You seem quiet all of a sudden."

"I'm fine."

She patted my knee. "My baby's getting married in three days. I still can't believe it."

"Neither can I."

"They'd better be nice to you or I'll come over there and raise hell."

"They're nice to me, ma."

"Good. They liked the brisket, huh?"

"Yeah, they liked it." Morty took the stage and the crowd hooted with delight as if Frank Sinatra had arrived to sing "Fly Me To The Moon." Morty smiled with some cockiness, ignoring the fact that the warm reception was strictly about gambling and not even the slightest bit personal. He certainly wasn't greeted with hoots and hollers when he arrived at his job at the Kosher butcher shop, so why would he think every woman in northeast Queens wanted him when he took the stage on bingo night?

Morty sat down beside the big metal canister and with slightly arthritic fingers he pulled the first number from within. "B thirteen," he called, leaning too closely into the mike. There was a healthy mix of cheering and booing, and he leaned forward slowly to shush the energetic crowd. "Before I forget, I have an announcement to make." The crowd groaned its disapproval. Morty ignored the rudeness and pulled a piece of paper from his shirt pocket which he unfolded carefully, then adjusted the glasses on his large, pockmarked nose. "This coming Sunday, August twenty-second, Rhona Gail Lipshitz and Stuart Martin Weiner will be married right here at Temple Beth Shalom." He looked around the crowded bingo hall. "I understand Rhona is here tonight. He paused to scan the crowd. "Rhona?"

Please let me die right now and get it over with. Sadie, to my immediate left, enthusiastically grabbed my arm and raised it high in the air. "Ouch," I said.

"Shhh."

"You did this," I sneered at her.

"It's a special time. You deserve a little recognition."

"Rhona, stand up and take a bow already. We've got a bingo game going on here." I looked up at Morty's table and imagined the chuppa there in its place, covered in colorful flowers. The eternal blue light of the Torah Ark would illuminate Rabbi Marks, and the bridesmaids and ushers would stand tall in their designated places. All heads would turn as I walked down the aisle in my wedding gown and picture hat. Stuie would be waiting for me in front of the chuppa, his big head turned toward me. No one would suspect we were two people who shared nothing, not even friendship. With every step I'd be plodding toward my execution and the organist would play a funeral dirge instead of the customary wedding march.

"Stand up," Sadie hissed and I did as she said, terrified to disobey. A few of the women clapped and I nodded my appreciation and sat back down.

"Okay, Morty, pull your balls already," someone shouted from the other side of the room. The crowd broke into spontaneous applause with a lot more enthusiasm than they had displayed for me.

"Come on, people, take it easy," Morty said, reaching into the canister. He smiled a big, toothy smile. "Here it is, ladies and gentlemen. O-sixty-nine." My mother grabbed her whistle and blew into it with all her might, the shrillness piercing the air and slicing right through me.

"Ma, you just broke my eardrum," I said with some annoyance.

"Oh, be quiet, you," she snapped back, scanning her cards and thumping loudly with the flat-topped marker. "I got O-sixty-nine in seven places."

It was too late for the good luck O-69 might bring. In seventy-two hours I would be a married woman whose husband the animal would be breathing down her neck for three minutes, twice a week.

Saturday,
August 21, 1971

I spent all day Friday alone in my room, reading two of Marsha's juiciest novels from beginning to end, writing poetry and avoiding everyone. My latest poetic effort was called, "Arriving at Death's Door In A White Dress," and I rather enjoyed its sardonic tone, modeling it after 'The Raven,' copying Poe's uniquely haunting rhyming scheme, A-B-C-B-B-B. Pleased with my work, I took a long walk, gazing into the open windows of my neighbors' apartments, watching as they washed dishes or watched television. *But are they happy?* I had a feeling they didn't give happiness much thought. Life was about survival, bread and death, as my sage grandmother would say. When I passed Stuie's building I turned away, repelled by my new home and not wanting to go near it any sooner than I absolutely had to. The notion of marrying Stuie reminded me of the polio booster shot I was forced to endure in the sixth grade, when Dr. Gold chased me around my apartment and I hid in the bathtub behind the shower curtain, frantic and shaking and screaming until my throat was sore. I felt precisely the same way on the day before my wedding. I wanted to hide in the bathtub and shriek so loud they'd hear me out in south Jersey.

This was my final chance to cancel the wedding. As I lay in bed staring at a tiny and delicate spider on the ceiling, I waited for a sign. Any sign. Anything.

"Why don't you just drop dead already?" It was Herbert Sinitzky screaming at Florence in what was sure to become another knock-down, drag-out fight.

"Shut up, you stinking son of a bitch," came her shrill response. "Don't you dare tell me how to spend my money."

"Oh, now it's *your* money?"

"You're damn right it's my money. If I had to wait for you to make any I'd die a pauper."

"Why don't you say it a little louder? A couple of people in Staten Island didn't hear you."

"Kiss my ass, Herb."

"That's all I've been doing for thirty years." There was a loud and violent slamming of the front door.

"Where are you going?" Florence yelled from the stoop. "Get back here. Herb!" I sat up in bed and peeked through the Venetians. Herbert was climbing into his old Ford parked along the curb. He turned the engine over a couple of times before it connected, then took off down the street, the tires skidding in the gutter.

I lay back down and put the pillow over my head, groaning so loudly I could feel the vibration of the foam against my face. This was the sign I'd been looking for. This was a glimpse into my future, stuck in a marriage that would deteriorate to nothingness, to a point where all intimacy, which never existed to begin with, would be permanently lost, anger and resentment hardened like concrete. If only Morty hadn't made such a scene, I could be on the next train to anywhere. But now everyone in the neighborhood, not just the sixty-four invited guests minus Selma's diabetic Cousin Shirley but absolutely *everyone* knew I would be married at Temple Beth Shalom the very next afternoon.

I stumbled out of bed and made my way to the kitchen where

SATURDAY, AUGUST 21, 1971

my mother was drinking coffee and eating a cream cheese sandwich on raisin toast. She had taken the day off to go to the beauty parlor and make last-minute arrangements with the caterer. Her hair was teased into an unnaturally high bouffant which gave her the look of an alien from the outer edges of the Milky Way. The hairdo was so severely laden with hairspray she could barely balance her heavy head on her shoulders and it looked, in a word, ridiculous, more like cotton candy than human hair. She glanced at me mid-bite, hoping I'd notice.

"They did a nice job," I said dutifully.

"You think? I was afraid it's a little too teased."

"No, not at all. I like it."

"Tell me the truth. I can go back and have her flatten it a little on top." She reached up with her freshly manicured hand and lightly tapped the top of her head. I couldn't help but giggle. "What?"

"Your head's even bigger than Stuie's."

"That bad?" She caught herself. "I mean, does it look bad?"

"It's okay to admit he's got a big head. Why do you think everyone calls him Skully, even Sam?"

"It still bothers me we cooked them a beautiful meal. I would rather have given it to charity." She paused. "Are you sure they liked it?"

"They loved it. They said the meat was cooked to perfection." She gazed out the window silently, a faraway look in her eyes. "What?" I asked.

"Could you believe he went a whole night without once calling G58? I came this close to winning the jackpot."

"I know. Seventy-five dollars."

"That's three dinners at your wedding, big shot." She stuffed the rest of her sandwich into her mouth and threw the napkin into the garbage can. "Do me a favor and throw out the garbage," she said through a mouthful.

"Come on, ma, it's the day before my wedding."

"So look at the bright side. This is the last time I'll be asking." We were quiet for a minute, digesting the weight of that. Although I looked forward to moving away from my parents, they were nevertheless an enormous improvement over the Weiners.

"Did you hear Florence and Herb screaming at each other?" I asked. "It had something to do with money, I think."

"He's been out of work since last winter. Every time she buys a can of tuna fish he asks how much it cost."

"How do you know all this?"

"How do I know. They live next door, that's how I know. That reminds me, I got you something when I was at the beauty parlor."

"What is it?"

"Wait here." She stood up, balancing her head on her shoulders, and walked into her bedroom, returning with two wrapped boxes, one large and one very small.

"More presents? You already got me that nice apron."

"You'll like this even more."

"Are you sure we can afford it?"

She nodded toward the enticing boxes. "Open them."

I went for the big one first, loosening the pink ribbon and tearing open the paper. "Oh, ma, it's gorgeous," I said as I lifted up a white satin nightgown with delicate silk straps. "Can I wear it tonight?"

"It's not for tonight, it's for tomorrow," she said. "You want to wear something special for your husband." My smile froze. It hadn't occurred to me to look special for Stuie. It hadn't even crossed my mind. "Open this one," she instructed. I picked at the Scotch tape on the tiny box and removed the wrapping paper.

"Oh my God. How'd you know...?"

She smiled modestly, pleased with herself. "A mother always knows her daughter. One day you'll understand."

"But it's so expensive," I called as I ran to the bathroom mirror and uncapped the Mary Quant burgundy lipstick, Rochelle's signature color, the one I coveted but would never actually buy, not at three-fifty a tube. I twisted it all the way up and sniffed the lightly scented cylinder, so creamy and red and flawless and inviting. I carefully applied the rich color and tapped my lips together, then pursed them, blowing a little kiss into the bathroom mirror, ready to wow the congregation on Sunday morning with my radiant beauty.

SATURDAY, AUGUST 21, 1971

"Go take out the garbage," my mother called from the kitchen. "Enough looking in the mirror."

"You know what, ma?" I called, loving how the color of my lips brought out the blue in my eyes. "This is the first time I'm actually feeling a little excited. Would you believe it?"

"Of course I believe it. Every bride gets excited the day before her wedding."

"All those people telling me how beautiful I am." I walked into the kitchen with my hair neatly combed and my lips a deep shade of red. "How do I look?"

She put down her broom and took me in, her eyes moist. "Like a grown woman," she said. She cleared her throat. "I don't mind if you have questions about you-know-what. Just don't ask anything about your father and me because I won't answer those."

"Are you talking about the S-word?"

"Quiet. Don't say it before you're married."

Married. The very mention of the word threw me back to reality, a reality even Mary Quant couldn't alter. I sighed, the familiar sadness crawling back into my body and curling up somewhere in the vicinity of my stomach.

• • •

At five o'clock I wandered into the kitchen in search of a snack. A little pickled herring in sour cream, maybe, or some prune Danish from Cappy's bakery. I was about to bite into a sour pickle when Rochelle and Marsha breezed into the apartment unannounced, saying we had somewhere special to go. "I don't want to go anywhere special," I said.

Marsha nodded toward the mysterious crystal gift that sat on the floor by the couch. "Nice jelly jar," she said.

"What did you call it?"

"A jelly jar."

"What's it for?"

"What do you think? You put jelly in it."

"But jelly already comes in a jar."

"Yeah, but you're not supposed to bring it to the table. You put it in a jar when you have company."

"Why?"

"I don't know. It looks nicer."

"I thought it was for baby food," Rochelle chimed in.

"Uh uh. *Jelly*," Marsha said.

"You realize that makes absolutely no sense," I said.

Marsha shrugged. "It makes sense if you're married, I guess. It's the kind of thing married people use." A slow chill crept up my spine. The jelly jar was living proof I was on my way to becoming Mrs. Weiner, married lady and collector of useless items.

"Notice anything new about my face?" I asked, striking my most dramatic pose. Rochelle's eyes narrowed as she moved closer.

"Is that my Mary Quant?"

"Very good, Sherlock. You guessed it."

"You stole it from my room, didn't you?"

"Did not. It was a gift from my mother."

"It looks good. But now we have to go." She grabbed my arm. "Let's get her out of here," she said to Marsha, who took my other arm. Together they lifted me off the shag carpet and out to the street where the Kotners' Pontiac Gold Duster was waiting at the curb. "Don't even ask because we won't tell you," Rochelle said before I could get out the first word.

"We've been planning this all week and we're not going to let you ruin it," Marsha added. I was happy they had formed such a nice relationship with each other. Who would've thought my tragedy would bring together my two best friends after so many years of mutual indifference?

"Get in the car," Rochelle said, and we all piled into the front seat, me in the middle. Rochelle put a blindfold around my eyes, one of her little neckerchiefs that reeked of Chanel Number Five.

"I know where we're going," I said into the darkness.

"No, you don't."

"Yes, I do. We're going to drive straight into the Hudson River because you know it's the only thing that will make me happy."

"We're not going to talk about stuff like that," Marsha said as

SATURDAY, AUGUST 21, 1971

she pulled out into the street. "Tonight we're gonna have nothing but fun."

I tried to guess the direction in which we were headed but I was too disoriented with the blindfold up against my eyes, cutting off my circulation. "How about a hint?"

"It's exactly what you need."

"Even more than Marsha does," Rochelle laughed. Marsha reached past me and slapped Rochelle on the arm, then she turned on the radio and Rochelle started to sing, off-key, not unlike the way my mother sang on Thursday evening en route to bingo. Soon the two of them were laughing and singing while I sat between them, jealously guarding my somber mood. Rochelle tapped the buttons back and forth on the dial, switching stations, the breeze from the open window blowing through the car. Rochelle pushed Marsha's hand away from the radio, turned up the volume, and began to wail.

"Shut up already, Chelle," Marsha said.

"No, you shut up. I love this song." Marsha sighed and joined Rochelle, her voice a bit sweeter, as they drowned out the voices on the radio.

"I can't handle this much fun," I said.

"Sure you can."

"You're not the one getting married tomorrow, Marsh."

She turned the volume down just a little. "We're not going to talk about anything unpleasant. Tonight we're gonna forget our troubles and get happy."

"Cause we're headed for the promised land," Rochelle added, and the two of them broke into new peals of giggles.

"Hey, let's play a game," Rochelle said when the laughter subsided. "Everyone pick one good thing about tomorrow. I'll go first." She bit her lip, thinking hard. "Give me a minute."

"I have one," I said. "For the first time in my life everyone will tell me I'm beautiful."

"People tell you that all the time," Marsha said.

"Yeah, but not sixty-three people all in one day."

"I'm proud of you for being so positive," Rochelle said. "Here's another one. You're about to get hundreds of dollars to spend on anything you want. Maybe we can go to Bergdorf's next week, huh?"

"You're supposed to *save* the wedding money," Marsha reminded her.

"Says who? It's hers, isn't it?"

We continued driving, reflecting on the good things my wedding would bring, and for that fleeting moment I felt happy, scrunched and blindfolded between my two best friends, anticipating how pretty I would look on Sunday afternoon. But my happiness began to fade when I realized the truth about Sunday: once the white gown was taken off and hung in the closet, once I'd washed off the make-up and put on my regular clothes, I would be left with Stuie as my husband. Adjusting the neckerchief that was cutting into the bridge of my nose, I settled into the seat and into a funk, my hands folded in my lap.

After what seemed like a long time, the car came to a halt. "We're here," Rochelle said, excitement in her voice. "Welcome to your last night as a bachelorette."

She pulled off the blindfold and I tried to focus, but I was disoriented and couldn't get my bearings. I soon realized we were outside a seedy club somewhere in the vicinity of Jackson Heights. The flashing marquee read, 'Live Nude Male Dancers,' and underneath, 'Complete Dinner, $2.99.'

"Let's go," Rochelle said, jumping out of the car. I looked over at Marsha who was rolling up her window, eager anticipation in her eyes. Marsha's friendship with Rochelle was having a definite impact on her, to the point where I barely recognized her from the bookworm she used to be. Her red hair was wild and curly and free and she wore green eye shadow and black eyeliner. I couldn't be sure but it seemed as if her breasts were larger and pointier than they had been just a week before; perhaps Rochelle had talked her into wearing a padded bra.

"Time to face the music," Marsha said, grabbing my arm as she opened the car door. I followed her into the darkened, air-conditioned lobby where Rochelle was giving our name to the host, a muscle-clad man with black-rimmed glasses and short, glossy hair.

SATURDAY, AUGUST 21, 1971

"You girls are twenty-one, aren't you?" he asked.

"Of course we are. My friend Ro's getting married tomorrow," Rochelle said.

He looked at me appreciatively. "That's too bad."

"Thank you, that's exactly how I feel," I said.

The host led us to a booth that faced a small, raised stage. "This is so exciting," Marsha giggled as we sat down. "I've never done this before."

"Sal and I do it all the time. Except the dancers are always women."

"Well, I've never been to one of these places, either," I said to Marsha. "Stuie and I don't go anywhere together, especially if it means spending money on something other than drugs."

"No talk of Skully, please. Tonight we're going to have a wonderful, fabulous dinner and look at a bunch of gorgeous nude men. Compliments of me and Marsha, your friends till the end."

Marsha opened her menu and scanned both sides. "Everything looks great. Oooh, they have prime rib. That's what I'm having. Prime rib with mashed potatoes."

"And I'm going to have the extra large sausage with a side of meatballs," Rochelle said with a sly smile. They laughed and joked until the waiter arrived, a tall, handsome man with a dancer's lithe body. Their enjoyment of the evening was contagious and I found myself laughing along with them. We placed our orders — steak for me and Rochelle, prime rib for Marsha, and ordered three glasses of burgundy wine, the first alcoholic beverage I'd ever had, not including the sip of brandy I'd taken in Jeffrey's frosty library so many days ago.

"To match our burgundy lips," I said to my best friends as I raised my glass in a toast.

"To liberated women," Marsha said, her glass high in the air.

"And naked men," Rochelle added.

"Amen." I took a sip, tentative at first, and found the taste to be mildly pleasing. We cleaned our plates of the delicious meal and unlike my friends, I ordered a second glass of wine and then a third glass, feeling better than I had in a long time. When my third glass had been drained and I'd finished off the remainder of Marsha's first, I turned playfully to Rochelle. "I've got a secret."

"Oh yeah, what's that?"

"Guess."

Rochelle ripped a piece of bread from the loaf in the basket. "You're really a man and tonight you're going to prove it by dancing in your jock strap."

"Nope." I leaned in close. "Remember the other morning when I came over, before we went to Jamaica?" Being drunk was fun. I could say anything I wanted.

"Yeah."

"Well, when you and Sal were waltzing into the bedroom he went like this." With an unsteady finger I showed her how Sal had beckoned me and blown a kiss and then winked.

"He wanted me, Chelle. For real. You think I should've said yes?" Rochelle sat straight upright, her smile and the festive mood at our table gone in a flash.

"You're full of shit, Ro."

"Why are you telling her this?" Marsha asked angrily, having overheard everything.

"Yeah, why are you telling me this?"

My brain cleared temporarily, long enough to realize what I had done. "Oh, my God. I'm so sorry, Chelle. I shouldn't have said anything."

"It's too late now," Rochelle said angrily. She paused for a minute. "He's such a little shit."

"I'm sorry, Chelle," I repeated as best I could.

"Let's just drop it," Rochelle spat. The announcer of the evening's festivities took the floor in a pair of hip hugger bell-bottoms and a bare chest. Marsha leapt up from her seat and whooped right along with every other woman in the room who had shown up to forget her troubles and get happy.

One by one the dancers took the floor, dancing and clapping and enjoying themselves, it seemed, as much as the women who beckoned them with neatly folded dollar bills, the better to slip into leather jock straps. Rochelle did her best to get back into the swing as she opened her purse, removing two bills and handing one to Marsha.

"What's this for?" Marsha asked.

"What do you think? Come on, let's get crazy!" Seeing the hurt in her dark eyes, I reached for her arm but she pulled it away, getting up from her seat and heading for the dance floor as I followed on unsteady feet. I stood off to the side, watching the tight masculine bodies and the adoring women who pushed and shoved to get up close. Suddenly a wave of warm blood rushed through me. Maybe it was the wine or the anticipation of the wedding or the plethora of emotions that had swirled through me these past twelve days. Whatever caused it, something giddy and terrifying and painful rushed through my body with lightening speed, shorting out all my emotions. I tried to call for help but my throat closed up and my legs were deflated tires.

"Ro! Answer me!" Rochelle was kneeling over me, screaming into my face, trying to be heard over the pounding music and the shouting women.

"Somebody help," Marsha shouted. It took a few minutes before the ones in charge realized there was actually a medical crisis going on right under their noses. People gasped and moved away. The manager and one of the waiters lifted me to my feet and placed me on a nearby chair. It took a few minutes before I remembered where I was, the room spinning around me, the blare of the music and the dancers and the audience blurring into one cacophonous drone. Marsha's voice stood apart from the others and I cringed when she shouted into my face.

"Ro, you okay? Ro..." I nodded, taking a deep breath, desperate for oxygen. That's when my eyes rolled back into the recesses of my skull, my body growing limp once more, my tortured soul preparing to meet its maker.

Sunday, August 22, 1971

I was alone in the middle of a vast ocean, a hot sun blazing down, my head aching and my blistered lips parched and cracked. I was treading water but my arms and legs were so heavy, so tired that I could no longer continue the paddling. My head fell beneath the cool surface, the salty water filling my nose, my ears and my mouth. There was a persistent banging, loud and determined. I tried to ignore it but the banging wouldn't stop and I found myself slowly rising to the surface, fighting for every breath, moaning, needing oxygen, floating up higher and higher until I finally came out of the water. I forced my eyes to open and realized I was in my bed and someone was banging on the closed door.

"Go away," I said, plastered to the mattress, unable to move.

"It's nine o'clock," my mother said. "Come on, we have a million things to do." I tried to sit up on my elbows but my equilibrium wouldn't cooperate and I fell backwards, crashing onto the bed with full force, the pain in my head echoing down to my shoulders. *This is what a hangover feels like.* I was in a miserable mood. I was tired and achy and thirsty and the last thing I wanted to do was get married. I leaned up slowly and peeked out of the Venetians to a dark, gray morning, a steady, hard rain bouncing off the asphalt in the street, the perfect Sunday to stay in bed.

"Ro, come on," my mother said from the other side of the door. "It's late already."

"Start without me," I called from beneath the covers. "I'll meet you there."

She rattled the knob with such force I expected the door to separate from the jamb. "Stop it," I yelled, bringing an unsteady hand to my forehead. I leaned over to the dresser and opened my sock drawer, removing the sacred student ID with Jeffrey's smiling face. I kissed the picture gently and placed it back under my folded socks alongside the poem and my last will and testament, just in case I were to die before the end of the day, which now seemed entirely possible.

I climbed into the bathtub to take a shower in slow motion, lingering an extra couple of minutes while the hot water beat down on my aching neck. As I toweled off and rubbed a little Johnson's baby cream into my skin, the thought struck that on this very night I would be having sex for the second time in my life. I wondered what it would be like with Stuie. Perhaps he would surprise me and be every inch the lover that Jeffrey was. Maybe he had learned the proper way to kiss since I'd seen him in the playground on Wednesday night. *Yeah, sure.*

I opened a new package of nylons, fastened them to my garter belt and slipped into my white pumps. Wearing just this and a lace bra I applied my make-up, first the pancake, then the cream rouge, brush-on mascara, blue eye shadow and the grand finale, my burgundy lipstick, but even that couldn't cheer me up. *I hope Jeffrey will be safe in the rain.* I fastened a couple of rollers to my damp hair so it would flip along the bottom. *I hate to think of him on that airplane in such lousy weather.* As I clicked the last roller into place, I pictured him high in the air, soaring further and further away from me.

I put the white dress over my head, then looked in the hall mirror for a long time. I was to brides what Pagliacci was to clowns,

SUNDAY, AUGUST 22, 1971

heartbreak worn on my sleeve. With great reluctance I slipped the purple, orange and green love beads over my head and held them in my hand. I placed them lovingly in my sock drawer next to the school ID and the poem.

The door to my parents' bedroom was ajar. My father was slouched on the bed, sleeping soundly, his head leaning on the headboard. He was dressed in charcoal gray slacks and a white shirt opened at the neck, his red and black herringbone tie clutched in his fingers. My mother, meanwhile, was admiring herself in the mirror, talking non-stop to her sleeping husband, undaunted by the fact he was snorting and snoring while she spoke. "I wonder what the bitch will be wearing," she said as I walked in. "How do I look?" she asked without missing a beat, changing the subject before I could scold her for bad-mouthing my future mother-in-law yet again, even though I hated her, too.

"You look very nice, ma."

"You don't think I'm too fat?" She sucked in her gut, ensuring the response she was hoping for.

"No, you don't look fat at all."

"I should've gone with a darker color. Pink makes me look like a balloon. Don't you think?"

"You don't look fat, ma," I said. She glanced from her reflection to mine.

"You're beautiful, ketzie," she said.

"Thanks, but I don't feel particularly beautiful."

"Why not?"

"I don't know. I guess I'm just not in the mood."

"To get married?"

"Yeah."

She chuckled. "You'd better get in the mood before the night is over, if you know what I mean."

"That reminds me. I have a question about the S-word."

Her body stiffened. "What?"

"Is it okay if you don't do it on your wedding night?"

"I already told you, no questions about me and your father. I won't answer those."

"I'm not talking about you. I'm talking about me. What if I don't feel like doing it?"

She adjusted the pearls around her neck. "Tell him you have a headache. He might as well get used to hearing it now."

My father snorted so loud he woke himself up with a start. "What?" he asked.

"You scared yourself," my mother said.

"Was I sleeping?" he asked stupidly.

"Yes, and it's time you woke up. Take a look at your daughter, Mel. Isn't she beautiful?"

He turned to me and smiled, his sleepy eyes trying to focus. "Look at you. Yesterday you were pishing all over me and today you're a married woman."

"Not yet, dad. Don't rush it."

"Make sure you never deny your husband what every man needs. You be a good wife, you understand?"

"Dad, stop."

My mother frowned. "Get up already, Mel. We're going to be late."

"What's the big hurry?" I asked.

"Are you kidding? I have a million things to do." She raised a manicured fist in the air and counted off on her fingers. "The flowers, the caterer, the katuba, the license, I have to pay for the Temple and the band and pick up the kiddush cup, I have to make sure all the tables are right. And remind me not to forget the little bride and groom for the cake. We don't want to forget that." She patted my hand. "That's Stuie and my baby girl on top of that cake."

I rolled my eyes and left the room but she kept talking. "Let's see. If everyone starts showing up around two, maybe a couple of minutes before, we should be there by eleven thirty. Ro? Are you ready?"

"It's not even ten o'clock," I called from my bedroom where I was sitting on the bed in my white dress, the sock drawer open, Jeffrey's picture in my hand.

I stalled for another hour, playing with my make-up and administering a quickie manicure. We were in the midst of a torren-

SUNDAY, AUGUST 22, 1971

tial downpour and my mother paced the apartment in her pink dress and perfectly dyed-to-match pink shoes, tsking and grumbling about the sheets of rain ruining our clothes. "Did you speak to Stuie this morning?" she asked.

"No. Should I?"

"You might want to give him a fast call."

"Why? Are you afraid he won't show up?"

"To say good morning, wise guy. In a few hours he's going to be your husband, you know."

"So?"

"So. Get used to speaking to him. He's the first person you'll see every morning starting tomorrow for the rest of your life." A flash of lightening tore through the slate-gray sky, followed by an enormous crash of thunder. "Such a day to get married," my mother said, shaking her head. "But who knows? Maybe it'll bring luck."

"Don't count on it," I said dryly.

"What is it with you? Here it's your wedding and look how you're talking."

"Ma, haven't you heard anything I've been saying to you? I'm not ready for this."

"Every bride feels that way."

"No, they don't. Most brides are in love with the person they're marrying."

"Give it time. Love comes over time."

My father put a raincoat over his gray suit and went to the front door, umbrella in hand. "I'll bring the car around."

I pulled an old jacket from my closet and draped it around my shoulders, then opened the front door and gasped at the fierceness of the rain, which was coming down sideways. My mother, in a plastic rain hat and plaid coat, squealed all the way to the car. I held my breath and followed her, my picture hat and overnight bag in my left hand, the bottom of my dress scrunched up in my right. I slammed the door hard, realizing I had closed it on the hem of my dress. I opened the door again and jerked the wet fabric inside. "We did it," I said breathlessly.

My father slowly pulled the car into the street, the windshield wipers slapping back and forth, the car humid and musty. "Open a window, my hair's gonna fall," my mother said. "I don't mind the heat, but I can't take the humidity."

"We can't open any windows, Sylvia. The rain's coming down too hard."

"Such a day for a wedding," she breathed, shaking her head sadly. When we arrived at the Temple the halls were hushed in Sunday morning reverence and the lobby smelled of ancient prayer books and lemon cleaning fluid. A maintenance man was mopping the floor of the sanctuary.

There was something about that sanctuary when a bingo game wasn't in progress that gave me a warm chill, making me proud of my heritage, this tribe of which I was a member. I felt accepted here, part of a greater whole, moved by the power of the Torah, which stood erect behind smoked glass doors on the bima. I closed my eyes and let the feeling linger in my body, but the sound of my mother's shrieks as she came in from the rain disturbed the sanctity of the moment.

"Where's Rabbi Marks?" she called, her voice echoing in the front room.

"Probably in his study downstairs," my father said, shaking out his umbrella onto the freshly mopped linoleum floor.

"Jesus, I bet my hair is ruined," she said, gingerly removing the plastic rain hat and tapping her head to make sure everything was intact.

"Stop worrying about your hair, Sylvia."

"Easy for you to say. A man just runs a comb through and boom, he's finished."

"Stop yelling," I begged, rubbing my throbbing temples, reminding myself never to drink again. I leaned against the wall, the hem of my dress wet and muddy, my hair a frizzy mess. *I hope the guests still think I'm beautiful.*

At eleven-thirty the caterer and two workers arrived in a large white truck and began to set up tables in the reception room. My mother fussed and followed them up and down the stairs, asking a million questions for which she received one-word responses. "The diabetic plate's been canceled?"

"Yes."

"And we have four children's portions."

"Yes."

"And fifty-nine regular portions?"

"Yes."

Suddenly she gasped and put a hand to her heart. "Oh my God, Mel. Mel, where are you?" She dashed around the upper level in search of my father, nearly slipping on the slick tile floor. "Mel, listen to me, I forgot the bride and groom for the top of the cake."

"Jesus, Syl."

"It's your fault. You rushed my kishkes out this morning."

"I rushed *you*? You're kidding, right?"

"Don't argue with me, Mel, there's no time."

He blew out a breath and squinted toward the window where the rain was pelting against the glass. "Where'd you leave them?"

"In a shopping bag in the kitchen, on the floor near the Fridgidaire. Thank you."

She hurried downstairs just as the Bernsteins entered the Temple and shook out their wet umbrella in the entranceway. I glanced at my watch. It wasn't even twelve-thirty.

"You look lovely, dolly," Gertie said, grabbing my chin and planting a wet kiss on my forehead. "Tell me, where's mommy?"

"In the reception room telling the caterer how to do his job." Joe smiled knowingly, then followed his wife downstairs. A slow wave of anxiety crept through my body, taking me by surprise. My mouth became dry and I could feel adrenaline pump through my wrists to the tips of my clammy fingers. This was it, it was really happening. August twenty-second was more than a date on a printed invitation. I rubbed my arms, chilled to the bone and desperate for someone to talk to. I needed Rochelle and Marsha, and I needed them now. I found a phone booth near the ladies' room and dialed.

"Chelle? It's me."

"Where are you?" Something cool and distant had crept into her voice overnight.

"At the Temple. It's torture. I've been here since the crack of dawn and if you don't get over here I'm going to die, I swear it."

"I have to wait for Sal. Ask Marsha to do it."

She hung up abruptly. I deposited another dime and dialed. "Marsh? It's me."

"Why aren't you at the Temple?"

"I *am* at the Temple, but I'm having a mental breakdown. I thought I'd be okay but I'm not. I'm scared, Marsh. I might actually die for real."

"Give me a couple of minutes."

I thanked her and hung up the receiver, resting my head against the black metal pay phone in that muggy booth, my eyes closed, forehead pressed to the phone, trying to breathe deeply without inhaling the rancid traces of stale cigarettes. A tapping on the glass made me jump out of my skin and out of a fitful, fevered sleep. I looked up and there was Stuie in his reconditioned Bar Mitzvah suit. The sleeves, waist and cuffs had been let out but the shoulders were a couple of inches short, making his neck appear smaller and his head even bigger. His curly hair was flattened to his head with some Dippity-Doo gel, and his voice was muffled through the glass. "Ro? I've been looking all over for you. What are you doing in the phone booth?"

I opened the door slowly. He didn't kiss me hello. "Calling Marsha."

"Marsha's been upstairs for ten minutes already."

"Then I guess I was sleeping." I walked past him, hiking up the gown, not telling him about my colossal hangover, and went upstairs to the front room. My mother was in a swirl of activity, even more so now that Selma and Sam had arrived. It wasn't easy to ignore the Weiners and annoy the caterer all at the same time.

Selma, in a long brown beaded dress, was holding Marsha's hand in both of hers, her back to my mother who was still having difficulty walking on the slick linoleum. I rushed to Marsha and hugged her so tightly I thought I'd never let go. "Let me see," Selma said, turning me around to face her. "That's your wedding dress?"

"Yes."

"You bought it used?"

SUNDAY, AUGUST 22, 1971

"No, of course not."

"Then what happened? It's all dirty."

"We're going to fix it right now," I said, tugging the sleeve of Marsha's pink gown and dragging her to the ladies' room. We grabbed a handful of paper towels, saturated them with hot water and soap, and began rubbing the daylights out of the hem of my dress.

"It's not so noticeable now," Marsha said, admiring our efforts.

We left the ladies' room and I pretended not to notice Stuie hanging around the cloakroom with Buffa, who looked silly in an ill-fitted suit and sloppily-made tie. "Hey, Ro," Stuie called as I headed for the stairs. I turned around. "C'mere, I want to ask you something."

Marsha gave me a little push and I followed him into the bowels of the cloakroom where damp raincoats were suspended from sagging wire hangers. "I thought maybe we'd have time for a quick creampuff to relieve some of the tension?"

"You're out of your mind, Stuie. People are going to be walking in and out of this place any minute."

"We'll close the door. Come on, Ro, I need something to relax me."

"Breathe. That'll relax you." I patted him on the shoulder of his too-small jacket and headed upstairs, where Rochelle and Sal had just arrived. Sal looked great in his tight black suit and snakeskin boots with Cuban heels. Rochelle was radiant in her pink gown, her eyes and skin luminescent. I assumed they'd just had sex before arriving at the Temple. I hugged her tightly and brushed a few strands of hair from her face, desperate to make up with her. She pulled me aside, her face serious.

"I told Sal and he said you're out of your mind. He said he's not attracted to you and he'd never in a million years ask you to go in the bedroom with us."

"Okay, I take it back. Maybe I imagined it."

"Yeah, maybe you did." Her voice was cold as she looked me up and down. "So how are you doing?"

"Stuie just asked for a creampuff down in the cloakroom. Need

I say more?" Marsha walked over and Rochelle slipped an arm around the narrow waist of her new best friend. Hurt, I glanced around the front room of the Temple where my mother greeted friends and relatives at every turn, her co-workers Mildred and Rita, my Aunt Henrietta, Uncle Benny and cousins Artie and Sharon, Tanta Ida in a sequined low-cut dress and too much make-up, Sadie and Gertie and Millie and their husbands who tugged uncomfortably on the ties around their necks. Sadie planted a kiss on her husband Lou's cheek and made a smug little face for my benefit.

My mother's Cousin Elise came toward me in a shiny black pantsuit encrusted with multi-colored jewels, a plastic cup of wine in her hand, her fingernails long and sharp and blood red. Elise was a woman who never, ever cracked a smile, and I could understand why, at age forty-three, she was still single and the cause of her mother's premature death from the dreaded C-word.

"Mazel tov," she said flatly in a deep, nasal voice before moving off in search of single men.

Stuie, meanwhile, was downstairs smoking a joint in the cloakroom with Buffa and Larry and Tony and Howie and Danny and Joel, guys from the schoolyard I disliked with great intensity. I chatted with some of the girls I invited, Karen and Debbie and Ellen and Ilene, who were happy and cheerful and had no idea how much I didn't want to be at the Temple. I wondered if it was too late to fix Stuie up with Ilene Grossman.

My mother grabbed my arm and said urgently, "Ro, find your fiance. Rabbi Marks wants to see you both in his study." I went to the cloakroom where Stuie and his friends were horsing around, the pungent smell of pot hanging in the stale air. Someone had brought a condom and had blown it up like a balloon and now they were letting the air out and watching it fly amid the wet raincoats and dripping umbrellas, guffawing like a bunch of idiots.

"Stuie, the Rabbi wants to see us," I said.

"Hey, guys, bad news," he called nervously to his friends. "The Rabbi found out about the scumbag."

The condom was retrieved and hurriedly tucked into Buffa's pocket for safekeeping as Stuie followed me to the closed door that

SUNDAY, AUGUST 22, 1971

said 'Rabbi Aryeh Aaron Marks' in carved wooden letters. I knocked softly.

"Come on in," said the voice of supreme authority. We walked timidly into the comfortable room that was piled with religious books, important looking papers and family photographs. Rabbi Marks stood up. He was wearing his tallis, even in the privacy of his office. A small velvet yarmulke covered his graying bald spot.

"Sit, sit. I wanted to have a minute with you before we get started upstairs." He looked into my guilt-ridden eyes and I turned away, ashamed to be seen in a white dress, the universal symbol of purity, a dress I had no right to wear. The Rabbi stroked his beard. *Here it comes. He's going to punish me for sleeping with another man, I just know it.*

I kept my eyes focused on my hands, peeling off the fresh coat of pink nail polish and brushing the little shards from my lap. Stuie, meanwhile, looked as guilty as me, his eyes downcast, fearful of being punished for smoking pot and abusing a condom on Temple grounds. Rabbi Marks sat back in his brown leather chair and looked at us, his thin lips forming a straight line beneath his gray whiskers.

"How long have you two known each other?" he asked, unable to make eye contact with either of us.

"All our lives," I said, knowing Stuie was too stoned to calculate the numbers.

"And when did you start...going steady, for lack of a better expression?"

"In third grade," I said. "At our friend Howie Berman's Passover seder." I remembered the evening well. Mrs. Berman had organized a seder for the children in the class. Stuie and I were alone behind the sofa, searching for hidden matzoh. Suddenly he leaned over and kissed my cheek as if he'd planned it the whole night. He asked me to be his girlfriend and then announced my acceptance at the table while sponge cake and macaroons were passed around. I glanced at him now but he seemed unfazed by the mention of our first prepubescent tryst on that Thursday evening in April. *He doesn't remember.*

"So by the time Stuart became a Bar Mitzvah you were practically engaged."

"Yes. I lit candle number three, after his parents and his grandmother, she should rest in peace."

"And now, what is it, five years later? Here you are back in the Temple, all of eighteen and getting married."

"Yes, we are."

"Never having dated anyone else, I presume." He looked into my face. *Oh, God, he knows everything.* Stuie shrugged without looking up. I shrugged, too, turning away from the Rabbi's probing eyes. "I imagine you've given this marriage a lot of serious consideration, and that you see it as a commitment between two adults," the Rabbi said. I glanced at Stuie briefly but he was playing with his shoelace, his left leg crossed over his right knee. "I'm correct in my assumption, aren't I?"

"Yes," Stuie said. The Rabbi put his index fingers to his lips and tapped them together slowly. We sat in his study like that, the Rabbi nodding his head and rocking in his brown leather chair for what could have been ten or fifteen minutes. I was beginning to sweat. "Let me tell you a little story," he finally said. "Rabbi Kaufman is walking home from Shul one evening when he sees a woman hunched over in the street. He asks her what she's doing and she says she's looking for her gold necklace. But the sun is setting, says the Rabbi. How do you expect to find something as small as a necklace on a dark street? And the woman says, I didn't lose my necklace in the street. It's somewhere inside my house, but my house is so dark I'll never find it."

Rabbi Marks paused and looked at us. Stuie snickered. "Pretty dumb chick. Why's she looking in the street if she lost it in her house?"

Rabbi Marks cleared his throat. "So Rabbi Kaufman says, don't you realize you're looking in the wrong place? Instead of looking out here, why don't you shine some light *inside*? That's where you'll find what you're searching for."

"Meaning what?" Stuie was really struggling to understand and I found my heart aching for him.

"Do you want to answer that for him, Rhona?"

SUNDAY, AUGUST 22, 1971

I took a cautious breath, praying it wasn't a trick question. Surely the Rabbi wouldn't swoop down upon me now and expose me for the liar and the cheat we both knew I was.

"I think the story means that the best place to find whatever you're looking for is inside yourself."

The Rabbi nodded. "We're individuals first. Before we can make sense of any relationship, we need to know ourselves." Stuie still seemed confused, staring out at the rain with a blank expression that wasn't lost on Rabbi Marks. "Now I'm going to give you both a little assignment." Stuie recoiled at the word. Assignments reminded him of school, and school was a place he was finished and done with. "Tonight, after the wedding, I want you to find a few minutes to talk about the story. Tell each other what it means to you."

"What for?" Stuie wasn't following.

"It's a good habit to get into, discussing important things with your partner. It will help you grow as individuals *and* as a couple." The Rabbi stood up. "Let's not keep your guests waiting too much longer." Stuie rose and walked out of the study with great concentration, one foot in front of the other, trying not to fall down. I followed, and as I walked through the doorway I looked up at the Rabbi's kind face. "Is that it?"

"Actually, there's one more thing I want to say to you." *He saved it for the end. I knew it.* "Come see me anytime you want to talk. I have a feeling there'll be lots to talk about."

We made our way upstairs and my mother waved to the Rabbi across the room, letting him know the photographer had arrived and we were ready to begin. Everyone filed into the main sanctuary, everyone except the bridal party who stayed back so Rabbi Marks could show us how to walk in rhythm with the organist, left foot together, right foot together, until we had reached the bima. He entered the sanctuary and we followed. I could feel my heart pounding in my ears and my chest and my stomach, the rich sound of the organ obscured by the steady thump-thump of blood rushing through my head. Buffa pushed Larry, nearly knocking him down, forcing him to make his way down the aisle, his feet shuffling awkwardly in time to the organ. Nola was by his side, her hair in banana curls, wearing the pre-teen version of the pink bridesmaid dress. Rochelle and Buffa came next, followed by Marsha alongside Stuie's cousin Barry. After a beat the Weiners made their way, then it was my parents' turn, my mother sucking in her belly all the way to the chuppa. Stuie counted to five and I watched the back of his big, glossy head as he lumbered left together, right together all the way down the aisle. It was my turn now. I started counting, four, five, six...my heart beating so fast that the sanctuary started to spin around me. I reached out for something to grab onto and found the back of a folding chair for support. Still counting, eight, nine, ten...I forced myself to let go and begin my final walk, every step taking me closer to where I didn't want to be.

The guests oohed and aahed as if they were seeing me for the first time that day. I wished I felt even a little beautiful, but I was dizzy and weak and hopelessy hung over. My mouth felt dry and my eyes were glassy. I must've looked like the bride of Frankenstein coming down that aisle, one leaden foot in front of the other, two clammy hands gripping a bouquet of summer flowers, four little words echoing in my head, *I don't love him, I don't love him...*

At last I reached the Rabbi who nodded at me as I took my place beside Stuart Martin Weiner, my betrothed, our parents and the wedding party forming a semi-circle around us beneath the chuppa, nobody making eye contact with anybody else. The Cantor began to sing, holding the last note for an impossibly long time, and the room fell into a reverential silence. The Rabbi waited a beat before speaking. "Ah, to be eighteen," he said. "With everything ahead. No mistakes and no regrets. Such an enviable place to be."

I glanced briefly at Tanta Ida in the front row, aware of the wistful look in her moist gray eyes. "Stuart and Rhona," the Rabbi said, "your lives have barely begun. You're just starting to understand yourselves and the world around you." He looked at us before continuing, the silence in the sanctuary palpable. "Allow me to offer you this blessing as you begin your journey. May you always treasure the quiet moments. That's where you'll find your greatest joy, where you'll learn the most about yourselves. And may you grow like two trees planted firmly into the earth. Side by side, but also independent."

Stuie shifted his weight from his left foot to his right. "I'd like you to join hands," Rabbi Marks said after a beat of silence. Stuie and I found each other's fingers. There was no magic, no current of electricity when we touched. "Stuart, do you take Rhona to be your wife, to have and to hold from this day forward, in sickness and in health, for better or worse, richer or poorer, for as long as you both shall live?"

As long as we both shall live. A chill ran up my spine like a flash of cold light. It seemed absurd to ask such a thing of two teen-agers who barely knew how to cook breakfast, let alone how to function in a marriage. *Why isn't somebody stopping us? They're the adults. What's wrong with them, anyway?*

"I do," Stuie said. He looked at Buffa who was crossing his eyes and sticking out his tongue.

"And do you, Rhona, take Stuart to be your husband, to have and to hold from this day forward, in sickness and in health, for better or worse, richer or poorer, for as long as you both shall live?" I opened my mouth but nothing came out. I tried again. My mother's pink lips turned downward and the lines around her mouth deepened. Marsha raised an eyebrow for encouragement.

"I do," I said hoarsely. *You've all lost your minds. I'm eighteen years old. What do I know about any of this stuff?* The Rabbi lifted the kiddush cup that my mother had provided and offered it to me. I waited until he finished making the prayer, then took a sip of the syrupy Kosher wine. I handed the cup to Stuie and he took a healthy gulp, wiping red wine from his chin with the sleeve of his white shirt.

"Stuart, may I have the ring?" Licking his lips, Stuie reached into his pocket and handed over the simple gold band his mother had gotten wholesale from her friend the jeweler in Bay Terrace. The Rabbi made a quick prayer in Hebrew, then placed the ring back in Stuie's hand and nodded for him to slip it on my finger. Touching our shoulders, the Rabbi positioned us so that we were facing each other. "With this ring," Rabbi Marks said slowly so that

Stuie could repeat it phrase by phrase, "you are consecrated unto me as my wife according to the law of Moses and Israel." *This is crazy. Two months ago I was in high school.* I held out my finger, but Stuie couldn't move the ring past my knuckle. I had given Selma an incorrect ring size, perhaps intentionally. The Rabbi's face showed concern. "Just go slowly," he whispered. There was a distinct hum of apprehension in the room. "We're having a little problem getting the ring on the bride's finger," Rabbi Marks said lightly to the crowd. "But we'll be patient." Frustrated and stoned and not knowing what else to do, Stuie lifted my hand to his mouth and licked my finger, then shoved the ring over my knuckle in one quick motion.

"Ouch," I said.

A light bulb wrapped in a cloth handkerchief was placed on the floor. Stuie drove his heel into it hard, shattering the glass. "In the eyes of God and the State of New York, I now pronounce you Mr. and Mrs. Stuart Weiner, husband and wife. Mazel tov." He smiled. "Go ahead and kiss the bride, and make it a nice one. That's everybody's favorite part." I lifted the brim of my picture hat so Stuie could get his big head under it without knocking it to the floor. We kissed briefly, nothing romantic, nothing memorable, just his wet lips on mine, the smell of pot and Marlboros and Manishewitz wine apparent as he breathed roughly through his nose.

"Mazel tov!" Millie Rosenblatt shouted from the crowd. Our guests began to clap along with the organ music as Stuie and I walked down the aisle without touching each other or making eye contact. The photographer popped one flash after another, capturing the moment for all eternity. We formed a receiving line at the exit of the sanctuary, Stuie and my parents, then Sam and Selma and finally Nola at the end of the line. I forced a wide, distorted grimace as I kissed the cheeks of the well-wishers, the old and the young, people I'd known my entire life and the few I'd never seen before. I inhaled the sickly sweet smell of my Aunt Fanny's Shalimar perfume and the scent of pot on the hair and clothes of Stuie's disgusting friends. Marsha approached and gave me a long, tight squeeze. Rochelle hugged me, too, and I held onto her, hopeful we'd be able to mend

SUNDAY, AUGUST 22, 1971

our friendship but fearful she would blame me forever just as she blamed Denise Silver (even though Sal had made the first move on both of us).

Rochelle moved on to hug my parents as Sal took me in his arms, tilting my face to his and kissing me with his soft lips. Glancing over his shoulder to make sure his girlfriend was lost in the crowd, he opened his mouth and quickly darted his tongue around mine, then winked and moved on, leaving me in shock, the sweet taste of his peppermint breath lingering in my mouth.

The crowd eventually thinned and we filed down the stairs for lunch. I did as I was told, waiting outside the reception room with Stuie. I peeked in to watch Murray and the Dialtones prepare their instruments for an afternoon of lively entertainment. They started off with their rendition of "Hang On Sloopy," Murray leaning into the microphone as his fingers glided over his accordion. He closed his eyes and belted out his second number, "Blues in the Night," beads of perspiration on his upper lip, while our guests hunted for their tables. Finally, he finished his last line, "Clickety clack, echoing back the bloooo-ooose, in the niiiiiiiight," and he held the high note with such intensity that I thought he was going to bust his gut. "Thank you, ladies and gentlemen and welcome to the Grand Ballroom of Temple Beth Shalom," he said at the end of the song. "Right now I'd like to introduce the two reasons we're here on this beautiful, sunny Sunday afternoon." There was a tiny smattering of laughter drowned out by Murray's own hearty bellow. "It gives me great pleasure to introduce for the first time anywhere, Mr. and Mrs. Stuart Weiner!"

He pointed in our direction while the drummer did a rim shot and we walked in, not knowing where to go or what to do. Stuie followed behind, discreetly giving the finger to his motley collection of friends gathered at table seven who shouted and whistled as we moved toward the dance floor. "Kids, this is just for you," Murray said in his most seductive voice, then he squeezed his eyes shut and began to sing "People, people who need people..." I held my arms open while Stuie awkwardly put a hand on my waist, gazing over my head at his friends who were smoking cigarettes and flicking ashes into the ashtray. He watched longingly as Tony and Howie and Danny and Joel tried to impress Karen and Debbie and Ellen and Ilene. I could see the jealousy on Stuie's face as he stared at his friends, these single boys who could flirt and hang out wherever and whenever they wanted, no questions asked by a bossy wife. Stuie's eyes narrowed enviously as Danny pinched Debbie under her ribs and she slapped him playfully on the shoulder. Stuie kept his eyes glued to that table while he swayed back and forth on the dance floor with his brand new wife, the old ball and chain who was going to stop him from having the fun he deserved.

The music ended and everyone applauded. I walked absently to the head table and sat down beside Marsha, Rochelle and Sal, across from Buffa, Larry, Nola, and Stuie's cousin Barry. I kicked my shoes off and took a sip of water, removing the big picture hat and placing it under the table by my stockinged feet, careful not to make eye contact with Sal. Marsha patted my left hand, which wore the plain gold band over the new diamond ring. She raised a questioning eyebrow and I nodded back. *Yeah, I'm okay, at least for now. But I can't make any promises about later.*

Murray cleared his throat and tapped the open mike. "All right, parents of the bride and groom. Now's your chance to show your kids how it's really done." He winked and began his next number, 'Come Rain or Come Shine,' snapping his fingers and nodding his head, imitating Tony Bennett whom he must've seen do the same thing on the Ed Sullivan Show. I turned quickly to tables two and six and saw the surprised expressions on the four faces. "I'm waiting," Murray said mock-impatiently between lyrics. The two couples reluctantly left their tables from opposite sides of the room and walked to the dance floor without so much as a passing glance at each other. Murray interrupted his lyrics one more time to say, "This song's for all of you who got a little wet on the way over to the Temple today." He wiped the sweat from his cheek with his forearm without missing a beat on the accordion.

My parents began to dance, looking in every conceivable direction except where the Weiners did a slow waltz, eyes downcast, gazing at their feet as they moved back and forth in time to the music.

SUNDAY, AUGUST 22, 1971

Without warning Murray leaned into his microphone and said, "Beautiful. Now everybody give the parents of the bride and groom a big hand as they switch partners." An audible gasp rose from the Grand Ballroom as the two couples froze on the floor. Apparently everyone but Murray knew about the pinochle game from twelve years ago and how it had created this permanent schism between the Weinstocks and the Lipshitzes. All breathing stopped but Murray seemed oblivious as he removed his fingers from the keyboard that was strapped to his chest and indicated for the couples to switch with each other. "Don't be shy," he said good-naturedly, "You're all one big, happy family now. Let's start behaving like machetunem." My mother turned tentatively to Selma who never looked quite so mortified as she did in that moment. "That's it," Murray said, coaxing them along. "Sheesh, have you ever seen two women so unwilling to let go of their own husbands? I wish *my* wife would hang onto me like that." He paused. "On second thought..."

There was a smattering of nervous laughter as my father took Selma's hand and my mother moved into Sam's open arms, all four of them desperately trying to find the eyes of their rightful mates across the dance floor. And then, either the humidity or the music or the sheer tension of the moment got to Sam because all of a sudden he spun my mother into an exotic whirl, dipping her backwards with her head inches from the floor, then pulling her back into his arms. There was a spontaneous cheer from the crowd as my mother, flushed and dizzy and just a little breathless, continued to dance with Sam, looking deeply into his eyes, possibly for the first time in twelve years. She held the eye contact, her right hand resting gently on Sam's neck as he pulled her close, his large splayed fingers just above her hips, drawing her closer and closer still, their lips an inch apart, eyes half-closed, their breathing shallow.

It was in that moment, the sexual energy between my mother and Sam plain as day, that I realized it wasn't pinochle that had caused so much grief between the two families all those years ago. It was something much more important, much more primal than a game of cards. There had been a passionate affair between Sam Weiner and my mother that ended before either of them was ready.

Good God, no wonder my father spit on the ground every time Sam walked down the block, no wonder Selma hated my mother with such fierce bitterness, and no wonder she hated me, the daughter of her arch rival. No game of pinochle could elicit such raw emotion, such unbridled rage. It had merely been a cover-up for the deeper truth: My mother and Sam Weiner had loved each other for well over a decade and by the looks of the two of them on that dance floor, the embers were still burning bright.

Suddenly I understood why Selma rejected the brisket and why she rejected me. All that talk about not respecting tradition, about hurting her family, wasn't about the ring at all. She was speaking to Sylvia through Sylvia's daughter. My mother had betrayed her, had pointed out that Selma's marriage to Sam wasn't even a friendship, it was loveless and passionless, forcing Sam to find solace in the arms of another woman, Sylvia Lipshitz from down the block.

I thought about the story my mother told me while we prepared the brisket. I had misunderstood her message because I didn't have all the information. Alan Ladd was her glorified, idealized fantasy, but Sam Weiner was the man who actually visited her bed. It was safe to fantasize about Alan Ladd and chat about him openly because he didn't live in the next building, he never traced his soft lips along her breasts and her thighs the way Sam did. Alan Ladd was the fantasy; Sam Weiner was flesh and blood. How difficult it must have been, knowing Sam was right there on the same street but not within her reach.

My mind racing, I remembered the words she'd chosen, that my father was a good husband but could never give her what she ached for. She was repulsed by his touch, worsened by the fact she longed for the touch of a man who already thrilled her, who showed her what she was missing. How delicious and forbidden and exciting their lovemaking must have been, breathless arrangements, backwards glances to ensure no one suspected a thing. I wondered if they talked about a future together as husband and wife, or if sneaking around in the shadows of Walnut was all they expected and all they needed.

How terribly tragic, I thought, that my mother and Sam couldn't have each other forever. When the romance ended they must have been left with the ashes, the terrible realization that something beautiful was gone and not coming back. My mother was forced to continue her life with Mel Lipshitz, all the while wishing she could live in the apartment I would be moving into tomorrow afternoon, the one above the garbage room with needle pointed Judaica on every wall. Perhaps that was why my mother insisted I marry Stuie. It was her way of keeping Sam in her life, of sharing the important milestones that were sure to come, births and Bar Mitzvahs and weddings and deaths. My marriage to Stuie was the only way they could be of the same family, bonded forever in a legitimate way that even Selma couldn't prevent. I was the pawn in my mother's scheme, but I couldn't hate her for sacrificing her only child, throwing me to the proverbial lions because of her own boundless love for the man she couldn't have. Spitting on him, indeed. She would have taken Sam back into her bed in a minute if only she'd had the opportunity.

I looked over at Stuie to see if he, too, had seen into our parents' souls and made the connection, but Stuie was tossing lit matches into the ashtray, bored and stoned and wanting to get out of the Temple and his too-small Bar Mitzvah suit. I decided to take my mother's tragic secret to my grave. I would never share it with anybody, not Marsha or Rochelle and certainly not with Stuie. In that moment I realized how much I loved her, how my heart ached for her and how deserving she was of happiness.

So many things made sense now. Nola was born eleven years ago, less than a year after the affair ended. Impregnating his wife was Sam's way of finding the road back to his family. He had appeased Selma with a baby girl. And my mother's job at the hospital started that very same year, when I was still in kindergarten. It was important for her to get out of the house and off the block, to engage her mind with thoughts other than Sam.

I wondered about the circumstances surrounding the end of the affair, if my father had found a single cufflink in his bed, if Selma had found a stray earring in her car. Or perhaps my mother or Sam became weary of all the lies, tired of hiding out and moving between the shadows. One thing was for sure: the affair didn't end because the passion had cooled. That was pretty clear, watching them hang onto each other ferociously on the dance floor, their eyes locked together, fingers clamped onto shoulders and hips.

Soon my mother was back in her husband's arms, dancing listlessly, the fleeting moment of truth gone forever. Murray was segueing into his next song, "Stop in the Name of Love," sung slowly, like a ballad, and I watched sadly as the two couples went their separate ways back to their tables, leaving me in a state of amazement from which I would not soon recover.

Sylvia Lipshitz and Sam Weiner. I tried to picture them in the throes of a hot embrace, kissing deeply with open mouths, Sam gripping my mother's ample breasts in his big hands, rolling on top of her, her legs wrapped feverishly around his waist. While my father was downtown cutting dresses, slaving away in some Seventh Avenue sweat shop, she and Sam were moaning and gasping behind the closed door of her bedroom, perhaps even while I was jumping rope or playing jacks out on the front stoop.

Empty plates were removed from the tables and couples got up to dance, enjoying the musical stylings of Murray and the Dialtones. Rochelle led Sal to the center of the floor and pressed her thick lips against his, hips grinding, her fingers laced into his. I turned away before Sal could know I was staring.

The afternoon dragged on in the windowless basement reception room, Murray beckoning and cajoling the guests to join in the Hora, the Bunny Hop and the Hokey Pokey. My mother made the rounds, greeting the people she'd invited, Selma greeting her own guests, the photographer snapping away, until Stuie and I were summoned to the dance floor by the irrepressible Murray. We sliced into our three-tier cake adorned with the plastic bride and groom who looked nothing like us. I fed Stuie a piece that symbolized, I suppose, the meals I would feed him in the future.

Slices of wedding cake were distributed along with the coffee service and finally, mercifully, the wedding came to a close and our guests began to leave. I graciously accepted the obligatory pecks on my cheek while Stuie collected the sealed envelopes, putting them into his jacket pocket as his father had shown him on his Bar Mitzvah

SUNDAY, AUGUST 22, 1971

Day.

In Walnut an appropriate gift for a Bar Mitzvah, wedding or bris was a check in a denomination of chai - eighteen, the number of life. The typical gift from a friend was one times chai, from a very good friend, two times chai, from a relative, three times chai. Except for the jelly jar given by my father's Gentile co-workers, all of our gifts would fit neatly into Stuie's lapel pocket, to be tallied later in the evening.

Maybe I can get away with just a creampuff tonight. I waved goodbye to our guests and watched as they ran through the relentless rain, heads bent against the summer wind. Stuie turned to me as the Dialtones packed up their equipment and settled the bill with my parents. "I told Buffa and Larry to meet us at the hotel in an hour," he said. "I hope you don't mind."

• • •

We spent the majority of our wedding night sitting on the queen-sized bed, me, Buffa, Larry and Stuie, eating cheeseburgers and fries from room service and watching the color television. At around ten-thirty Larry fell asleep, drooling on my pillow, one leg hanging off the bed. He rolled over and Buffa shoved him out of the way, whining, "Get offa me, schmuck."

"Party's over," Stuie said, annoyed by his friends' antics. Buffa regarded me with a raised eyebrow and I almost slugged him, reading his disgusting mind and not finding it even a little funny.

"We know what *you're* gonna be doing tonight," Buffa said as he pushed Larry so hard they both fell right off the bed, which woke up Larry pretty fast.

"What the fuck's your problem?" Larry asked, jumping back onto the bed and wrestling his friend into a headlock.

"Hey, come on, quit it," Stuie said.

"Yeah, it's Skully's wedding night," Buffa said to Larry. "What are you, some kind of an ape?" Buffa staggered to his feet and Larry followed, both of them grabbing their ties and jackets and the leather shoes they borrowed from their fathers.

Stuie waited for the door to close, then took off his pants and shirt, stripping down to a pair of white boxer shorts and settling under the covers. He patted the bed, wanting to do this the right way, the way his father had told him. "I'll be right back," I said, grabbing my overnight bag and a few minutes time. I disappeared into the bathroom, slipping out of my shorts and tee shirt and into the soft and smooth satin nightgown. I stalled for another minute or two, not wanting to come out.

"Hey, Ro, did you fall in?" Stuie called. I left the bathroom with some reluctance and sat tentatively on the edge of the bed. "We don't need the cream tonight," he said mischievously. Then his voice got quiet. "I've wanted to have sex with you for a long time, Ro."

"I know you have. Since tenth grade."

"No. Since the first time I found out what it was." He leaned over and turned off the lamp on his side of the queen-size bed, leaving us in semi-darkness, the lights of the nearby airport casting shadows in the room. "Let's get under the covers," he said, pulling back the stiff floral bedspread before I could respond. Without warning he took off his boxers and flung them on the floor.

"Hey, Ro."

"Yeah?"

"You're done with your period, aren't you?"

"I think so."

"Good. But we should still use a condom."

"I don't have any. Maybe we shouldn't take a chance and just skip the whole thing."

He put his hand under the starched pillow, producing the foil packet he'd obviously planted while I was in the bathroom. "Surprise. You want to put it on for me?"

"Why, you don't know how?"

"I think it's something the wife's supposed to do." He handed it over and I sat up on my elbow, curiosity getting the better of me. I tore open the packet and took it out slowly, enjoying the silky latex between my fingers. I unrolled the thing all the way, letting it dangle limply between us.

"Like this?"

SUNDAY, AUGUST 22, 1971

"You're supposed to do it a little at a time."

"Oops." I tried to restore it to its original position but it wouldn't cooperate.

"Here, I've got another one." He reached under the pillow. "I went through a whole box last night practicing."

"I didn't expect them to feel so smooth."

He smiled. "At least I know you've never had sex before."

Oh, God. I swallowed hard, not looking at him, terrified he might read my mind and learn the truth. I removed the condom from its wrapper and pondered the mechanics of unrolling it. Stuie was right, it would have to be done slowly, the way my mother unrolled her stockings at the end of a long work day, wearing them around her ankles like fat nylon bagels. "You ready?" He pushed out his stomach in response so I could reach him more easily. We stared with deep concentration as I did my wifely job, both of us pleased with the outcome. "There. How does that feel?"

"Weird, but I'll get used to it."

I inhaled deeply. "Okey-dokey."

"You want me to get on top?"

"Either way. Whatever you want."

"It might be easier if I get on. Next time you can get on top, okay?"

"Okay," I said.

He took a deep breath and climbed on top of me apprehensively, squeezing his eyes shut and turning his face away from mine to make sure our lips didn't touch. He kept his hands on the mattress the whole time as if he were doing push-ups in gym class, eyes clenched tight from the exertion, lips pursed together. I gripped the floral bedspread in my fists and held on tight. It was fairly uncomfortable but there was no major physical pain. I gasped anyway, just to throw him off the track as Rochelle suggested. "Does that hurt?" he asked between grunts.

"A lot," I said. After another minute of thrusting he shook with a brief and vocal spasm, then collapsed on top of me before rolling onto his side of the bed. He gingerly removed the wet condom and flung it across the room toward the wastepaper basket, but it missed by a few feet. "That's disgusting," I said. "Go pick it up."

"See that? You're already telling me what to do."

"Please, Stuie." He got up with a groan and tossed the condom into the small basket, then jumped back onto the bed with a thud. "I've got four more under the pillow," he announced happily.

"Are we going to use all of them tonight?"

"Sure."

His voice was smug.

"Where'd you get them?"

"Walnut Drugs. My father bought me three boxes as a wedding present. So how'd you like it?"

"Nice. What about you?"

"I loved it. It's a lot better than a creampuff, that's for damn sure." He paused. "And just think, we can do it any time we want, even if my parents are home."

"I know."

"We don't even have to tell them. We'll just close the door and there's nothing they can do about it."

"Mmm."

"Was it different than you thought it would be?"

I hesitated. "A little."

"What did it feel like, you know, inside you?"

"Good. It felt real good, Stuie." *Is this a white lie?*

He breathed in, hands behind his head, staring out into the darkness. I could hear the smile in his voice. "I can't believe we can do it whenever we want." He turned over, his back facing me. "Good night, Ro."

"Night, Stuie."

"We're really married now."

"I know."

"I'm not so scared anymore."

I paused. "Stuie?"

He yawned loudly. "Yeah?"

"The Rabbi said we have to talk about that story."

"Can we talk tomorrow?"

"I don't think we should wait. He said it's an important assign-

SUNDAY, AUGUST 22, 1971

ment for tonight, remember?"

"Okay, you go first."

"Well. I think the story's about being happy with yourself, and not expecting someone else to make you happy, because when it comes right down to it, no one can really make you feel anything. It's like what he said about those trees, growing independently, you know?" I waited for Stuie to answer, staring at the back of his big head, which was stiff and sticky from all that styling gel. "Stuie?" There was no answer. "Stuie?" He lay there unmoving, snorting in through his nose, letting the air rush out of his sleeping mouth. "You know what else I think?" I was confident he couldn't hear me. "The Rabbi was talking to me in code. He believes the wrong person can actually stop you from growing. He was telling me to do some growing by myself."

I stared at the ceiling until deep into the night, focused on the quiet in the room and the voice in my head. I must've dozed off shortly after four, the early-morning sun stirring me awake at seven-fifteen. It took me a minute to remember where I was, to remember *who* I was, until I realized with a heaviness in my chest it was my first morning as Rhona Gail Weiner, *Mrs.* Weiner, the woman married to the man she could never love. I got out of bed and tiptoed over to Stuie's suit jacket that lay in a heap on a side chair. Retrieving a pile of white envelopes from the inside jacket pocket, I sat down at the little desk and dug through the drawer as quietly as I could. I found a white plastic pen that said "Holiday Inn" and a glossy post card, and made a mental note to bring the pen home to my mother so she could add it to her collection of souvenirs.

I ran my finger inside the flap of the first envelope and pulled out a gift card that said "Mazel tov from the Bernsteins" with a check for two times chai written in Sadie's fanciest handwriting. I wrote, "Bernsteins. Thirty six dollars," on the postcard and then opened the next envelope, one times chai from Anthony Marinelli. I smiled to myself, enjoying how Anthony's parents were familiar with the protocol of a Jewish wedding even though they were devout Roman Catholics. I continued adding checks, glancing across the room every now and then to make sure Stuie was still asleep, his left leg hanging off the bed.

I looked at his toes and amused myself with the realization that the stubby biggest one looked like Sam's face. Sam's face. A chill rushed through me as I thought about my mother and Sam on the dance floor, lost in their memories in that fleeting but oh, so important moment. Putting down the pen I traveled back in time, searching for a shred of evidence that would support my hypothesis, not that my hypothesis needed support.

And then I remembered. *Dear God.* I had been five years old, in Miss Rice's kindergarten class. It was after school, one of those fabulous autumn days when the leaves are crisp and golden, the air brisk and clean. Rochelle and I were playing with Barbies on her bedroom floor when we started arguing. I wanted my Barbie to wear the red shoes that matched the red striped bathing suit, but Rochelle wanted those shoes for *her* doll, which was clad in a red satin evening gown. Rochelle pulled the shoes out of my hand with such force that the sharp little plastic heel broke the skin on my thumb and I started to cry. "That's it," I said, picking up my barefoot doll and walking angrily to the door. "I don't want to be your friend ever again." I ran back to my building in the dappled afternoon sunlight and opened the door to the apartment, which remained unlocked during the day.

"Ma?" I called. There was no answer. I heard frantic whispering behind her closed bedroom door. "Give me half a sec," she called, and I was frightened by her urgency. She came out after a minute with only a bathrobe on, her hair messy and her lipstick askew. "What are you doing home?" she asked impatiently and I stammered, still mad at Rochelle and worried that now I had displeased my mother, too. I told her about the fight and she said I had to go back to Rochelle's and apologize right now and I started crying, wanting to know why *I* had to apologize when Rochelle was the one who cut my thumb. I showed her where the skin broke and where a tiny dot of blood oozed out. She marched me to the front door, a hand on my shoulder, and said I had to go over there this very minute and she closed the door behind me and I heard it lock. For a long time I wondered why the fight with Rochelle was my

SUNDAY, AUGUST 22, 1971

fault, why my mother forced me to make up with Rochelle when *she* was the one who had been so wrong.

On the morning after my wedding I understood why I needed to get out of the house so quickly. My mother must've watched from the window until I was gone, then called to Sam to get his pants on and get out while the going was good. Like my father, Sam was a dress cutter who couldn't always find work, leaving him in the dangerous position of having too much time on his hands.

I wondered how the affair had actually begun. Did he seek her out at the grocery store and whisper into her ear that his body ached for her touch? Did he grab her from behind in the kitchen while the men's weekly pinochle game droned on in the other room? And what was her reaction? Was she filled with guilt or did she push the indiscretion from her mind the way I had done with Jeffrey, justifying her actions in the name of love? I wanted to know every thought that crept into her head. Did she relive the details over and over in her mind, the taste of his mouth and the scent of his neck and the weight of his body on top of hers?

How unfulfilled she must be, I thought sadly as I opened the next check, two times chai from Stuie's Aunt Rebecca and Uncle Leo. I forced away the picture of my mother as a lonely, longing woman, and concentrated instead on the twenty-seven envelopes on the desk in front of me. I opened them all, carefully noting their contents, adding up the numbers on the postcard, carry the eight, carry the two. One thousand twenty-six dollars, or a total of fifty-seven times chai. Not a bad haul. I would take it to the bank the next morning and open an interest bearing account in both our names, knowing full well that if Stuie had sole access to that much cash he and Buffa and Larry would surely allow it to go up in smoke behind the schoolyard.

Stuie opened one eye and was disappointed to find me at the desk and not in the bed. "Come here," he said drowsily. He smiled and patted the pillow. "I got four left." It was the happiest I'd ever seen him, like he'd been given a new toy for Chanukah.

I sighed and moved to the bed dutifully. He handed me a foil packet from beneath the pillow and watched as I unrolled the condom, having mastered the technique after only one use. He mounted me for a repeat performance of what we did the night before, but this time he tugged at my tee shirt so he could grope my body while reaching a quick and silent climax. The whole ordeal lasted under three minutes, including the removal of my shirt. When it was over we lay on our backs, staring at the cracked ceiling. Stuie was wide-awake. "Are we going to do it again?" I asked, holding my breath.

"When we get home," he said. "I've got two whole boxes in my drawer and we can get more whenever we need them."

We skipped breakfast since it wasn't included in the twenty-two dollar room charge and took the bus back to Walnut, hiking the four blocks from the bus stop to Stuie's building, gripping our cumbersome overnight bags. "Let me go home and get my stuff," I said. "I'll meet you at your house later, okay?"

Opening the door to my parents' empty apartment, I went straight to my bedroom. I crawled under the covers, Keds and all, and fell asleep, exhausted from my previous sleepless night and the remains of my hangover. I woke up mid-afternoon, wanting to stay in my warm little bed forever but knowing it was time to leave. Like it or not I was a married woman now who belonged beside her husband in the trundle bed with the cowboy hat engravings on the headboard.

I collected my most important things, clothes and socks and my FM radio, make-up and bath oil and my favorite hairbrush and stuffed them into a brown paper grocery bag. From the bottom of my empty drawer I lifted the beads, the poem and the ID card from Washington University and brought them to the closet where I kept my notebooks. There would be no hiding places at Stuie's house; all my secrets would remain here in my bedroom, safely hidden in the narrow closet. I hauled the grocery bag to the front door and looked around the empty living room. "So long," I said, taking a deep breath and opening the door with my pinkie, the only finger available what with the heavy bag in my arms. I went one step at a time down the stoop and onto the sidewalk. None of the neighbors were out which was just as well as I stepped carefully, the overflowing bag obscuring my vision, in the direction of the garbage room and into Stuie's building.

I knocked awkwardly with a knuckle, the package in my arms growing heavier by the second. Stuie opened the door after a couple of minutes. "You need help?"

"I'm fine. Where should I put everything?" I asked, following behind him, dropping the grocery bag onto the faded shag carpet in his bedroom and rubbing my arms.

"There should be room in the closet. My mother took Nola's stuff out this morning." I opened the tiny closet and found the left half completely empty except for a few wire hangers and a pair of metal roller skates in the corner. I busied myself emptying the paper bag and putting my dresses neatly on the hangers while Stuie reclined on the bed, watching the baseball game, slamming his fist against the wall and yelling "Damn it!" when his team screwed up.

"Where's your mother and Nola?" I asked, trying to make pleasant conversation with this person I was married to.

"I don't know. They went out. Damn it!"

"What happened?"

"This game sucks."

I took my two pair of shoes, an extra pair of Keds and my fluffy blue slippers out of the bag and lined them up at the bottom of the closet. I opened the top drawer of the dresser, surprised to find it filled with Stuie's underwear and assorted junk. "Which drawer is mine?"

"The bottom one."

"Can I take the second one from the top?"

"I don't care. Just don't talk. The Mets are up shit's creek. You want to watch it with me?"

"No, thanks." I opened the second drawer, which housed Stuie's pajamas and underpants and folded them into the empty bottom drawer. It seemed strange touching his personal things. I didn't know him well enough for such an intimate gesture. While he focused on the game I worked silently, arranging my own stuff in the small second drawer. As I placed my hairbrush next to the nightgowns I heard the key in the door followed by an angry slam.

"I wish I was an orphan!" Nola said loudly and angrily.

"Do you know what an orphan means? That means your parents are dead!" Selma was weary and upset, and I wondered if she had woken up on the wrong side of the bed, images of her husband and Sylvia Lipshitz filling her head. She walked heavily and with purpose towards Stuie's room. "You want to hear something?" she asked him with annoyance. "I take her to Korvette's to get her a pair of go-go boots..."

"You said I could have them." Nola was right behind her mother.

"And they're out of her size until Friday."

"The four and a half were just as good, ma. I even tried them on."

"Where do you come to a four and a half? You'll kill your feet in boots so small."

"They're my feet, what do you care?"

"Don't open a mouth. Now you're not getting them even when they *do* come in."

"Shut up, I'm trying to watch the game!" Stuie finally shouted. Selma dismissed us with her hand and went into the kitchen, while Nola turned on the television in the living room, the volume up all the way. "Make it lower!" Stuie yelled. Selma went into the living room to turn down the television, then came back into Stuie's room, a half-eaten onion bagel in her hand.

"We're going out for pizza tonight. You want to come?" She looked directly at her son who was absorbed in the ball game, ignoring me as if I weren't there. "Hey. You coming with us to the pizzaria tonight?" This time she asked it with a tad less patience.

"No, thanks," Stuie said.

"What're you gonna eat?"

"Ro will make me something, won't ya?"

"Yeah, sure."

Selma made a face before leaving the room. "There's some bologna and eggs you can scramble together, and a couple of bialys in the freezer."

Stuie watched the rest of the game in relative quiet and when it ended at four o'clock he turned the volume down and went into the hallway. "Ma," he called into the living room where Selma and Nola were busy with their soap opera, "don't come in my room, okay? Ro and I are gonna be in there."

"Not now. Dr. Spencer is all hooked up to life support and he's about to die for real this time."

Tell Dr. Spencer I'm next. Stuie locked the bedroom door, unzipped his pants and pulled off his tee shirt. I tried to ignore him, fumbling with the contents of the second drawer of the dresser, folding my socks and stalling for time. "Why don't you take your clothes off?" he asked.

"Can't we do it tonight?"

"Sure we can do it tonight, but we're also going to do it now." He noticed my hesitation. "Come on, Ro, why else do people get married?" I nodded dutifully and allowed him to lead me to the bed. The whole thing lasted just under four minutes, including the fifty-seven seconds it took for him to fumble with my bra. He put the used condom in a tissue and handed it to me for disposal, then he promptly fell asleep.

I got dressed and sat on the floor, skimming through an article about Mary Tyler Moore in the *TV Guide*. As soon as Selma and Nola left the apartment I went to the kitchen to make bologna and scrambled eggs with two toasted bialys. It was my first attempt at a real dinner without my mother's help. The eggs were undercooked, the bialy burnt, but it seemed edible enough to present to my husband. Stuie sat up drowsily when I walked into the bedroom, the aroma of his dinner having stirred him from sleep, and we ate on the bed, watching reruns on channel eleven. Stuie drained his plastic cup. "Can you get me some more soda?"

"In a minute," I said, but I didn't get up. At eight o'clock the family arrived home, Nola carrying a large shopping bag from May's department store, a self-satisfied smile on her face.

"Guess what, I got my boots," she announced as she came into the bedroom and plopped down on the bed to try them on. "They had my size at May's and I don't even have to wait till Friday." She zipped them up and paraded around the room, doing a whirly little dance. "I have to call everybody and tell them."

"Get out of the way," Stuie said as she ran from the room, craning his big head to see the television screen. Selma walked in and removed our dirty plates from the foot of the bed. "Can you get me some more soda, ma?" Stuie asked. He held out his empty plastic cup and she took it into the kitchen, returning a minute later with it filled to the brim. Stuie chugged it down and put the cup on his dresser. After a few minutes he wandered into the living room to sit beside his parents on the sofa where they were watching "Let's Make A Deal." I eventually followed and leaned against the wall, not wanting to sit too close to my in-laws.

"That's what we need, a new car," Sam said as Door Number Three opened to reveal a shiny blue Buick. I looked at Sam from across the room, peering at his arms which were still strong, even in middle-age. I looked at his hands resting on his belly and pictured them tenderly caressing my mother. I turned away shamefully, as if I'd peeked into her bedroom and witnessed their lovemaking.

At eleven o'clock Stuie got up and pulled me to my feet. "We're going to bed," he said with a wicked little grin, right in front of his parents, who were still on the couch. There was a pause. "Did you hear what I said?"

"Good night," Sam replied, eyes on the television screen.

"We're going to *bed*," Stuie repeated, trying to get a rise out of them. But they seemed unfazed. Disappointed, he led me to his room. "You want to do it again?" he asked, brightening as he closed the door. "I'm super horny tonight."

"Actually..."

"What?"

"I'm a little tired. We've already done it three times since yesterday."

"So? We're married. We're supposed to do it a *lot*."

"I counted the wedding gifts," I said as I opened the trundle bed, hoping the subject of money would deflect his mind from sex. I could hear the squeak of the sofa bed opening in the living room.

"How much we got?"

"Fifty-seven times chai."

"How much is that?"

"One thousand twenty-six dollars. I thought we'd put it in the

SUNDAY, AUGUST 22, 1971

bank."

"No way. I want half of it here."

"Stuie, you know what'll happen. It'll get pissed away and we won't even know where it went." I was starting to sound like Florence Sinitsky who humiliated her husband for being out of work and kept track of every penny.

"Tomorrow I want you to cash the checks and keep five hundred in the house."

"That's not a good idea."

"I'm not talking about money tonight. Right now it's time to open scumbag number four," he said in his Monty Hall voice.

"How about a creampuff instead?"

"Creampuffs are history. We're married."

"Stuie, I'm not in the mood, okay?"

He looked at me with narrowed eyes and I could see the hurt in his face. "I'm going to the schoolyard."

"But it's after eleven."

"So what? I'll see you later."

"Come on, Stuie, don't be mad."

"I'm not mad, I just want to see my friends. You said you wouldn't stop me from seeing them, remember?" He walked out, leaving me alone at the foot of the trundle bed.

I parted the plaid curtains and watched Stuie walk down the block, a lit Marlboro in his hand. *I wonder what Jeffrey's doing tonight.* I pictured him wrapped in his girlfriend's long, graceful arms, moaning into her blonde hair. Or maybe he was alone, unpacking his books and settling into his room, preparing for his final year of college. I started thinking about Jeffrey's green eyes and quiet voice and that broad smile with the dimples at each end of his mouth, and then I remembered how his mouth had laughed at me and how cold his voice had been when he wished me luck and hung up the phone. This was another side of Jeffrey, a side I had barely gotten to know. I wondered what he would have been like as a husband, if he'd turn cold without warning

Just then the sound of soft crying in the living room brought me back to reality. I waited a minute or two for the crying to stop, and when it didn't I went quietly to the darkened living room, passing the master bedroom where Sam and Selma were fast asleep in front of the TV, their faces illuminated by the monochromatic glow.

Nola was hunched on the open sofa bed, head in her hands, her body wracked with sobs, wearing a Smurfs nightgown and her new go-go boots. I sat down beside her and put a hand on her leg, but she immediately jerked it out of my reach. "Nola? I'm really sorry I took your bedroom away." I patted her back gently but she arched that away, too. "Nola, listen to me, it won't be forever even though it seems like forever right now."

"I miss my room," she said.

"I know you do."

"It's not fair."

"I know."

She turned over and looked at me. "Does it feel different to be married?" she asked, the crying just about gone.

"Not really, not yet, anyway. But I've only been married for a day."

"Does it hurt to have sex?"

I started to answer but stopped myself. She wasn't even twelve and certainly didn't need to know the ugly realities of my life. "It can be very beautiful," I said softly, my mind floating back to a mere ten days before.

"Yuck," she said. "With Skully?"

She had me there. I smiled and touched the tip of her nose. "You'd better go to sleep," I said. "It's late."

"I'm not tired. Can we go somewhere? You're eighteen so it's not against the law."

"I don't think so."

"Where'd Skully go?"

"The schoolyard. With Buffa and Larry."

"Isn't he supposed to be with you?"

"He'll be back soon."

"But if he went out, why can't we?"

"It's late. It's time to sleep."

"Will you stay with me all night?"

SUNDAY, AUGUST 22, 1971

"I can't. I have to sleep with your brother."

Nola thought about that. "So you can have sex."

"Not necessarily."

"Are you going to have sex tonight?"

"I don't think so. No, definitely not tonight."

Nola was quiet for a minute. "I don't mind that you live here, Ro. I'm just scared to sleep alone in the living room."

"There's nothing to be scared of. Your whole family's here."

"Yeah, but sometimes there are zombies inside the walls."

"No, there aren't."

"They only come out if you're alone in the room."

"Look on the bright side. The TV in here is the biggest one in the house."

"I don't care about that."

"And you're closer to the kitchen."

"So?"

"So you can get cookies any time you want. And it's nice and private, like having your own room."

"I don't want my own room. I want the one I used to share with Skully."

"I think you'll like sleeping in here when you're older."

"But I thought you guys were getting your own house by then?"

She had me again. She was pretty smart, this kid. A lot smarter than her brother. "It's really late," I said for lack of a better response. I started to climb off the sofa bed.

"Don't go yet," she said. "Just sit here, just tonight so I won't be scared, okay?"

"Okay," I whispered, "but only if you close your eyes and go to sleep."

She shut her eyes but peeked out through the cracks. "We're kind of like sisters now, aren't we, Ro?"

"I guess we are."

She tried to stifle a smile. "Give me chills," she demanded, her eyes still shut. "Do X marks the spot."

"I'll tickle your arm for a couple of minutes but then you have to sleep."

Nola turned onto her side and relaxed her eyes. I leaned over and tickled her arm lightly for several minutes until my back started to ache. "Don't stop, Ro. That feels good."

"Good night, Nola." I started to get up.

Eyes still closed, she said, "Ro? Iris Sinitsky told me a secret and I haven't told anybody."

"What's that?" I asked hoarsely.

"She said you love another boy."

"Did she."

"Yeah. She said he was the ice cream man and she saw you kissing him in his car."

"Iris Sinitsky doesn't know what she's talking about. Don't listen to her."

"But she's my best friend and she's two years older than me."

"That doesn't mean she can't make up a story."

"But she saw you from her window." She paused. "Do you love that other boy? I won't tell anybody, not even Iris."

She yawned again, curling up into a ball in the corner of the thin mattress. I pulled the blanket up around her neck and rubbed her back softly. "To tell you the truth, Nola, I used to love him." Her eyes began to close. "Nola?"

"Yeah?" Her voice was quiet.

"This is our secret, okay?"

"Okay," she whispered and turned over. I sat down on the sofa bed for at least an hour before getting up slowly and quietly, tiptoeing into the bathroom to brush my teeth before climbing back into bed. I lay there in the dark, staring at the ceiling, listening to the occasional car drive down the block, the wind softly rustling the leaves outside of Stuie's window. At about two-thirty Stuie came home and moved around the room as quietly as he could, his hair and clothes reeking of cigarettes and pot. I shut my eyes tight and pretended to sleep. He carefully climbed over me and got under the blanket. As an afterthought he leaned up and kissed me softly on top of my head before turning over toward the wall.

I stayed on my side of the bed, eyes open, body unmoving, until the clock displayed five-thirty and the first pink light came

SUNDAY, AUGUST 22, 1971

through the plaid curtains. I got up and found my way to the closet, listening to the rumble of metal as the garbage men emptied the cans below the window into their truck. I slipped into a checkered sundress, stepped into a pair of sandals and quietly placed my belongings into the brown paper grocery bag. I removed the envelope of checks from my bag and counted five hundred four dollars, which I left on the dresser. I put the remaining five hundred twenty-two dollars worth of checks into my purse, making a mental note to return eighteen dollars to Stuie so we'd be even. It would be my gift to him, one times chai, a sweet life filled with sweet things, a life that wouldn't include me.

I moved silently to the living room and saw that the sofa bed was empty and that Sam and Selma's bedroom door was ajar. I smiled at the thought of Nola fast asleep in the warmth of her parents' bed and how happy she'd be later that night, back in the bedroom she'd known all her life, safe and sound where the zombies couldn't get her. I turned the handle of the front door quietly and stepped out into the fresh early morning air. The windows on the block were dark except for the ones belonging to those men who worked the early shift in the city, the men who needed to be on the subway by six-fifteen in order to get to work by seven-thirty.

Standing there alone with nothing but my paper sack I remembered an old movie I'd once seen where a prisoner is released after a twenty-year sentence, emerging into the first light of day with just a paper bag under his arm. With the big house looming in the background he looks up at the pink sky, fills his lungs with the air of a new day and in that wondrous moment, we know — and he knows, that everything's going to be all right. He's got a lot more than a paper bag full of old clothes to call his own. He's got his life, and he's got himself, and there's nothing more he needs.

• • •

The marriage was annulled later that morning in a process that was simpler than I anticipated. I stopped at a pawn shop, picked up a handy hundred twenty-five dollars for my dear little diamond ring and the plain gold band which I could barely get off my finger, and added it to the five hundred twenty-two dollars in gift money for a total of six hundred forty-seven dollars, minus eighteen for Stuie, leaving me with the net amount of six hundred four dollars. I figured the guests at the wedding would have so much to talk about when news of my escape hit the streets that they'd forget to ask for their money back.

I found a one-room furnished apartment in Flushing for ninety dollars a month and landed a part-time job as a junior secretary for an insurance salesman who was elderly and kind and reminded me of my Grandpa Morris. Later that week I took the bus to Queens College to enroll in a couple of classes, delighted to learn I would qualify as a part-time student, even with my commercial diploma. The two classes I wanted were full but they promised to notify me if a cancellation came in. So I busied myself with my new job and my new apartment, using some of my earnings to buy posters and a bunch of candles shaped like unicorns, rainbows and daisies.

My parents had mixed feelings about my leaving Walnut. On the one hand they would miss me terribly and were concerned about my living alone, but on the other they were looking forward to turning my room into the den they'd always wanted, complete with wood paneled walls, two reclining lounge chairs and a brand new color television set they were paying off on their Sears credit card. I sent a note to Marsha wishing her well at Albany and a note to Rochelle who was still too angry with me to reply, even though I mentioned in the postscript that I had every intention of returning her panties. Stuie's letter was more difficult than I thought it would be. I rewrote it nine or ten times, hand-picking every word so as not to hurt his feelings. He wrote back several days later, insisting he wasn't mad at me even though his parents were. He seemed pleased to announce he'd landed a job in the stockroom of Walnut Drugs, ensuring him a ten per cent discount on all over-the-counter items, including every brand of condom. Now that Stuie was an experienced man, having moved beyond creampuffs, he would be showing off his sexual acumen to any of the Walnut girls willing to participate.

SUNDAY, AUGUST 22, 1971

In the second week of the fall term I got a letter from Queens College saying that a spot had opened up in English Composition and Introduction to Philosophy. They were both early morning classes, allowing me to get to work before noon, thereby pleasing my boss.

I walked into my philosophy class for the first time on a gray and blustery Thursday, ten minutes early despite the fact I was lost on the sprawling campus and had to ask for directions to the Arts and Sciences Building. With a racing heart I climbed the stairs to the second floor, marveling at the soda and candy machines along the wide corridor. I came to an open door, room two-sixteen, my classroom, already half-filled with students.

Taking a deep breath I crossed the threshold and chose a seat way in the back, took out my notebook and clicked my pen into position. *So this is college.* I glanced at the students who looked like the kind of people I might see on the bus or at the movies or in the pizza place, but with one major difference: these people were here in search of a better life. *Please, God, let me fit in. Let them think I'm one of them.*

Having no one to talk to, I sat in my seat and squinted at a large bulletin board on the side of the room, which was covered with colorful notices. Study Abroad. Graduate School Opportunities. Work-Study Programs. Transfer Applications to the State University of New York. So many possibilities.

After a few minutes Dr. Dorothy Welles, tall and slender with large glasses and short, graying hair, bounced cheerfully into the room and placed her briefcase on the podium, snapping it open as she must have done every morning for her entire adult life. She smiled to her students as she took out her notes and scanned them quickly. All the while people wandered in, some sipping coffee or hot chocolate from Styrofoam cups, munching on Snickers bars and filling up the remaining seats until the room was full.

Dr. Welles waited patiently until the rustling of books and bags and papers quieted down before speaking in her confident voice. She began her lecture with an introduction to common experience in the Aristotelian view. The class had already covered Socrates and his prodigy Plato in the first two weeks and now, much to my delight, we were moving on to Aristotle.

For the past several nights, alone in my apartment, I devoured the textbooks whole, stopping only to call Ziggy and asking him to play "I'm Free" by the Who. I turned the radio up full blast and at exactly seven-twelve my requested song came on. When it was over, Ziggy said in his patented velvet voice, for all of New York to hear, "I've never dedicated a song before, but that one was for my very special friend, Rhona Lipshitz from Queens."

As Professor Welles lectured about happiness and human desires, I wrote down every word she said, thanks to my knowledge of Gregg shorthand. Just before class ended, Dr. Welles scanned the roomful of students. "How can we make the most of our lives?" she asked. There was silence in the room. "Come on. Take a chance." She looked from face to face, but no one was willing to risk humiliation. Finally, I raised my hand high in the air and she acknowledged me with a nod.

"Here's one way to do it," I said with trepidation. "Just shine the light inside for a change, instead of looking everywhere else. Maybe then we can figure out who we are and what we really want." Dr. Welles looked at me with curiosity. I blushed, knowing I'd mutilated Rabbi Marks' story beyond recognition.

"Have you been here since the beginning of the semester?" the professor asked. "You don't look familiar."

"Today's my first day," I said shyly.

"And your name is...?"

"Rhona Lipshitz."

"Well, thank you, Rhona. That was an insightful response." Another hand shot up. Dr. Welles pointed with a piece of chalk, while I suppressed a satisfied grin.

When class was over, I walked quickly to the cafeteria in the Student Union, having just enough time for a quick bite before going to work. I opened the heavy door and stepped inside, fixing my windblown hair and rearranging my sweater. "It's sure blowing up a storm," I said as I held the door for a young woman I recognized from class.

SUNDAY, AUGUST 22, 1971

"Yeah, it's really the end of the summer now." We took our places at the back of the long lunch line. "I like what you said about shining the light," she said. "I never thought of it that way before." As we inched our way toward the counter, we talked about Dr. Welles and how much we liked her, how effortlessly she made the material come alive.

"By the way, I'm Rhona," I said.

"Nicole."

By the time it was our turn to order, I learned that Nicole was also a freshman. She lived in Forest Hills with her mother and brother and was hoping to transfer to Albany in her junior year.

"My best friend Marsha goes to Albany," I told her.

"Maybe you and I can take the bus up there sometime for the weekend."

"I'd love that," I said. "Wow, doesn't everything look great?" I placed two slices of pizza, a large order of fries, a jello with whipped cream, a chocolate brownie and a cherry Coke on my tray.

"You sure you've got enough?" Nicole asked as we sat down at an empty table.

"At least for the next hour," I said, popping a golden French fry into my mouth.

Nicole bit hungrily into her hot dog, tucking stray bits of sauerkraut back into the bun. She wiped mustard from her chin and looked at me shyly. I had been staring, no doubt making her uncomfortable, but it was the joy with which she ate that hot dog that had me riveted. "Aristotle wanted us to take large bites out of life," I said.

"Well, score one for Aristotle," she replied through a full mouth.

"Look at that," I said, pointing. "Do you realize what that is?"

"A bun?"

"It's not just bun, Nicole." I did my best imitation of our professor. "It's the representation of the external world, and the meat represents our inner lives. You can't get the full flavor of either without having equal parts of both."

Nicole laughed. "Whose philosophy is that? Oscar Meyer's?"

"No, it's mine," I said in my regular voice. "I just made it up."

217

She thought about that for a minute. "You are a true philosopher, Rhona, to see that much in a hot dog."

"You really think so?"

"I do."

"I know people who bite into the roll and actually believe they're getting it all. They go through their entire lives without even realizing what they missed." I glanced at my watch. "Speaking of which, today's Thursday, isn't it?"

"Yeah. Why?"

"No reason." I took a sip of my Coke and thought about my mother and Millie and Sadie and Gertie, all of whom would be piling into the brown Chevy Biscayne in just a few hours, all four of them talking at once. Soon they'd be spreading their bingo cards on the long table, applauding Morty as he stepped onto the stage. "B-sixteen," he'd call into the microphone, and the women would boo or cheer as they scanned their cards with the tip of their flat marking pen. Just another Thursday night at the Temple. But this night would be different from all other bingo nights, because on this night I knew with absolute certainty, I would not be at the table with any of them.

"How about a fry?" I asked Nicole, pushing the plate her way. "They're really amazing."

"Thanks, Rhona. Do people ever call you Ro?"

"As a matter of fact, they used to," I said, "but I think I like Rhona a lot better."

Acknowledgements

I'd like to thank these amazing women (and a few good men) whose support for this book has meant everything to me:

Judi Farkas, Tanya McKinnon, Richard Simon, Corie Skolnick, Terri Farnsworth, Joan Aguado, Louretta Walker, Kaja Blackley, Ron Furst, Maia Danziger, Adele Levine, Linzi Glass, Patti Sirulnick, Lisa Meyer, Eva Sumerlin, Barbara Jacobs, Geoffrey White and Dave St. John.

I am forever indebted to my son, Andrew Lieberman and my daughter, Jamie Lieberman, for their incredible wisdom and unconditional love. And to my husband Ron, there are no words to adequately express my love for you.

Printed in the United States
1489300003B/123